THE RIGHT TIME

The Lahaina Mystery Series
by Barbara E. Sharp

THE LAST SMYTHE
THE THIRD SPY
THE RIGHT TIME

Coming Soon:
THE WIND MISTS

THE RIGHT TIME

A LAHAINA MYSTERY

By
Barbara E. Sharp

To order more Lahaina Mysteries
or to find out when the next book in the series
is available, check out,
www.lahainamysteries.com

Hignell Printing Edition

This is a work of fiction. Although some Maui locales are real, others are ficticious. The characters, incidents, and dialogues are products of the author's imagination and are not to be construed as real. Any resemblance to actual events or persons, living or dead, is entirely coincidental.

Cover Design by Steve Sharp

Printed in CANADA - 2007

This book is printed on 100% recylcled material including 20% post-consumer waste. This-acid free paper is oxygen bleached, an environmentally friendly process.

ISBN 0-97-14277-2-0

Mahalo

Special thanks to my son, Steve, for his graphic skills in setting up the book and for designing the beautiful covers, and to Penny Garrett for meticulously editing every page.
To both of you, mahalo for your constructive and valuable input.

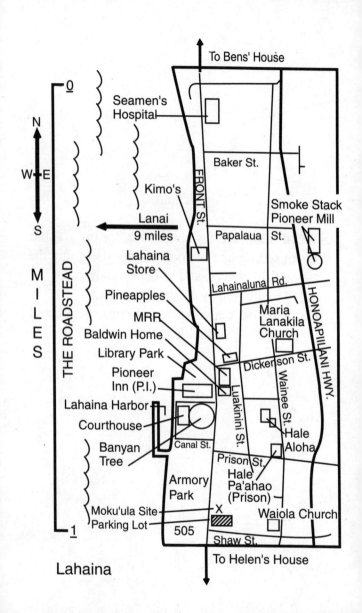

Lahaina

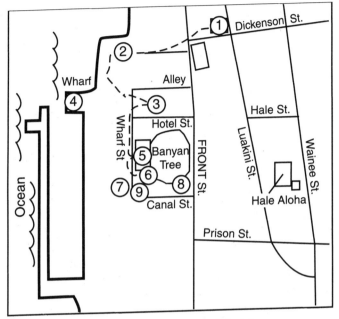

Lahaina Halloween Night

1. Pineapples
2. Library Park
3. Pioneer Inn
4. Pier
5. Court House
6. Tom O'Connin
7. Helen (Mustang)
8. Lani
9. Justin on Fort Wall

A Note from the Author

In this novel I have paid tribute to a real person named Larry Windley, who in his short life did a great deal to preserve the written history of Lahaina. Following a debilitating accident in 1959, he began organizing the restoration and protection of Lahaina's historic sites. The details of his life are as accurate as possible, taken from interviews with his friends, and from his obituary.

Another real person mentioned in The Right Time is Arthur Waal, whose highly regarded reminisces and vignettes of Lahaina at the turn of the century, are quoted.

All information about the Plantation Era was researched from historical archives or from interviews with long-time residents. Descriptions of historical sites in and around Lahaina, are also accurate.

The Right Time is, however, a novel, so with the above exceptions, the story and its characters are purely fictitious.

THE RIGHT TIME

"Be patient, when the time is right, it will happen."
Jim Luckey, Executive Director of The Lahaina
Restoration Foundation, 1972-1997

CHAPTER 1.

Sunday, October 17th
Lahaina Maui, Hawaii

"September is way too humid to suit me – October, too. This hammock by the lapping surf is the only place without air-conditioning that feels cool. As much as I love my house in town, it's way too hot there this time of year. There's no breeze at all! It's like a pause that won't go away. How would you feel about me and Windy moving in for a while?"

This said, Ben glanced over to see what reaction if any, Helen had to his question. Finding no sign that she was even on the same planet, he continued: "Why didn't I bring Windy along today? She would have loved it out here on your patio. Just look at Mambo, contentedly staring at the surf. Have you ever seen a happier cat? I'll bet he misses Windy; after all, he saved her life. Do you think the name Windy sounds like she has gas? Maybe Sandy would be a better name. I'll never forget that stormy night when Mambo came up on the patio, carrying the small kitten in his . . ."

Helen, who was sitting at the glass-topped patio table, face to face with a laptop computer, looked up and said: "Did you say something, Ben?"

"Say something? Oh let's see, I was just rambling on about Windy's and my future plans, struggling to find her a suitable name, and arranging a visit with Mambo. Nothing important."

"Oh, good. Tell me, which of these beginnings do you like best? Once upon a time, long, long ago . . . or: Once, long ago, upon a time before . . . or: Once before, long ago, there were . . .

"Do I have any other choices?"

"No."

"Well, then let's see; I think I've heard the first one somewhere before . . . like in: *Once upon a time* there was a beautiful princess. The second one seems plagiaristic of the first, and the last doesn't make sense."

"Plagiaristic is not a word, Ben. I just ask for a little help, and you have to start making up words?"

"Helen, I believe that this frustrating conversation is due to the weather. It's making us testy, and too easily stressed out over minor things. It's a balmy

Sunday in Hawaii - let's go have some fun. Then later we can stop by my house and pick up Windy."

Helen gathered up her papers, tamped them several times on the table, slid them into a folder marked Windley, and said: "It's not a minor thing to write a story about such an important person as Larry Windley but you may be right about my stressing out. Let's take a walk into town."

One of the nice things about Hawaii is that you hardly ever have to fuss around getting dressed up. With the temperature usually hanging around 82 degrees year round, there's no need for sweaters or jackets, something that Helen and Ben, who are both from the Mainland, have never gotten used to. Lahaina sits on the leeward side of the island of Maui, known as the Valley Isle. It's always been a vacation spot, from the time of the ancient kings and queens. Today, visitors come from all over the planet to visit the historically important town.

Most days are sunny, cooled by the trade winds, but in late summer when the trades stop, humidity rises, making it feel very hot and sticky. As Helen and Ben prepared to walk into town, it was one of those days - the air was still, the sky and ocean a flat steely gray. Ben, dressed only in a pair of old khaki shorts, hoisted himself up out of the hammock, reached for his tank top and stuffed his feet into his sneakers.

"This is as ready as I get. You going like that?"

Helen glanced up and said: "We look like twins. Maybe I'll change to a pink tank top instead of this blue one. But on the other hand it's too hot to go to all that trouble. I'll just take these papers and my computer inside and grab my purse."

Waving goodbye to Mambo who was hiding behind the potted palm eyeballing a tiny green chameleon, they headed up the beach towards Lahaina town.

Trekking along the sandy beach hand in hand, Helen looked up at Ben and smiled. "Move in? With Mambo and me?"

"Ah, then you did hear me."

"Of course I did. I can do two things at the same time, you know."

"Like make cookies and carry on a conversation? Listen to a lecture and plan your grocery list? Drive your car and invent cold fusion?"

"Yeah."

Ben paused to take a look out at the calm silver-gray ocean and the clearly visible reef. Helen sat down and patted the sand next to her, indicating that he join her. "What will you do with your house while you and Windy are gone?" she asked.

Sitting down beside her, he said: "Then you wouldn't mind putting up with the two of us for a while?"

"Are you kidding? The only problem I can see is that our friends will jump to the conclusion that we are finally going to do it."

"Do what? Don't you suppose they already suspect we have done it?"

"I don't mean that "it." I mean the other one."

"Oh, marriage! Why would we want to go and do a thing like that and risk spoiling what we have together?"

"Exactly what I told Mrs. Sylva when she asked why we don't tie the knot."

"Maybe we should let them speculate - speculation is good, keeps 'em guessing and keeps us from becoming dull and boring."

"Right. As though two people who get involved in murders, stolen art, arson and mayhem could ever become boring."

"My dear Helen, even without all that intriguing fun you could not possibly bore me. You have a mind similar to mine. I think we may even be soul mates."

"What kind of a mind do you have, Ben?"

"Could we go into that another time? I'm starving!"

Following a leisurely lunch at Lahaina Coolers, they strolled up Dickenson Street to the intersection at Wainee, and stopped to admire Maria Lanakila church. The first Catholic mass held on Maui was held here in 1841. The lovely building standing today is a replica of an earlier church, built in 1928.

"Let's hang a left and head past the Seamen's Cemetery and then make a pit stop at the wine store."

"Sounds good to me, Ben, but how about we pick up wine on the way back from our walk, so we don't have to carry it."

"Your common sense overwhelms me."

"I take it that remark is sarcastic? Meaning that common sense is not one of your favorite personality traits?"

"Common sense is not a personality trait, it's a deep seated personal attribute. You either have it or you don't. It is neither likeable or unlikable – it is only logical."

"You sound like Spock."

"I take that as a compliment, and suggest that it would be logical to stop conversing and get on with our exercise; it is hotter than hell today, and will only get hotter this afternoon."

After making it all the way to the Seamen's hospital and back to the wine store, Helen said: "Let's head over to Pineapples for a glass of iced tea with Justin, and hear all the latest news."

"Great idea. We haven't seen Justin since we ended the Valdera caper. I wonder if he's still in love with Kari Byrde."

Pineapples restaurant is in the heart of historic Lahaina town, just across the street from the Research and Preservation Society, known as RAPS, where Helen is the Historian/Research Director. Pineapples is a small family run business, specializing in delicious homemade food, gourmet coffee and fresh donuts. As an added bonus, they have fresh pineapples, papayas and Maui onions, all boxed and ready for visitors to take home.

Justin Takamura, eldest son and manager of Pineapples, is known for greeting each customer with a smile, and for spreading good cheer like sunshine. But today he seemed different, like there was a cloud hovering over his head.

"Mrs. G. and Ben, good to see you guys. Find a table and I'll join you in a minute."

Returning with frosted glasses of iced tea and an assortment of exotic donut holes ranging from pineapple/guava to chocolate/macadamia, Justin pulled up a chair and sat down, staring at his friends with uncharacteristic seriousness. "How long have you two lived in Hawaii? Ten years maybe?"

Ben answered: "Five for me and eight for Helen."

Justin continued his questioning. "Where from? Some far off place I suppose. Some place where there's snow and ice and raccoons and squirrels?"

"Are you okay Justin?" Helen asked. "I think there are raccoons here in the zoo."

"Oh sure, that's easy for you to say. You probably come from a town loaded with them, where they run around loose! My family has lived here in Lahaina for generations and none of us has ever seen a chipmunk!"

"Actually I come from Seattle," Helen said, "and yes we had raccoons in the woods near my house; chipmunks and rabbits too. My daughter, who is grown up and married now, has a tailless squirrel that drops by her house every day for his supply of peanuts. Why aren't you happy with the local mongeese, Justin?"

"It's mongooses, Mrs. G." Turning to Ben, Justin asked: "Where you come from Ben, there's ice and snow, isn't there?"

"Yes indeed Justin, Colorado is a snowy place in the winter. Even in the spring it can go from warm and sunny to a sudden snowstorm, taking everyone by surprise. Why do you ask?"

"I ask because I have hardly been anywhere, seen anything, except when I went to college in California, and all I saw there was the surf and palm trees. Sound familiar?"

"And?"

"And I want to have an adventure. I want to feel cold, see fir trees, snowy mountains, raccoons and squirrels."

Helen looked thoughtful. "Could this have anything to do with Kari Byrde?"

"Maybe, . . . well, yes. Remember a few months ago when I cased the Valdera mansion and had lunch with Kari?* She talked about her job and all the traveling she did. It started me thinking about my life. Oh by the way, did you hear that her grandfather, old Valdera, died?"

"Yes, read about it in the paper." Helen answered, "No great loss there I'm afraid, although I do feel sorry for Mrs. Valdera, she was a very nice lady."

"Right, Mrs. G., she is a nice lady. When I heard the news I phoned the mansion to give her and Kari my condolences, and Kari told me she was moving to California to live with her sister."

"Well," Ben said, "that explains your mood. I'm sorry, Justin, I know how careful you were to protect your relationship with Kari, even giving up sleuthing when we went after her grandfather, the old spy."

*The Third Spy

"Yeah, well that's the way it goes, and I don't mind that I took a chance with her. What really gets to me is that now I feel trapped here. I feel like my life is going nowhere."

Ben's eyes lit up and with a smile, he asked: "How does this sound, Justin . . . a cabin at a ski resort in Aspen, high in the mountains with ice and snow, ski lifts, a fireplace, and possible raccoons?"

"Sounds wonderful but impossible, Ben. First off, I have my responsibilities here at Pineapples, and I don't have any skis or cold weather clothes, and I probably couldn't afford a cabin in Aspen anyway."

Ben, still smiling, said: "Winter is still a few weeks away, so you have plenty of time to think it over. The cabin belongs to my brother and comes free. It's equipped with skis, ski boards, warm jackets and such. You can always rent boots or whatever else you need. All you have to do is get there. Think it over. You could take some friends along and you'd all have a great time, maybe get this squirrel thing out of your system."

"Thanks for the offer, Ben, I'll give it some serious thought. It does sound terrific."

On the walk back to her house, Helen smiled and said: "I think you pulled Justin out of the dumps with your offer of a ski trip to Aspen and I hope he takes you up on it."

"So do I. Justin's one of the most cheerful people in town. It's awful to see him so down in the dumps.

However, not that it is any of my business, but I've thought all along that Kari Byrde was wrong for him."

"You're not alone, Ben, I know Nacho feels the same way. Do you realize that it's been over a year since we met Nacho and got involved with him and Justin in the murders? Where has the time gone?"

"Where it always goes, Helen. Time is only important because it keeps things from happening all at once. Time flies like an arrow – fruit flies like bananas. So to ask where it has gone, is irrelevant. Time marches on, after all."

"You do have a way with words. Where do words go?"

"Are you nuts?"

"Well, you had such a ditzy answer for where time has gone, that I wanted to know what you think about where words go. Personally I think they fall to the ground and become a part of the earth."

"That's possible, though it's more likely that they float up into the atmosphere where they freeze and are preserved forever."

"Every word since people began to speak is up there?"

"Yes, way up there."

"Wow."

As they approached Helen's cottage, engrossed in conversation, they failed to notice Mambo, who was pacing impatiently back and forth on the edge of the patio. A token pat on the head from Helen caused a yowl of protest and an angry swipe at her sneaker. "I think he's hungry, Ben."

"If he attacks your shoe when he's hungry, I'd hate to see how he acts when he's starving! Windy wouldn't do anything like that."

As she fixed Mambo's snack, Helen turned to Ben with a smile and said, "Windy is just a baby, she hasn't learned adult cat behavior yet. Let's go pick her up, then when we get back we can marinate some ribs and then sit on the patio and watch the sunset."

Ben's house, in a residential section of Lahaina, is only a few miles from Helen's seaside cottage. It's a beautifully renovated cane house, but because of its location it lacks that wonderful ocean breeze.

Windy, who sometimes acts more like a puppy than a kitten, was sitting on the kitchen windowsill, apparently keeping a vigil for Ben's return. She purred up a storm on the ride to Helen's house. Did she know she was going to see Mambo, they wondered?

Mambo, who was waiting by the front door, greeted Windy with purring and a cat grooming session, followed by a nap on Helen's favorite chair. "Look at them curled up together, sound asleep. Where's my camera? I have to have a picture of this."

After mixing up the rib sauce, Ben opened a bottle of wine and headed out to the patio to watch the late afternoon sun sink towards the horizon. In comfortable silence, he and Helen sat side by side enjoying the peaceful time of day.

Staring out into the Pacific Ocean for several minutes he sighed, and actually said the following words: "Pale turquoise waves, trimmed with delicate pearly foam, marked only with bat wings of deep purple shadow, reflect the glittering gold of the suns last gasp."

Helen took a sip of wine and said: "Huh! Funny, that's exactly what I was just thinking. I would only add that the darkening velvet sky hosts a herd of pink sheep clouds, while a golden fan unfolds shafts of light for a brief moment, announcing the arrival of the first diamond in the sky."

"Pink sheep clouds?"

Before Helen could respond, Mambo hopped out through his cat door, which is set into the screen door, leaving Windy on the inside looking out.

"Ben, you'll have to open the screen door for Windy until she learns the hang of the cat door. It's hard at first, for a cat to open a swinging door by banging it with his head. It's something they have to get used to."

Ben retrieved his kitten, holding her on his lap while she squirmed to get down and follow Mambo. "Don't you think Windy is a little young to go out for a nocturnal hunting trip, Helen?"

"I think its fine as long as she's with Mambo. After saving her life in the storm, he'd never let anything bad happen."

Setting the kitten down, Ben said: "Okay Windy, but stay close to Uncle Mambo, and don't go too far."

Windy pranced after her hero, who was waiting patiently at the edge of the patio near the dark bushes.

"Before I light the barbie, Helen, tell me more about the Larry Windley story – the one that starts out, *Once upon a time . . .*"

"Hmmm, *Once upon a time* does sound a little over used, I may have to come up with a better opening line. As for writing the story about Windley, it was a decision I made after entering all 3000 pages of Lahaina's history into the computer. He was the one who researched most of that material in the 1960's, and I feel as though people should know more about that and about all the work he did to preserve the historic sites in Lahaina."

"I remember you telling me about him when he was a young man in his twenties. Didn't he get the bends?"

"Right. It happened while he was diving for black coral, which was very popular in the making of jewelry in the 50' and 60's. The coral grows deep in the ocean. On the day he got the bends he was more than two hundred feet down, and with the equipment they had at the time, diving to those depths was very dangerous. Fortunately an American submarine rescue ship was nearby with a decompression chamber and one of the Navy's top medical experts on the bends. Windley was brought aboard unconscious. He lived, but was never able to dive again. It must have been devastating for such an active young man."

Ben poured more wine. "Is that why he gathered all that historical information about Lahaina? To keep himself busy?"

"Exactly. He saw that something had to be done to draw attention to the deteriorating condition of the old buildings and sites here. He got other concerned people together, which ultimately led to the beginning of RAPS. Then he and several friends went to all the repositories in Oahu, and copied everything pertinent to Lahaina's past. All this information, dating from the late 1700's to the early 1900's, came from journals, inter-island memos, letters, newspapers, magazines, government, school and church files, etc. It's about as close as you can get to what actually happened without the opinions and agendas that are written into most history books."

"Like the glossed-over history we learned in school?" Ben asked.

"Right. That's why having all the memos and information directly from that time is so important. Neither Larry Windley nor I changed one single word of what was written by the people of the past. After Windley and his friends gathered this information they typed it onto 5"x 7" pieces of paper and put it all into categories, like Shipping, Hawaiian, Missionary, Diseases, Schools, and many many more. It's such an amazing collection; it filled three drawers of a file cabinet!"

Ben smiled and said, "Then along came Helen, thirty some years later, and put it all into the computer. How long did it take you to do that?"

Interrupted by the phone, Helen said to Ben: "Two years." And to the phone: "Hello? – Sam! How have you been? – Sure I can. – Okay, 8:00 A.M. at Pineapples. See you then. - Bye!"

"Ah, having breakfast with Sam, eh?"

"Yes, and I can't wait to hear what her big news is. She sounds so excited about something, I'll bet her parents are coming to visit."

CHAPTER 2.

Monday, October 18th

Up at dawn, as usual, Helen fed Mambo and straightened up the house, which really doesn't take long. Other than the master bedroom and bath, guest bath and laundry room, the cottage is just one big room. The kitchen faces east and is separated from the dining area by a sit down counter. There's a fair sized dining room table and four chairs adjoining the main part of the living room, which contains an L-shaped couch, two comfortable chairs and a coffee table, all facing the view of the ocean. One third of the room is raised up one step. Helen's desk, computer, and printer are tucked in one corner, surrounded by bookcases and partially hidden by a Japanese screen. The opposite corner is cozily fitted out with foldout futon, small coffee table, fan back rattan chair and TV.

Chores done, Helen left Mambo on the patio with instructions to leave the birds alone, and started her mile long walk up the beach into Lahaina town, deep in thought about the day three years ago when she first met Samantha Fields. In those days Sam was a very confused young girl who had recently run away from her home in Nevada. What a culture shock it must have been to arrive in old historical Lahaina town.

Sam's first day working for a local caterer was at the RAPS annual brunch meeting, attended by Helen and one hundred and fifty other residents of Lahaina, many of whom witnessed the almost dance-like recovery attempt Sam made after she tripped over someone's foot. Her dance started with one gigantic step forward, then a sudden lift of her heavily laden tray in a misguided attempt to erase the inertia of the uncontrolled forward motion. Plates of food crashed to the floor, as the empty tray soared into the air and Sam fell backwards onto the lap of the guest speaker.

Helen felt that the poor girl was not entirely to blame – after all, the man's foot had been sticking out right in her path. So she took it upon herself to explain this to the head caterer, with such success that it saved Sam's job. From then on, she became a sort of substitute mom to the awkward girl with maroon hair, and black lipstick. Today, three years later, Helen looked across the restaurant at Sam, and saw the beautiful woman she had become.

"What in the world did you swallow, Sam . . . a canary?"

"Sit Helen, Justin is bringing coffee. I can hardly wait to tell you my news."

Justin arrived with mugs of steaming coffee, took Helen and Sam's breakfast order, then sat down in the third chair. "What's up Sam? I can tell you are bursting with information."

"It's not information Justin, it's news; the biggest news on the planet! Could you put our breakfast order in now, I'm starved."

Reluctantly Justin headed to the kitchen.

"Sorry Helen, I don't mean to be rude to Justin, it's just that I want to tell you the news and watch your reaction without any interruptions."

"Okay, shoot!"

"Woody and I are getting married!"

"Oh, Sam, I am very happy for you. Woody is a fine young man; probably the best of the whole Byrde flock. When is the wedding?"

"In two weeks. Yes, I know it is a short time to plan such an event, but my parents are here and it's probably the only trip they will ever take to Maui. I hadn't seen them since I left home four years ago, during my troubled time, when I had my nose ring, fake tattoos and purple hair. They were very surprised to see that I've become a solid citizen with a terrific job."

Justin arrived with their breakfast order. "Two-egg herb omelet and rye toast for Mrs. G., and pineapple pancakes and bacon for you, Sam. Now, are you going to tell me what's the biggest news on the planet?"

"Sure, Justin; sit, pour some coffee. Are you ready? Woody and I are getting married!"

Justin paused for just a second. "I'm happy that your luck with the Byrdes was better than mine, Sam. Woody's a neat guy, and he's lucky to have you."

"Thanks, I know you're feeling sad about Kari moving to California. If things had worked out for you two, we might have been brother and sister-in-law."

"I guess Kari and I weren't meant to be. It's okay – I'm okay, and I am really happy for you and Woody."

Justin made sure Helen and Sam had fresh coffee, then went back to work.

"Are you heading to work, Helen?"

"No, I'm off to the grocery store to get stocked up with kibbles and tuna."

"I have the day off too," Sam said, "and I'm going to spend it with Woody. We're going to check out some romantic spots for our wedding ceremony."

At Foodland, Helen wandered from aisle to aisle trying to remember what it was that she had written on the grocery list she forgot to bring along. Recalling two items, she made a sudden U-turn in the snack aisle and collided with a very large Hawaiian man. "Oh, I am so sorry!" Helen exclaimed.

"No harm done, Mrs. Grant."

"You know me? I'm sorry, I don't remember your name."

"Keoni Sanford: fisherman, diver, and connoisseur of fine food and beautiful women."

With a big smile, Helen said: "Keoni Sanford! Yes, you are all of those things and also a saint to the homeless and downtrodden, and last but not least, a friend of Ben Anderson's. Ben speaks of you often and he laughs about some the adventures you two have had – but he never tells me the details. Why is that? And where did you and I meet?"

Keoni leaned on his grocery cart and laughed. "Ben and I only get into small trouble, we're too old for the really memorable stuff. As for where you and I met, it was a couple years ago in the Master's Reading Room when you first started working on Larry Windley's stuff. I brought you a box of his personal papers that had been stored in my attic for thirty years."

"Now I remember. You and Larry were close friends who shared a beach house near 505."

"Yep. Those were fun days, the days when the trouble we got into was worthwhile. Did you ever finish putting all that info in the computer?"

"Yes. It took two years, but it's done. Now I'm trying to write a story about Larry. Could I interview you some time?"

"Tell you what, phone that rogue you date and tell him that you two are attending a feast at Keoni's place, Wednesday night - we can talk about Larry then. Now, if you will excuse me, I have to go catch something fabulous for your dinner. Come about 5:30. Ben knows the way."

Ben is the Regional Manager for Maui's three Visitor Centers, and the hands-on manager at the busiest one, located in Lahaina's old Courthouse. Thanks to competent local managers, the Kihei and Hana Centers require only monthly visits from Ben.

When Helen arrived on her way home from the grocery store, she found him seated at his desk staring at his computer screen.

Ben, guess who I ran into in the grocery store." He looked up and rubbed his chin. "Newt Gingrich?"

"No, although I think I saw him riding a bike, carrying a surfboard and wearing a Panama hat, but that was yesterday. Guess who I ran into today?"

"Keoni Sanford."

Helen looked dejected. "Swell, now you've taken up mind-reading! Or, more likely, Keoni told you all about it."

"Not Keoni - it was Mrs. Sylva. I ran into her just a few minutes ago, walking down Front Street with a heavy bag of groceries, so I carried them to her house for her. On the way I learned that the Kealoha's are expecting their ninth grandchild, the Basket and Bucket restaurant is going to be closed for a few days while it is tented for termites, and that you were seen flirting with Keoni Sanford at Foodland."

"Funny, I didn't see Mrs. Sylva at Foodland - I guess I was just too involved with my flirting to notice

her. Seriously, Ben, I do have something to tell you –
Keoni has invited us to dinner Wednesday evening."

"Oh my God! Do you realize what this means?
Keoni is a fine cook; we have to head to the gourmet
wine store and find a zesty Zin or a perky Pinot, or
whatever is touted to be the best . . . maybe a snappy
little Shiraz from Australia. Let's head out now!"

An hour later, as they were putting the groceries
away, Ben said: "You won't believe what a fabulous
cook Keoni is. He's got a beautiful wife, a daughter
who lives at home and two sons who are away at
school. They've got a house near the beach. His
younger brother, Henry, and his family live nearby."

"So, where is their place?"

"Olowalu."

Helen took a giant step over Mambo who was, as
usual, right in the middle of things. "I've met Keoni
before, you know. It was several years ago when he
dropped by my office with a box of Larry Windley's
personal papers. They were close friends when they
were younger, and when Larry died Keoni stored the
box in his attic. It was there for nearly thirty years."

Ben detoured around Mambo, who was now spread
out full length across the kitchen, and opened the fridge
to put lettuce and tomatoes in the produce bin. "Why
is Mambo here, spread out wall to wall? Never mind,
don't answer that, I know he's doing it to get attention.
Windy's watching and I'm afraid she is learning
annoying cat behavior from her notorious savior." Ben
gave the elongated cat a nudge with his foot and

instantly found his sneaker the object of a playful attack. "Helen, get this clinging clown off my foot!"

"Mambo, behave yourself. Here, come and have a slice of Gouda."

Giving Ben a little nip on the ankle, Mambo, still in a devilish mood, hopped sideways and eagerly accepted his cheese snack from Helen.

"As I was saying before devil cat attacked me - what was in Windley's box?"

"I know this sounds terribly irresponsible of me, but I honestly don't know. After Keoni dropped it off I got so involved with all the information in the file cabinet, that I forgot all about the box. I think I shoved it under the desk . . . I'm pretty sure it wasn't tossed out. My guess is that it got put into storage up at Hale Pa`i during the Pacific Rim Conference last year when I had to clean up the Reading Room for an orientation meeting."

"Aren't you curious about what's in the box?"

"I sure am, especially now that I am writing the story about Windley. I'll head up to Hale Pa`i first chance I get, and see if it's there."

CHAPTER 3.

Tuesday, October 19th

It was early when Helen arrived at work. Traffic on Front Street was light, Lahaina seemed to be waking up slowly. She climbed the stairs to her office, deep in thought about Sam's wedding and about Woody's grandfather, Ricardo Valdera. The old Nazi sympathizer was dead now, his stolen treasures returned to the rightful owners without a media frenzy. Thank God Woody and Kari and their family of innocent bystanders had not been dragged through that scandal.

Still absorbed in her thoughts, she unlocked the padlock, opened the office door and turned on the light, failing to notice the broken window opposite her desk until she sat down at the computer. Pieces of glass and splatters of blood covered the desk and keyboard. With a flicker of fear, she quickly turned to check out the room. It was empty, but the trail of blood led to the file cabinet, microfilm storage drawers and across the room to the two small closets. Feeling shaky, Helen slowly pushed back her desk chair, and without touching anything except the doorknob she left the room, replaced the padlock and headed down to the office to phone the police.

Chief Johnstone and two other officers arrived in minutes. "Looks like your intruder cut himself up pretty badly, Helen."

"What do you think he was after, Chief Johnstone? I mean, there's no money here, only archival material. All of the Research and Preservation Society's resources are available to the public, so except for the computer equipment, I see no reason for anyone to break in.

The Chief, a massively large man, knelt down to examine a bloody smear on the lower file drawer. Two other officers were present, one looking for fingerprints and the other getting blood samples.

"Well, Helen," the Chief said, as he hefted himself up off his knees, "I was going to ask you the same question, since your computer and other tech stuff is safe; what was our intruder after?"

The rest of her unsettling day was spent watching the police dust for fingerprints and search for clues. No one was allowed to enter the room, so she hadn't seen Ben or anyone else all day long. When he arrived at her house that evening, promptly at 6 P.M., and said, "Where to my dear?" she hugged him, thankful for his comforting presence.

"You know, Ben, I think the Pioneer Inn would be just perfect. We can get a nice potent drink, watch the sunset, and then eat dinner."

"Not like you to think about potent drink, but I must say it's probably a good idea. We'll head to the P.I. and discuss this disturbing event that took place in your office while we get bombed."

"Swell."

After Helen had told Ben all the details of the police inspection, she started on her second Mai Tai. Feeling more relaxed, she said: "Did I mention that the officers might have gotten a couple of thinger prints."

"That's finger prints, and yes you did. Are you sure you can handle that second Mai Tai? I've never seen you drink more than one at a time."

"Yes, I can handle it, although I don't know why I feel the need to have a second one. Doesn't seem that I should be so upset over a mere break-in. I wasn't this upset when Mambo was nearly disnembered."

Ben hid a smile. "As I recall, you and I along with some friends, polished off several bottles of very special wine that night to celebrate Mambo's safety and the capture of a double murderer. What I do not recall, is you getting tipsy."

"Are you saying that I am tipsy now, Ben?"

The waiter arrived as if it was scripted, carrying plates of hot spicy shrimp with rice and sautéed vegetables. "Will that be all Mr. Anderson? Perhaps a bottle of wine?"

"No thanks we're fine, Freddie. Maybe we'll have an espresso later."

After dinner, which was followed by coffee drinks and lime sherbet, they left the historic old Pioneer Inn and walked past the library to Front Street. It was a balmy Hawaiian evening; tourists and locals strolled along the seawall, past the shops and art galleries, taking in the exotic window displays, while a steady stream of cars cruised by.

Looking in the window of a memorabilia shop, Ben said: "Helen, take a look at this. Isn't that a piece of black coral?"

"Yes, I think it is. It's unbelievably lacey and fragile looking. I didn't know it grew that big. Let's go in and see if we can find out more about it."

Standing behind the counter was a large tanned man, in his 50's. Ben introduced himself and shook hands with Hans Albright, the owner of Hula Han's Sandwich Island Treasures, a collection of Hawaiian memorabilia.

"Did you bring that beautiful piece of coral up yourself, Mr. Albright?"

"Make that Hans, and yes I did, many years ago; but because of its size I had a little help. Back in the 50's we kind of dove by the seat of our pants, not knowing exactly how to get things done, but amazingly we didn't make too many mistakes, and we found some treasures for sure."

Helen wandered along the glass case checking out the collection of ash trays, shot glasses and swizzle sticks; all with the name of a restaurant, bar, or hotel; many of which were gone now. She recognized several of Lahaina's favorite old spots: The Whales Tail, Banyan Inn, Lahaina Broiler, Blue Max, Boat House, Blackbeard's, Lani's, The Wind Sock, Whalers Pub, and Alex's Hole in the Wall. The shelves were lined with hula girl lamps, old bottles, glass floats, and ancient lanterns.

"Hans, back in the 50's, did you ever meet a guy named Larry Windley?"

"Yes, Larry was a friend of mine, and a hell of a diver too until he got the bends, which could have happened to any of us on any given day. Why do you ask about Larry?"

"I'm the Research Director at RAPS and recently I entered all the historical information he collected about Lahaina into the computer – three thousand pages!"

"Wow! I remember that Larry and his friends used to work on some history stuff, but I never realized the extent of it."

"Most people don't know the extent of it, but I'm planning to correct that by writing a story about him. Can I make an appointment for an interview with you?"

"Sure Helen, just give me a call and I'll spill my guts!"

"Thanks Hans, see you later."

When Ben pulled his van up in front of Helen's house later that evening, they noticed that Mambo wasn't pacing at the front door as usual. "I wonder where your roommate is. I suppose the great hunter is out catching a nice juicy mouse for you. I'll see you to the door, then I'm off to give some TLC to the hunter-in-training, Windy."

"Wait Ben, something's wrong - look, my front door is open!"

"You stay here Helen, while I go see if anyone's in there."

"Oh, no you don't. I refuse to be put in the position of having to identify your body! We have cell phones, so wait while I call the cops."

"Okay, go ahead. I'll just go take a quick peek while you're on the phone. Never fear, I know what I'm doing."

With that, Ben slouched down and made his way to Helen's front door. Only a dim kitchen light was on, but he could see some soft flashes of light coming from the bedroom, probably from a flashlight, meaning the intruder was still there. Quietly Ben tiptoed across the tile entry floor and onto the living room carpet. The bedroom door was only a few feet away when he was stopped in his tracks by a piercing shout from the direction of the front door: "Ben, are you in there?"

From the bedroom came a loud crash, three expletives, and the sound of the sliding door opening. Ben raced into the bedroom in time to see a large, probably male, figure dash across the patio and disappear into the bushes.

"Well really Helen, that was unlike you! Why in the world would you yell at a time when I was nearly apprehending the culprit?"

"Once again you're talking like an old time detective, Ben. I think you picked that up from James. The reason I yelled was in an attempt to save your life. After all, the "culprit" could have been, and probably was, armed. He could have shot, stabbed, choked, or clubbed you!"

"You forgot poisoned."

"Not funny. Now give me a hug, and say that you understand that when someone loves someone, they are protective."

"When someone loves someone they are protective, that is why I told you to stay in the car!"

Ben folded his arms around Helen in a bear hug. They stood quietly for several seconds, parting only when a deep voice said: "I thought this was an emergency, not a meeting of the lovers club."

"Oh, Chief Johnstone." Ben said, with a rather sheepish grin. "Yes, indeed we had an emergency situation a few minutes ago; an intruder. He was in the house when we got back from dinner, but he escaped through the bedroom sliding door and ran across the patio and disappeared."

"Ben, I want you to describe this intruder in as much detail as you can. Helen, go take a look around and see if anything is missing. Try not to touch anything, we may be able to get some prints."

Helen found drawers pulled open, her desk rifled, and several things knocked over, but nothing missing that she could see at a glance.

Chief Johnstone, standing in the now well-lighted living room, scratched his head. "This break-in and the one at your office could be connected; I don't believe in coincidences. There is one difference this time though, the intruder didn't break a window to gain entry. It looks like he somehow opened your front door. Did you lock it when you went out earlier?"

"Oh yes, I almost always lock the doors. Sometimes I forget to close the patio doors, but I usually lock the front door. I have a really strong lock, you know. It's only when I'm in a hurry or distracted that I would ever forget to lock up." Helen said.

"Then it's possible that you did not lock the door?"

"Well, it's not likely, but if you put it that way, I suppose it is possible."

"I see."

Under the bushes that border Helen's patio, Mambo lay with his front legs extended like the great Sphinx of Egypt, waiting for the strangers to leave. Then, with his usual panache, he hopped in through his screened cat door and deposited a piece of black leather at Helen's feet.

Ben, in the kitchen fussing with some tea bags, was in mid-sentence trying to decide if he should take tomorrow off to make the move to Helen's house. "I won't let you be alone here with some maniac around. Tomorrow Windy and I will pack up our little suitcases, Wok, cat dish, and telescope, and become your roomies for a couple months."

"Ben look, it's Mambo. Oh my poor baby; how are you? Did the awful bad man scare you?"

"Oh really, is that any way to talk to him? He looks like he is going to gag. Come on Mambo, my man, I'll fix you a midnight snack. What's that you have in your hand, Helen?"

"It's a piece of leather that Mambo brought in. You're right, Ben, Mambo is smart and brave. He probably bit the intruder, and tore off a piece of his pants as a clue to his identity."

"Are you serious? I only meant that as cats go, Mambo is not the type that likes baby talk, I did not mean that I thought he was smart enough to . . . but, yes, that could have come from the intruder. Let me take a look."

Handing Ben the torn piece of leather, she said, "Okay, you examine the evidence, while I finish making tea. Then we'll go get Windy, and spend the night here curled up together."

"All of us?"

CHAPTER 4.

Wednesday, October 20th

The disturbing events of the previous night disappeared in the sunny light of the Hawaiian morning. In fact, if it weren't for the piece of torn leather laying on the patio table like a black widow spider, Helen could have forgotten the break-in ever happened.

Munching on a piece of toast, Ben watched Windy and Mambo rolling around on their backs on the sun-warmed tiles of the patio. When Mambo stopped, Windy stopped. "Have you noticed that Windy apes everything Mambo does? Maybe she thinks Mambo is her mother."

"More likely her father. More coffee? Actually, why don't you finish it off and I'll make another pot. Sam is going to come by, and I think Chief Johnstone may drop by too."

"I have to get going, Helen. I'm interviewing new volunteers for the Lahaina VIC today. I have to find someone to replace Marjorie Bayview, or perhaps I should say, Mrs. James French."

"Marjorie was one of a kind and I miss her. I hear she and James are cruising the Greek Islands. Oh, and speaking of marriage, I forgot to tell you that Sam and Woody are planning a wedding in two weeks. Her parents are here and Sam is so excited."

"I like Woody and I think he and Sam make a great couple. Why don't you ask her if her parents would like to baby-sit my house while they're here? I hate to leave it empty."

Sam and Helen spent an hour discussing wedding plans.

"Hawaiian weddings are so lovely and I can't think of a better place than the chapel by the sea."

Sam smiled and said: "Did you ever think that your klutzy friend would end up with a gem like Woody Byrde? It's a dream come true, Helen, and all I ask now is that the wedding take place without a hitch."

"Don't worry Sam, things seem to be going forward just fine so far. I take it that Woody's family is okay with the marriage?"

"They are. No problem there, although Pastor Byrde wants to marry us in his church in Kula. What worries me is my family. My parents, to be specific. They're like a train wreck waiting to happen. Helen, you have no idea what havoc they can create just being themselves. They mean no harm, but like the weather, there seems to be nothing that can be done about them."

Since Helen had never met Sam's parents, she felt at a loss for the right worlds to say, so she changed the subject. "Have you chosen your wedding dress?"

"Woody and I have agreed on an old fashioned wedding so I chose a simple white cotton dress trimmed in French lace with huge puffed sleeves, and topped off with a wide brimmed hat."

"Sounds beautiful. How can I help?"

"There is just one thing I ask of you, my friend. Will you be my maid of honor?"

"Oh yes, Sam, I would be delighted."

"Okay then, how about wearing something in either pale periwinkle blue or pale yellow. Maybe the blue would be best, my other two bridesmaids are wearing pale yellow so that way you, as maid of honor, will stand out."

"Pale periwinkle it is. I'll start looking around for just the right dress; maybe Makawao would be a good place to start. By the way, where are your parents staying?"

"With me. I know that sounds a little crowded since I only have a small room, but they don't have much money and they refuse to let me pay for their accommodations."

"Perfect. I have a deal for you . . . Ben is moving in with Mambo and me for a while, until the weather cools down, and he said he would be willing to let your parents stay in his house while he is gone."

"Wow, Helen, that would be great! It would be so much better than staying in my tiny room."

Helen walked Sam to the door; they hugged and Sam grinned. "Ben's moving in, huh? So, you guys finally going to do it?"

When Chief Johnstone arrived, Helen took a tray of iced tea and cookies out to the patio. Once seated in a comfortable chair, the Chief sighed and said: "You got the best little cove for privacy I have ever seen. I love sitting here, just watching the surf roll in."

"I know what you mean. This patio is where I live most of the time. Ben and I watch the sunset here nearly every evening. It's hard to believe that an intruder ran across this very spot. Which reminds me, look what Mambo brought home after you left last night."

"Looks like a piece of somebody's leather jacket or pants that was ripped off rather violently."

"I'm sure Mambo attacked the intruder."

"Attacked the intruder? Well, I guess that's possible, I mean he did attack a murderer, after all. He's a big cat. Wouldn't want to be on his shit list, that's for sure!"

"He's a real pussy cat most of the time, but occasionally he does get riled up."

"I'll hang onto Mambo's clue in case we catch a perp with a hole in his pants. It might come in handy. Did you find anything missing, yet?"

"Nothing so far."

Leaving Windy and Mambo safely inside the house, Helen locked both the front and patio doors, and walked into town along the beach - one of her favorite times for creative thinking – a time to find answers. Why did someone break into her office and her home? What was the intruder looking for? Certainly this was no ordinary thief, but a person desperately looking for something specific - but what? If he was after jewelry or art objects, not that she had anything of real value, he would have just broken into her home, not into her home *and* her office. So what was the common denominator? Maybe if she asked Nacho and Justin, they could help her piece it all together – they seemed to have a straightforward uncluttered approach to life.

She found them at Pineapples having a cup of coffee at one of the back corner tables. "Hi you two, I had a feeling I'd find you here."

"Hi yourself, Mrs. G. Were you looking for us?"

"Yes, Nacho, I have a little problem and I was hoping for some of your down to earth advice. Maybe something your mother taught you back on the plantation."

"Oh yeah, the plantation. You mean when I was a slave? Jeez you are so deep into history that I fear for your sanity."

"I was only jesting, my friend, I know you're from Philly and I know you have a brother named Nathaniel Plantrinette, who's living there. Which reminds me, how is our investment doing?"

Justin spoke up. "That's *my* brother's department. Oki has invested the $30,000 we "liberated" during the Valdera caper, quite wisely. The market is down some, but still, we're way ahead of the game. Someday soon we'll have to get together and decide what philanthropic thing we're going to do with all that money."

Nacho reached for a chocolate donut hole, which he dunked into his coffee, and said: "Who would believe that we never meant to con Valdera? The whole caper was so weird that even I don't believe it."

Nodding her head in agreement, Helen said: "Speaking of weird, something has happened and I need some input from you two." She reached for the coffeepot and continued: "Yesterday my office was broken into by someone who entered through the window and bled all over the place. He took nothing. Then last night when Ben brought me home after dinner there was an intruder in my house. He got away, and again took nothing. So guys, what do you think?"

Silence reigned for a few minutes then Justin said: "Who have you offended lately, Mrs. G.?"

"No one, Justin. You know me, and I'm the poster lady for polite."

Nacho mumbled something.

"Speak up Nacho, you know you can say anything to me."

"Well, sometimes you are a little outspoken, Mrs. G. Not rude mind you, but, well, sort of opinionated. Frankly I like it. It's refreshing."

"Okay . . . Now, what could the two break-ins have in common?"

More silence, then a sudden burst of genius from Nacho: "Something you are working on at work?"

Justin nodded in agreement. "Right! Not a guy who's after the family jewels, but a guy who is after information. Maybe something you've been researching. When the intruder didn't find what he was after at RAPS, he tried to find it at your house."

"Not bad you guys, but I haven't been doing any real research for months, I've just been keeping up with the usual requests for genealogy information. For the past few days I've been writing a story about Larry Windley, but that seems innocent enough."

"He the guy who got the bends and dug up history?" Nacho asked.

"The very one, yes. He was a black coral diver."

"Ah, a soul brother."

"No, Nacho, the coral was black, not Larry. But you do have something in common with him - he was in a wheelchair too, after he recovered from the bends. To keep himself busy he went on a quest to find historical information about Lahaina. Nothing sinister or worth stealing there, I'm afraid."

"What do you know about this guy Windley? Where is he now?

"Larry died in a sailing accident in 1969. He and a friend went out on a small boat and never returned."

Justin looked pensive. "Wow, that makes it seem very unlikely that the break-ins are connected to him."

Helen nodded in agreement.

Nacho put his hand over Helen's, and said: "You take care, Mrs. G, I don't want anything to happen to you. This is the first time since 'Nam that I've settled down and made friends and become involved in their lives. You and Ben and Justin are my Lahaina family, my fellow sleuths, so if you need protection or help in any way, just ask."

With that said, Nacho pushed his wheelchair back from the table, smiled, and headed off to work.

Justin watched his friend skillfully wind his way through the tables and chairs, and said: "Wow, I never saw Nacho get sentimental before. I know how much he loves all of us but he usually doesn't come right out with it like that."

"I know, Justin, it surprised me too; I am honored to be a part of his Lahaina family."

As she got up to leave, Helen remembered something: "What have you decided about using the cabin in Aspen?"

"Oh yeah, I meant to tell you. I talked to Ben about making reservations for mid-November which is fine with Ben's brother, since no one else is scheduled to be there. My brothers, Oki and Calvin, are coming too and maybe my cousin Randy."

Wednesday evening:

Olowalu is a wide spot in the road, just a ten-minute drive from Lahaina on the two lane Honoapiilani Highway. There's a small grocery store, a gas station, and a tiny gourmet restaurant on the mauka side of the road, and a handful of homes hidden by large trees, on the ocean side.

Back in the forties and fifties the kids of Olowalu entertained themselves by lying in the middle of the tree-lined road looking up through the leaves at passing clouds in the blue Hawaiian sky, moving only when an occasional car approached. Today traffic is nearly bumper to bumper, which has done away with highway cloud-gazing.

The original residents of Olowalu, the Hawaiians, left an interesting collection of petroglyphs on a nearby rocky hill. For generations people visited and photographed the fascinating stick figures, until vandals sprayed graffiti on the ancient site causing it to be closed to the public.

Keoni stood waiting for Helen and Ben at the end of his tree-shaded driveway. He waved, pointing out a parking spot next to his carport, which housed a pickup truck and small fishing boat.

"Hi you two, welcome to my paradise."

Ben shook hands with his friend, and Helen got a big hug. "Lead the way Keoni, we're starving!"

A one-story island-style house was set among the trees facing the ocean with a vast slope of lawn to a pebbled beach. The overhanging roof covered a large veranda, much like an outdoor living room, where Keoni's wife Lani, a tall rather regal looking woman, sat watching several children and dogs run and play on the front lawn.

"Lani, meet the infamous Ben and his lovely friend, Helen."

After introducing his 11-year-old daughter Sara, his nieces and nephews, and the neighbor kids, Keoni smiled at the children and said: "Scoot you guys, it's time to hit the books." They sighed, complained a little and finally gave in, receiving their hugs and kisses, then ran noisily off to take one last race around the yard.

Lani gestured to the wicker couch and smiled at Ben and Helen. "Welcome to our home. Help yourselves to some taro chips and my grandmother's special dipping sauce. Can I get you a beer or some wine?"

"Beer for me, and if I know Helen, she'll have wine. This is one beautiful spot! I love your plantation style house; mind if we look around?"

After Lani gave them a grand tour of the house, Keoni was ready to put the mahimahi on the grill. "What do you think of the place, Ben?"

"My friend, I think you are one lucky guy. What I wouldn't give to pick up my cane house and deposit it in a setting like this. So this was your parents home originally?"

"This property has been in the family for several generations. My brothers and I grew up here but since Mom and Dad died ten years ago, Lani, the kids and I moved into the big house, as we call it, and my brother Henry, in the ohana house over there down near the beach. My older kids, the boys, are away at school on the Mainland, so it's just the three of us now."

Is there enough time for Helen and me to check out the beach before we eat?"

"Sure, but don't get lost, you only got fifteen minutes."

Darkness was settling in as they returned to the veranda.

"Sit here Ben, by Lani, and Helen next to me. It's time we attack this handsome mahi, a very cooperative fish who almost leaped into my boat. It's grilled and lightly salted and I have some toppers if you're interested: a green papaya salsa, or dill-cucumber-yogurt sauce with green onions. The salad is Lani's creation. It's fresh fruit, grown on our property - all of it, right down to the sweet oranges and strawberries. There's saffron rice and fresh young asparagus from upcountry, and last but not least, the amazing wine you brought. Wow! A Haut-Brion from France! Thanks, both of you. Now, lets dig in."

After dinner Ben insisted on helping Lani with the dishes, so they disappeared into the house. Keoni turned to Helen, and said: "Here's your chance to interview me for the Windley story. What would you like to know?"

"First off, what was Larry like? What kind of a person was he?"

Keoni looked off into space, as though he were viewing the past. "Larry was an avid sportsman. He loved everything about the sea. He loved to fish, sail, dive, swim – you name it. It was a good life; lots of partying, drinking, and a little pot smoking, and a girlfriend or two."

Helen looked puzzled. "Hard to believe he ever had a serious thought."

Keoni smiled and said: "Oh, I have only begun to describe the man. Along with what I've told you, Larry had a serious side. Back in the fifties and sixties Lahaina was a very different place, still very much a sugarcane town with most everyone employed by the Mill, but the tourist era was right around the corner, we could see it coming. Larry was passionate about the history of Lahaina and was worried about the deteriorating condition of her historic sites. He knew the town had to move fast to preserve them."

Helen interrupted: "You guys were fortunate to live here when Front Street was lined with local stores."

"I agree. I remember, as a kid heading to the Lahaina Bakery in the evenings for malasadas and a Howdy Soda."

Helen looked surprised. "I have one of those little Howdy soda bottles in my collection. Orange flavored wasn't it?"

"Yep, best orange flavor I ever tasted, and only a nickel! That recipe was guarded well by the Lahaina Soda Works. Oh, and I remember fry soup! That was such a treat; just a dime at Liberty Restaurant."

"What's fry soup?"

"Local name for Chow fun. Ah, those were the days . . . before the big grocery chains and discount stores ever dreamed of coming here. There wasn't much in the way of entertainment or nightlife, although there were two theaters, the Queen's on Front Street and the Lahaina Theater next to the Pioneer Hotel. There was a bowling alley in back of the Baldwin Home and a court for soccer and basketball in Campbell Park, right next-door."

"Was there ever any unusual excitement?"

"Once in a while something out of the ordinary would happen. I remember when the movie "Twilight of the Gods" with Rock Hudson was filmed in Lahaina . . . in the forties, I think. And who could ever forget Whale Spree! Larry headed the annual event for a couple of years. All of us guys were involved in the beard-growing contest and seeing how much beer we could consume. One year Richard Boone was the honorary Commodore, and Hawaii Calls, the radio show, was here along with the Marine Band and lots of homegrown entertainment. It was wild and fun until hippies arrived with drugs. The police thought there might be some major problems, so they cancelled Whale Spree. Most of the time, though, people made their own fun by getting together with family and friends for a luau or picnic. Life was simpler then."

"I heard that Larry lived upstairs in the Master's Reading Room, where my office is."

"Yeah he did for a short time, and he developed a love for that old stone building, as well as for the missionary house next-door. Even before his accident he began to organize a group of concerned people in an effort to raise money to restore the old buildings before they crumbled away."

"He was the first unofficial director of RAPS." Helen said. "I found a newspaper article from the 1963 Maui News about the restoration of the missionary house, which included a picture of Larry."

"Excuse me for a second, Helen, I'm going to get us some coffee."

When Keoni returned, he had two mugs of Kona coffee, and some of Lani's fresh baked coconut cookies. "Try one of these macaroons, Lani's a fabulous cookie-maker. Now where were we?"

"I guess we were in the 1960's, probably after Larry's accident."

"He got the bends in 1959 after diving more than 200 feet deep. I remember him telling me about being in the decompression chamber. He said: '*I had a lot of pain; so much pain it was incredible. I kept thinking that I've got to keep breathing, if I stop, I'm pau.*'

For a while he was paralyzed, with little hope of recovery, but he worked hard to revive his muscles. Slowly and painfully he regained the use a toe, then his legs, and then he began walking. But he was never able to resume many of his former physical activities, including diving. We all wondered what he would do with the energy he'd expended on sports, but he never looked back as far as I could tell. Before we could even worry about him, he got some lady friends together and they all headed to Oahu to the Mission Society, Historic Society, Archives, and the University Library, where they hunted down Lahaina history like they were after gold."

Munching on her second cookie, Helen asked Keoni: "What was it like when you two lived on the beach near 505?"

"That was one of the best times of my life. Larry and I shared a small cottage there, along with various ladies from time to time. We cooked whatever fish we caught over a fire on the beach, and then we'd drink some beer and talk story with the rest of the diving gang, who generally dropped by in the evenings. We had amazing conversations about Hawaiian history, the state of the old buildings, and about the stars and navigation . . . about everything at one time or another, I guess. There was a hammock tied between two trees near the beach and half the time I spent the night there, under the stars."

"Was Larry born in Hawaii?"

"No. He was originally from North Carolina. He came here in 1957 after a stint in Korea as a Marine in the Special Forces."

"Just one other question for now, do you know Hans Albright? Ben and I met him at Hula Hans Sandwich Island Treasures a few days ago."

"I know him. Known him for years, although we're not close."

"He said he knew Larry and knew about his work, gathering historic information. He said Larry was a hell of a diver."

"I don't want to dig up bad memories, Helen, so I will just say that Hans, and especially his brothers, are basically bad news."

Lani and Ben returned to the veranda; Lani giggling and shaking her head.

"What's so funny, Lani?" Keoni asked.

"Ben's been telling me stories about his volunteers at the Visitor Center and about a hilarious scam when he pretended to be a TV cameraman, and about Helen's cat."

"What's so funny about your cat, Helen?"

Before she could answer, Ben said: "It's not that the cat is so funny, it's the way women react to him. They either want to baby him or they're scared out of their wits by some little rodent he brings home."

"That's not fair!" Giving Ben a stern look, Helen continued. "I take it you didn't bother to tell Lani about Mambo locating the wallet that was a major clue to a murder - or about how he attacked the murderer, thus saving his life and mine."

Lani's eyes widened. "Wow, that sounds like some super cat to me!"

"Yes he is," Helen said, "and someday I'll tell you all about him, but right now I think we had better head for home. It's been such a delightful evening. Thanks Keoni, for sharing your memories with me. You've inspired me to document the history of Front Street during the Plantation Era. Thank you both so much for this special evening"

"Indeed!" Ben added as he gave Lani a hug. "Keoni, you are a master chef."

"Thanks, Ben. How about we head out early Saturday morning for some serious fishing?"

CHAPTER 5.

Thursday, October 21st

Ben dropped Helen off at RAPS, and headed his van to the highway for the thirty-minute drive to southwest Maui, excited to spend the day at the new Kihei Visitor Information Center. The lovely little building had turned out just as he pictured it would: roomy enough for a gift shop, restrooms and a small office, and surrounded by a wide veranda lined with benches. Today as he drove in, visitors were sitting in the shade looking at maps and brochures and planning their day. He smiled as he recalled the time he first showed the site to Helen, and they had laughed about the crumbling gas station that formerly inhabited the place.

Meanwhile, back in Lahaina, Helen sat staring at her blank computer screen, contemplating what life was like in Lahaina 40 years ago. She had almost enough information to finish the Windley story . . . just one more phone call to make.

"Hello, Mr. Albright? This is Helen Grant. - - Okay, Hans it is. Would it be convenient for me to drop by for a quick interview about Larry Windley today? - - Ten o'clock would be fine. Thanks, Hans."

Hans greeted Helen with a smile. Leaving his clerk in charge of the store, he said: "Come, Helen, let's head through the back room to my secret patio and try to catch a breeze from the ocean."

"Thanks Hans. I appreciate you taking the time to share some memories about Larry."

"That seems like such a long time ago, and yet in many ways the years have flown by. Let's see . . . I knew Larry way back in the 50's when a bunch of us began diving for black coral. I guess you could say we were a little crazy but we were young and thought nothing bad would ever happen to us. You probably know that Larry got a serious case of bends. Some of the other divers got the bends too, but nothing as horrific as what happened to Larry. But I remember good times too, like when he caught a big sea bass in Honokokua Bay. The thing weighed 345 pounds and was seven and a half feet long. Maybe if I scrounge around I can find that snapshot of it. It shows the bass and a bunch of us guys in front of the Pioneer Inn. That was about the same time we helped with the underwater filming of a John Hall movie . . .can't remember the name of it."

"Did he ever talk about his family?"

"Not much. I know he was from the south, but that's about all I know. We weren't terribly close. He ran around with Keoni Sanford and some other local guys. None of them liked my family, especially my brothers, Morton and Holden. I admit they're a couple of losers, but they are my brothers so I've always tried to help them out."

"So you weren't involved in the historical work going on at that time?"

"No. It never really interested me at all. All I thought about at that time was diving and fishing."

"Thanks Hans, you've been most helpful. I won't use up any more of your time, although I think I'll take a look at one of your hula lamps while I'm here."

Helen spent the rest of the afternoon finishing up the Windley story. Both Keoni and Hans had added some nice human-interest touches, and she was quite pleased with the result. Hopefully the local newspaper would be interested in printing the story. In any event, it would become a part of RAPS research material.

CHAPTER 6.

Saturday, October 23rd

Ben and Keoni headed out for their day of fishing, so Helen phoned Hillary, the first friend she made after moving to Maui, and invited her to join in the search for the Windley box. Hillary eagerly accepted, saying that she would pick Helen up in her big red convertible. An hour later they were heading up Lahainaluna Road toward the deep valley in the West Maui Mountains, with top down and wind-blown hair.

"Thanks for asking me along, my friend, it's good for me to get away from my art gallery for a while."

Hillary said.

"You are so welcome. I've missed seeing you for the past few months. How's business anyway?"

"Business is great. Right now I have a very successful showing of Hawaiian artists and a whole new line of jewelry. Personally speaking, things are great too. I've been seeing someone. I thought when Peter died that I'd never get involved again, but this new guy is intriguing. Just when I think he's too conservative and almost boring, he comes out with the most outrageous thoughts."

"Who is this fascinating guy? What does he do?"

"He's a writer. You and Ben know him, his name is Joe."

"Joe French?"

"Yeah. He said you guys have had some odd adventures together. How did you meet Joe? Do you know him well?"

"Oh, yes! Some time I'll tell you what I know about Joe French. Don't worry, it's good stuff."

Hillary looked puzzled, but settled for waiting until a later time.

"Helen, what does the Hawaiian word Pa`i mean? I know Hale means house, but what's a Pa`i?"

"Pa`i means printing; thus: Printing House. It was built a few years after the missionaries started Lahainaluna School back in 1831. The students, who were young Hawaiian men, printed all their books, bibles, tracts and newspapers in the Hawaiian language. A replica of the old Ramage Press is on display there now, and it actually works."

"So, it's a museum now?"

"Yes, and also a storage place for some of RAPS historical stuff. I'm on a hunt for a box of papers that I carelessly lost track of a few years ago."

They parked by the little bridge that leads to the front door of the old printing house and were greeted by Archivist, Carol Boxter.

"Hi Helen. What brings you all the way up the hill?"

Helen introduced Carol to Hillary and explained why they were there. Carol led them into the large main room, and said: "Before you get started on your search down in the basement, let me give you a quick printing lesson."

The little metal letters used to set up the page were stored in a printer's box on a long table along with rollers, ink, and paper. Carol explained that the box basically held only 12 letters; a-e-i-o-u and seven consonants; h-k-l-m-n-p-w, which make up the Hawaiian alphabet. She inked the set up page with one of the rollers and showed them how to tighten the old Ramage press and print one single page.

"It must have taken months to print out a whole book!" Hillary exclaimed. "They did engravings too? Look, Helen, there are maps and pictures of African animals!"

In the air-conditioned basement of Hale Pa'i, artifacts are neatly stored in boxes and bags with everything labeled and placed on shelves. Helen and Hillary went from box to box reading the labels.

"Look, here's a silver mirror, comb, and brush set that belonged to Charlotte Baldwin. I read about it in letters she wrote to her sister in New England. It was the only thing of value that she brought round the Horn when they left home. I would love to see it."

"Go ahead, open it up and take a look." Hillary said. "After all, it's survived all these years; I don't see how you could harm it."

"Okay, I will!"

Carefully Helen unfolded the tissue paper and removed the ornate little mirror. "This gives me chicken skin, Hillary, just to think that Charlotte Baldwin actually held this in her hands, 170 years ago. She was one of my favorite characters in Lahaina's history."

"Rev. Dr. Baldwin's wife, I presume."

"Yes, and the mother of his six children – eight actually, but two died when they were very young. They lived in Lahaina from 1834 to about 1868 in the old missionary house. I guess you know all about that, since it's just across the parking lot from your art gallery. He preached to a congregation of nearly 3,000 Hawaiians and he was the medical doctor for all of Maui, Lanai and Molokai."

"What makes Charlotte Baldwin so special to you?"

"Oh, most of all I guess it's because I identify with her as a mother. But there's so much more. Here she was, in a foreign place, so far from home and married to a man she met only two weeks before they sailed from New England. Fortunately it turned out they were made for each other and they had a long happy marriage."

"She sure spent a lot of time being pregnant. Makes us looks like wimps today, with all our high tech equipment, even sonograms that show us the sex of the baby. Charlotte probably didn't even have a hospital to go to."

"Right. All her babies were born at home. She was a tiny little thing too, and had terrible bouts with asthma, but she was tough. Along with all her family responsibilities she taught Hawaiian women how to read, sew, and make quilts."

Gently they replaced Mrs. Baldwin's treasures back in the storage box. After a half-hour search through the rest of the shelves, they had failed to find the box containing Windley's papers. Helen was about to give up when Hillary, who was down on her hands and knees, said: "Hey Helen, I found four boxes under the table labeled *Misc*.

The first box they pulled out contained a small sewing kit that had once been covered with velvet but now had only a few remnants of the original forest green fabric. Carefully they opened it and were delighted to find an ivory needle and a beautiful porcelain thimble with tiny roses painted on the sides. The next box was taped shut, but handwritten in pencil in the corner, were the faded words: *Keoni Sanford - (Larry's papers)*. Bingo!

Later, at Pacific'O⁵ restaurant at 505 Front Street, Helen and Hillary sat near the beach enjoying fresh crab salads. The trade winds had returned, lowering the humidity and clearing the sky. Looking out at the deep blue waters between Maui and Lanai, known as The Roads, Hillary sighed and said: "It's heavenly here Helen. Thanks for treating me to the delicious lunch."

"It's the least I can do for a friend so loyal she crawls around on her hands and knees in a storage basement. Wait! Wait a minute. Am I seeing what I am seeing? Look at that couple on the beach. What in the world are they doing?"

"Looks like they're setting up a hotdog stand! Isn't that illegal? Not to mention, tacky?"

"They look like a couple of tourists from the Mainland who are starting up business with just a card table, a small charcoal barbecue, and a pile of hot dogs and buns."

"They have pickle relish and mustard, too." Hillary added.

Out on the sandy beach between the softly lapping surf and the elegant restaurants the tacky, yet enterprising, entrepreneurs went about unfolding a few cheap aluminum chairs in a semi-circle in the sand facing the ocean. The male, a pale thin 50ish type, set a jar of mustard on top of the paper napkins to keep them from blowing away. Turning to the hibachi he gave his hotdogs a quarter turn and started unwrapping a package of buns, just as his female partner, probably his wife, slammed a case of soda pop onto the card table.

A line was forming, headed by two shapely girls in bikinis, followed closely by four surfer types who,

Helen figured, were more interested in the tanned buns than the hotdog buns. Behind the surfers stood a bearded man with a black dog that was wearing a flower lei and sunglasses. At the end of the line an obese family of four, Mom, Dad and two hefty pre-teen sons, all sported severe sunburns.

Smoke from the grilling hotdogs began to invade the restaurant area bringing loud complaints from the customers, but the busy entrepreneurs were blissfully oblivious as they handed the bikini-clad girls their hotdogs. Paying with a twenty-dollar bill, they waited for change but all they got was a nod towards the relish and mustard.

Quickly the surfers paid for their dogs, grabbed a couple cans of pop, and sat on the sand near the girls who were comfortably seated in the aluminum chairs.

Just as the bearded man and his dog were being served, three police officers arrived, including Chief Johnstone. Quickly they doused the charcoal fire, disbursed the crowd and began hauling everything away, while the confused vendors argued with them. Joining in the fray were the bearded man and the tourist family, all of who were hungry, tired of waiting, and angry. It was not a pretty sight.

After a lengthy discourse, the couple finally packed up their food, hibachi, and chairs, and trudged on down the beach leaving Chief Johnstone scratching his head. Spotting Helen and Hillary, he waved and walked over to their table. "Hi you two – mind if I join you for an iced tea?"

"Not at all, Chief." Helen said. "It looks like you let the enterprising entrepreneurs off with only a lecture."

"More like a warning that if they do anything like this again, I'll book 'em. I have a reason for letting them off so easy - and Helen, you are not going to believe this one - those people are Sam's parents!"

Later that evening . . .

"Hi Ben, how was the fishing trip? Did you and Keoni catch some big ones?"

"If you think a two inch by four inch striped fish is big, then yes. Since I was not willing to bring the cute little thing home to eat, I picked up some shrimp and a head of romaine in hopes that we have a lemon and some garlic. Why are you sitting on the floor? Why is Mambo rolling around in all those papers?"

"Dammit Mambo, Shoo! Now look what he's done. I've been trying to sort Windley's personal papers, but I guess Mambo thought I put them there for his entertainment. Sometimes I wonder what good cats are!"

"Here let me help you get things in order."

"Okay. 'Personal' goes here, 'Nothing Much' there, 'Unknown' here, and 'Plantation Era' there.

"Actually," Ben said, "I have a better idea. Since I wouldn't know 'Unknown' from 'Nothing Much,' why don't the kitties and I head to the kitchen, where I'll create a creamy sauce for the shrimp, toss a Caesar salad, and dish up some cat kibbles."

After dinner Ben set a small table between two comfy patio chairs facing the ocean. On it he placed the coffeepot, two mugs and a small tray of tiny pies.

"Where did you get those yummy looking pies, Ben? Don't even try to tell me you and the Kitties made them"

"I got them from a friend, a lovely lady, who baked them just for me."

"Oh."

Here, my dear, try one of the lemon tarts, they are perhaps the epitome of gastronomic experience."

"Mmm, you're right. Hand me one of the berry ones too. Thanks. Oh, and tell Lani the next time you see her that she's the best dessert chef on the island. Keoni is a lucky man!"

"So am I." Said Ben, "Thanks for being here. Thanks for being you."

"Wow! You are so welcome, and may I say that I too am thankful."

"What for?"

"For moments like this – for having you and Windy here with Mambo and me - and for the pies."

After a few moments of listening to the soft lapping surf and strange rustling noises in the bushes, Ben said: "Did you and Hillary have fun today?"

"Yes, it was a fun day, and also rewarding and it even contained an element of the unbelievable."

Helen related in detail the events of her day including the fact that Joe and Hillary were an item, which Ben already knew. That sort of took the fun out of Helen's story, but when she got to the part about lunch at Pacific'O^s and the hot dog stand, Ben shouted: "Sam's parents? Oh my God!"

"Is that your cell phone ringing? Oh, it's mine. Just a minute, I still haven't gotten used to this thing. Where are my glasses? Hello? – Oh, Hi Sam - - -Yes he's right here, I'll ask him. Sam wants to know if you and I can be at the Chinese restaurant near Safeway at 6 P.M. tomorrow. She wants her parents to meet her friends."

"Tell her we will be there with bells on. Oh, and ask her how her folks like my place."

"Ben says we'll be there with bells on, and he wants to know if your folks have settled in to his house okay."

"So, what did she say?" Ben asked.

"Sam said good and fine. Meaning it is good we will be there to meet her parents, and things are fine at your house."

"Okay now that that's settled, let's enjoy our dessert while you tell me about this Plantation Era thing you are writing. Why did Windley have Plantation information the box? Why wasn't it in the file cabinet with all the other historic information?"

"My guess is that he was in the process of adding that era to the history he had already collected, but died before he finished."

"So, are you going to add it to the Windley Files?

"Probably, although I think I'll take it a step farther . . . but I digress.

The plantation era began in about 1860. Whaling was declining because petroleum and kerosene were replacing whale oil; which is a darn good thing or we might not have any whales today! There were other factors in the demise of big time whaling too, like during the Civil War when the confederate ship, Shenandoah, came round the Horn and burned twenty-five or thirty northern whale ships in an effort to cause an economic slump. Then in 1871, thirty-one whale ships were completely destroyed in the Arctic when they stayed too long and got trapped in the ice."

Ben looked shocked. "Wow! Did everyone die?"

"No. Only one person died. All the men women and children on those ships walked across the ice dragging the long boats until they reached the shore There was enough unfrozen water along the coast to navigate their way south, where other whale ships picked them up and brought them to Hawaii."

"Lahaina must have been drastically affected by the demise of whaling." Ben said.

"I'll say! For forty years Lahaina had been a booming whale port, with most businesses tied to it, but by the 1860's there were only a few whale ships coming here. So all the whaling related businesses left town. Dozens of abandoned marine shops, grog shops, hotels and saloons closed, along with the market places, which put the Hawaiians out of business too."

"So, where did all the merchants go?"

"Most of them headed to Honolulu or San Francisco."

"Bummer! How about we have a little sip of brandy? Be right back."

When Ben returned, carrying two small brandy snifters, Helen was deep in thought, gazing up at the stars in the inky black night sky, distracted only slightly by the rustling noises in the bushes near the storage shed.

"Ben, I hope the kitties are just playing jumping games in the bushes, I'm in no mood to face a dead rat."

"Relax, Mambo's just giving Windy a hunting lesson, I don't think he'd start out with such a big project as a rat. Probably just a bug or something."

"Something? Like what?"

"Oh you know, like maybe a centipede."

"Swell. That's what I wanted to hear. Tell you what, If they come out of the bushes dragging anything - dead or alive - please warn me so I can go inside while you bravely stomp on it and dispose of it's body."

"It would be my pleasure. Now, before we close down conversation for the night and head to more romantic things, I want to know how Lahaina survived the end of whaling."

"Sugarcane was becoming a viable crop in 1860, so just at the right time Lahaina eased gently from booming port, to plantation town.

"Wow, I love history." Ben exclaimed. "Or maybe, I just love hearing you tell about history."

"I'll have more to tell after I check out Windley's info."

"Helen, I think it's time for you to go in the house." Ben said, as Mambo and Windy ambled onto the patio.

"Aren't you going to join me?"

"Okay, just give me a minute to get rid of the, ah, that little ole – maybe you don't want to know."

"Oh, gak! Is that a . . . never mind – I'm out of here!"

CHAPTER 7.

Sunday, October 24th

The vision of Sam's parents selling hotdogs on the beach would not leave Helen's mind. It was causing a gnawing feeling in the pit of her stomach . . . a warning? Was Ben's house in some sort of danger? Yes it seemed silly, but she just couldn't shake the uneasy feeling. So when Ben headed off to work, she cleared the breakfast dishes off the patio table, locked up her house and headed into town with a welcome gift.

Ben's house is just a few minutes away if you turn onto the highway, but Helen chose to take the scenic route through town, car windows down and sunroof open. Under the Banyan tree, the arts and crafts fair was crowded with Sunday morning shoppers. The Pioneer Inn looked freshly painted, its white trim glistening in the sun.

Caught up in Lahaina's magic charm, Helen momentarily forgot about her mission. Taking a deep breath of fresh sea air, laced with a slight aroma of fresh-brewed coffee, a smidgen of teriyaki, and just a touch of plumeria blossoms, she continued at a snail's pace down Front Street. Traffic slowed to a gentle stop in front of the Baldwin House while a group of newly disembarked cruise ship passengers crossed the street. Then a half a block later, just as she reached 10 mph, traffic stopped again. This time it was due to the unrelenting efforts of a driver trying to wedge an enormous van into an impossibly small parking space. No matter, it was lovely waiting next to the seawall, gazing at the incredibly blue ocean, the island of Lanai, and the humongous cruise ship anchored out past the reef.

It took her another five minutes to get through town, due in part to a group of Japanese tourists gathered in front of the Wo Hing Temple, taking pictures; some of them had backed up into the street to get a better shot. Noticing the stopped traffic they shyly smiled, bowed, and headed towards the old cookhouse for a showing of Thomas Edison's first motion pictures.

Helen continued the rest of the way to Ben's house, uninterrupted.

"Hi Mrs. Fields! I'm Sam's friend, Helen Grant. I came to welcome you and your husband to Maui with a fresh pineapple and some home-grown papaya."

"Homer! It's that friend of Sam's with some fruit!" she shouted. To Helen she said: "Come in and park your carcass. Want a shot of rum?"

"Oh, no thanks. I don't mean to interrupt. Were you heading to the beach?"

Just then a small wiry man, zipping his fly and tucking his shirt in, approached from the direction of the bathroom.

"Wha'd you say Flo? A friend of Sam's is a fruit? Mighta known she'd have a bunch of fairy friends."

"Shut up Homer, you putz! Grab the card table and take the cookies to the car."

"Going to have a picnic?" Helen asked, as she leaned back far enough to look into the kitchen.

"Oh, I see you've been baking."

"Twelve dozen brownies. Special brownies!"

Dismayed at the condition of Ben's newly renovated kitchen, Helen envisioned ten thousand ants marching four abreast to the sticky counter top.

"What are you going to do with all those 'special' brownies?"

"Sell 'em under the Banyan Tree, along with all the other stuff they sell there."

"Those are crafts that are sold under the Banyan, Mrs. Fields"

"Flo."

"Flo. You need a special permit to sell food in Hawaii. Perhaps I could find the name of the County Licensing Agency, so you can look into getting one."

"Jeez, get a life, honey. Haven't you ever taken a chance? Live a little!"

With that said, Flo and Homer piled into the brownie-laden rental car, and drove off, leaving Helen standing in Ben's living room wondering if she really wanted to tackle the mess in the kitchen.

Sitting at his desk behind the counter in the Visitor's Center, Ben was engrossed in explaining the rules of the Annual Poster Contest to his new volunteer. Helen stood in the doorway watching him as he patiently went over it one more time. He looked so handsome, she thought, and so refreshingly normal.

"Helen! I didn't see you standing there. What's up?"

He introduced her to the new volunteer, who then headed back to work.

"Did I ever tell you how much I appreciate you, Ben? What a wonderful man you are? How delightful you are, not to mention interesting, intellectual, funny and sexy?"

"Okay, what's going on? I know trouble when I see it. Come clean, lady!"

"Let me say that I am the last person to harp on cleanliness, or on intelligence, or the art of doing things right, for that matter."

"But?"

"But after meeting Sam's parents I just can't help being a little critical. I mean when I suggested she get a license to sell food, Flo said I should take some chances and get a life.

"Well that just shows you what Flo knows! After all, you've conned a preacher, made off with $30,000 that's not legally yours, lied to a murderer, impersonated a legal secretary and need I go on? Certainly these are chances you took, and are part of a life you have gotten. Sell what food?"

"They're selling loaded brownies at the Crafts Fair under the Banyan Tree. Flo baked them in your kitchen."

"Oh-oh!"

"I cleaned up the mess so you won't have 10,000 ants – or the DEA."

"Thanks. Aren't we supposed to have dinner with Sam and her parents tonight?"

"Yep."

Sunday evening . . .

The wedding celebrants were gathered around a large round table in the center of the Chinese restaurant, looking much like mourners. Woody, the groom to be, sat with his arm around Sam's shoulder watching Nacho and Justin as they tried to lighten things up with a toast. Three of Sam's friends from work were paused with their wine glasses ready to clink when Helen and Ben arrived. Ben pulled out a chair for Helen, gave Sam a kiss on the cheek, and said: "Hi guys! Woody, long time no see. Congratulations on your up-coming nuptials."

Justin poured two more glasses of wine and they all toasted the bride and groom to be.

"Sam, where are your parents?"

"In jail, Ben. Chief Johnstone said they'd have to stay at least until tomorrow. I warned Helen about my parents . . . they're loose cannons! Accidents waiting to happen! This time they got caught selling goofy brownies under the Banyan Tree."

Just then Chief Johnstone arrived. "Hi everybody. Sorry I'm late, and I'm sorry that I had to cast such a pall over this special occasion Sam, but I warned your parents when they set up a hotdog stand on the beach the other day that I would not be so lenient the next time. I hope you will accept my apology."

Sam smiled at the Chief and said: "I'm used to this Chief Johnstone. All my life they've been scamming and scheming to make a fast buck. Maybe that's why I took off for Hawaii when I got out of high school."

Woody stood up and tapped on his water glass. "Hey you guys, this is a special occasion. We invited you here because you are our friends, so let's order food and drink and get on with the celebration."

Following what turned out to be a relaxing and delicious dinner, everyone headed to the parking lot, laughing and talking about the vast array of Asian food they had just demolished. As Sam and Woody climbed into the yellow Ford, Chief Johnstone suddenly darted between Ben and Justin's vans and headed at full speed down the sidewalk, across the street and down the beach.

"What just happened Ben?"

"I'm not sure Helen, but I think someone was tampering with either my vehicle, or Justin's. Wait! Look here next to the door, I think someone was trying to break into the back of my van."

Nacho came over, parked his wheelchair, pulled out a flashlight and examined the scratches, confirming Ben's theory.

Justin was beaming. "James would be so proud to know that one of his 'children' just happened to have a flashlight at the time of the alleged break-in attempt."

"This is my headlight, my man. I've carried a flashlight since 'Nam, long before I met James, although it is sort of funny to imagine him beaming at us with pride. I miss that ole con man! Let's go have a cup of java at Pineapples and toast our old mentor."

"Okay Nacho," Ben said, "as soon as we've had a chat with Chief Johnstone, we'll meet you guys there."

Nacho and Justin were seated at their favorite table in the back corner of Pineapples, deep in conversation, when Ben and Helen arrived.

"What did the Chief have to say, Ben?"

"He caught the kid who tried to break into my van. Said his nickname is Perp, and that the name suits him. Apparently Perp has several minor misdemeanors on his resume. So the Chief, who is always willing to give a guy a break, lectured Perp and threatened jail time if he ever tries anything like that again."

Helen sat down and poured some coffee. "I guess it's useless to try to get that dumb kid to pay for the scratches on Ben's van."

"You know what I think?" Justin asked. "I think there are no coincidences in this world. I think that the break in at your office and your home are connected to this, Helen."

No one spoke for several seconds until Ben asked: "In what way, Justin?"

"Listen to this: A few days ago we deduced that someone was after something connected to Helen's work – maybe to her research. That's why he broke into both her office and her home. So, maybe this intruder figured out that whatever he's looking for might be in Ben's van."

"Perp?" Nacho shouted. "You think Perp is the intruder?"

"Not exactly, Nacho. I have determined that the double thief hired Perp to tackle the third job because he himself is not very good. I mean, think about it. He cut himself breaking into Helen's office, leaving smeared bloody fingerprints all over the place, then he nearly got caught in Helen's house and then he was attacked by a cat who chewed off a piece of his pants. On top of all that, he never found what he was looking for."

"Well," Helen said: "I, personally, am not comforted by the fact that the intruder is clumsy and inexperienced. This is getting out of hand. I do think Justin's on the right track, though. Here we are, a group of experienced sleuths noted for our innovative skills in getting the job done, so my friends, let's put our collective minds to work and catch the clumsy stupid thief."

Charged by the thrill of a new adventure, all four great minds clicked into gear at the same time, causing a positive charge that shorted out the electricity. (At least that's one theory).

"My God it's dark without lights! What happened to the power? Are you guys still here?"

"Where the hell would we go?" Nacho said. "It's. like the inside of a cow in here! I have an idea. Follow me!"

With his 'headlight' on, Nacho led the way out of Pineapples with Justin, Ben, and Helen following in a line behind him. They crossed Front Street, which was well lighted by car headlights, and ended up at Library Park where a concert was in progress. Tiki torches lined the shore, and due to the power failure, guitars were being played without amplification, giving the Hawaiian music a timeless quality."

"This is lovely."

"Sure is, Helen. I love it when the power fails."

A crowd was gathered, sitting on the lawn and humming along with their favorite tunes.

"Look, Ben; isn't that Keoni over on the right, playing a guitar?"

After the concert ended Ben invited Keoni over to meet Justin and Nacho, who were sitting along the seawall with Helen.

"You play a mean guitar - the music was terrific!" Nacho said extending his hand as Ben made the introductions.

"Great to meet you, Nacho. I've heard a lot about you . . .all of it unprintable! As for Justin, his family and mine go way back. How are you amigo?"

"Fine Keoni. Dad caught a big one and wants to brag, so could you give him a call?"

"Sure brah, be glad to. Hi Helen, you're looking lovely as usual. What's new with you guys?"

After they briefed Keoni on the latest robbery attempt, he said: "This is weird, you being hit three times. Seems like more than a coincidence to me. Speaking of which, here's another coincidence for you: Perp is related to Hans Albright. He's his nephew."

CHAPTER 8.

Monday, October 25th

"Ben, what do you make of Keoni's information that Perp is related to Hans Albright?" Helen asked, as she sat down at the patio table to watch him brush the cats. "By the way, did I tell you that Keoni said Hans and his bothers are bad news?"

Ben, who had a firm grip on Windy in an attempt to brush her tail, looked up and said: "Don't know what to make about Perp being related to Hans. I'm beginning think that the link to the break-ins is in the Windley information; it all began when you started looking for that box. Have you gone through all the stuff yet? What could be in there that someone would want bad enough to break in and steal?"

"Nothing so far. I'm in the process of checking out a small notebook; want to help? You aren't going in to work today are you?"

"No, the new volunteers are okay on their own. Besides, they have my cell phone number if there's an emergency."

"Are you finished brushing Mambo and Windy? If so, how about taking the cat hair out to the garbage can and getting them a snack - there's some tuna in the fridge. Then bring some iced tea when you come back? Oh, I think someone's at the front door – could you get that too?"

"Wait, I'll make a list so I don't forget anything. Would you like some caviar and crackers to go with your cold drink? Perhaps a small, but lavish, lunch of game hen and baby asparagus? Then for dessert, a few flaming. . . ."

"Sarcasm does not become you." Helen interrupted, as Ben headed towards the front door.

"Keoni and Lani! Wow, what a great surprise! Come on in. Helen's out on the patio. I just have to lose the cat hair, feed the spoiled, but well-groomed felines, and get us something cold to drink, and I'll be right with you."

After Ben set a tray of iced tea, cold beer, crackers and cheese slices on the table, Keoni observed: "You two have finally done it, haven't you?"

"It?" Helen said.

"What?" Ben asked.

"Moved in together, man. What did you think I meant? I mean jeez, everyone knows you did *that* a long time . . ."

"Keoni! You're being rude." Lani said, as she stifled a giggle. "I hope you don't mind that we dropped in unannounced; usually we call ahead, but Keoni has been worried about something and I encouraged him to stop by and tell you about it."

"Hey, Lani – no problem. You two are welcome anytime. What's got you worried, Keoni?"

"It's about Hans Albright. When you guys were over for dinner, I mentioned that Hans's brothers are basically no good. Now that you're having break-ins, and Perp is involved, I just can't get it out of my head that Hans could be involved too."

"Have you seen Hans lately?" Helen asked Keoni.

"Yes, as a matter of fact I saw him yesterday – even had a short conversation about the large Ahi that was caught that afternoon. Why do you ask, Helen?"

"I was wondering if he had a bandaged hand or arm. The guy who broke into my office cut himself pretty badly, judging from the amount of blood he left."

"No, I'm pretty sure he didn't. He was holding what looked like a shoebox in his hands, like maybe he was on his way to the post office to mail it. I think I would have noticed a bandage."

Lani was stroking Windy, who was asleep on her lap, and at the same time, petting Mambo who was sitting closely at her side. "What was in Windley's

box, Helen? Anything that would cause a break in?"
she asked.

Helen answered: "There were lists of repositories,
their addresses, phone numbers and names of the
curators, supervisors, or clerks; a list of local people,
and some personal notes. There was also a large stack
of organizational notes on the Files and a folder with
information on the Plantation Era; none of which seem
sinister. But I found a couple things in the box that
did peak my curiosity - a small notebook titled *Gayle's
Story,* and a sketch of a rather elegant locket."

Keoni suddenly looked up and said: "Gayle? If
that's the Gayle I'm thinking of, she was a real history
nut . . . a very serious sort of aloof person. I didn't
know her very well, but Larry enjoyed some long
historical conversations with her from time to time.
What's in the notebook?"

"I just started looking through it, but it seems to
have several hand drawn maps with big X's, and a
creepy sort of lament on the first page. Hold on and
I'll read it"

Helen reached for a small, orange spiral notebook
and read from page one: "*Almost gone, I leave only a
dim memory of my former self. Will anyone come to
my rescue, or will I crumble into oblivion? If only I
could be rid of my terrible secret I could die in peace.*"
Flipping to the next page she read: "*MRR was broken
into yesterday.* Talk about déjà vu . . . the MRR has to
mean the Master's Reading Room."

Ben stood abruptly, raised his arm, and with his forefinger pointed to the sky proclaimed loudly: "Hatchenschoozer!"

"Gazoontite!"

"God Bless you!"

"I didn't sneeze – I just gave you the name of an author."

"Hatchenschoozer, the author?"

"Right. He's the guy who wrote extensively about a series of break-ins that covered a span of 25 years. One particular house was robbed over and over. No matter who lived there, it was broken into at least once a year."

"So?"

"Well, I guess that's it. The break-ins at the Master's Reading Room reminded me of Hatchenschnoozer."

"Okay."

"Smiling sympathetically at Ben, Lani said: "I understand Ben, we all want to help. But I must say that two break-ins over a 30-year span, is hardly like one every year. Nevertheless I understand that you are probably thinking that if Windley's box had not totally disappeared for all those years, there might have been more break-ins. So, how did someone find out that the box had recently surfaced?"

Helen almost shouted: "Yes! That's it. You've asked the million-dollar question, Lani! How did the intruder know about the box surfacing recently? Who knew about it? How many people knew?"

They all sat in silence for a few minutes, sipping cold drinks, while Windy and Mambo wandered down towards the beach.

"Carol Boxter and Hillary knew." Helen said.

"Who is Carol Boxter?"

"You remember Ben, you met her at the last RAPS meeting. She's the archivist that works up at Hale Pa'i. That's where Hillary and I found the box last week."

"Another person who knows is my brother, Henry," said Keoni. "I told him the story about the box after I ran into you at Foodland. He's too young to remember Larry Windley, but he thought it was interesting that I had stored a box of papers for 30 years."

"That could be the answer to our question about how someone knew the box had surfaced." said Lani.

Keoni got up, stretched and began to stack the dishes, then remembered something. "Before we head out, I want to talk to you guys about something that has nothing to do with all this, but is very important. A bunch of us are interested in preserving an 1860 historic site that is about to be destroyed."

"You mean the Mill smoke stack, don't you?"

"Right, Helen. It's such an important landmark in Lahaina. Now that the Mill has closed down forever, it seems like some of its history should be preserved."

"I sure agree with that." Ben said. "Weren't you using it as a marker to locate certain fishing places when we were out on your boat the other day?"

"Sure was. It's been used for navigation by fishing boats and others, since 1860. The star that's lighted at Christmas time, is a beacon."

Helen frowned. "The first thing that needs to be done, is to organize a group of concerned people who are willing to go to work immediately."

"We're doing that now, Helen. I brought this up because I hoped you and Ben would join us. You'd be important members in our cause."

Both Helen and Ben agreed to help and even volunteered to host meetings, carry signs, hand out flyers, etc.

After Keoni and Lani headed back home to Olowalu, Ben and Helen hopped into Ben's van and drove up the hill to Hale Pa'i.

"Helen, what would you think of inviting Keoni and Lani to meet with us tomorrow morning for our brunch with Nacho and Justin?"

"You mean to discuss the case of the bumbling burglar?"

"Yes. I think it would be a good idea to phone Keoni and ask him to question his brother Henry, just as we are going to question Carol Boxter."

They found Carol giving a printing lesson to a group of tourists. "Hi, Helen. Be right with you."

Ben put his arm around Helen's shoulder, and they gazed out the window at the amazing view below. From two miles up the hill, Lahaina looked like a tiny village along the shore. The ocean spread out to the horizon, interrupted only by the island of Lanai, a smoky gray gem floating in the sun sparkled sea.

Ben broke the silence. "Once, back in 1980, I made a dreadful trip to Hawaii with my ex and her mother. We drove up here to see Hale Pa'i, but as I remember, it was condemned."

"Honestly Ben, I think your ex-wife must have been crazy! Maybe she got it from her mother. How could she have cheated on you? Well, no matter, that's all in the past . . . now you have me in your life."

"Thank God, Helen. I wouldn't take a single step back for anything."

"Wow, how romantic. Neither would I."

Seeming to hear strains of *Ode to Joy* played by a string quartet, they stood transfixed, in a warm embrace.

"Ehem. - - Excuse me? Hello! Could you two move over just a few feet so I can get a shot of the printing press from here?"

Instantly Ben and Helen obeyed the pushy tourist and wandered off, arm in arm, into Carols' office where Helen suddenly launched into another of her odd little historic stories. "RAPS restored Hale Pa`i in 1982, just a couple of years after you and ex were here. In the process they found miles of rat tunnels in the old stone walls; a massive collection of sticks and junk that nearly filled a Dumpster. After they dug out all the garbage, the walls were re-mortared and restored to their original condition."

Carol Boxter showed the last tourist out the door and joined Ben and Helen in her office.

"This must be Ben? I've heard so much about you."

"And? . . ."

"And, most of it good."

"Most of it, you say. What did you hear that was not good?"

"Ben, leave Carol alone. He's just kidding. He has sort of a peculiar sense of humor."

"That's what I heard."

Grinning at Carol, Ben asked: "Do you remember when Helen came here a few days ago to get a box from the basement?"

"Sure. Glad you found it, Helen. What a strange thing that is. Thirty years!"

"Yeah, it is sort of strange. I was wondering if you mentioned it to anyone."

"Well, let's see. I hardly talk to anyone except tourists these days. I am very busy with my work here. I live on the other side of the island, and with the half-hour commute each morning and each evening, I don't have much time to socialize. But I may have mentioned it to Tom the Restoration Manager. Why do you ask?"

"Oh, nothing serious. If you think of anyone else, would you please call me?"

As they climbed back into the van, Ben asked: "Where can we find Tom the Restoration Manager?"

"He could be at any one of the historic sites, but the best bet right now would be the Baldwin House, where porch repairs are underway."

Standing next to the Master's Reading Room, in front of the lovely New England-style Baldwin home, Ben shook hands with Tom O'Connin "Nice work you do, restoring these old buildings, Tom. This is one of my favorites. I love this old house."

"Me too, Ben. Imagine livin' here when there were no cars, busses, motor boats, or planes. It musta been so quiet; just the sound o' the birds, and the wind in the trees."

"Dream on, you guys. Twice a year, thirty or forty whale ships came to anchor here and hundreds of rowdy sailors roamed the town. It must have been just a little noisy then. And what about the gatherings of Hawaiians with drum beating and chanting? And horses galloping up and down Front Street? And dogs! There were so many dogs roaming the streets, along with cattle and . . ."

Ben interrupted Helen's speech: "Don't get her started Tom, or we'll be here all day."

"Looks like 9-0 has found a new friend. He loves to have his ears rubbed." Said Tom, smiling at Helen. She was kneeling next to a Benji look-a-like: a small light brown pooch with wiry fur sticking out in all directions. His lively brown eyes gazed at her with adoration as she continued to pet him and rub his ears.

"Is this the same dog you had last time I saw you?"

"No. I'm thinkin' you're referrin' to 8-0. She passed on a while back. Hit by a car, the poor wee thing. It nearly broke me heart. Once I began to feel better, I phoned the Kula farm where I had taken most of 8-0's last litter and after tellin' my sad story they agreed to let me pick one of the half-grown pups. He's a gem . . . just like his mother."

"So, did you start out with 1-0?"

"No lass, I started out with 5-0 when the famous TV series was so popular, so 9-0's me fifth pooch. The first three were beagles, then I found 8-0 who was pure mutt."

When Helen quit rubbing 9-0's ears he headed over to sit on Ben's foot, hoping for more attention.

"Tom, are you aware that I recently located a box of papers that have been stored for a long period of time?"

"Are you're askin' me if I know about Windley's personal papers? I've known for a couple o'years that they were up at Hale Pa`i. I'm in and outa the old buildings on a regular basis lookin' for bugs, rot, rats, and other of natures surprises so I often have to move stuff that's in the way. Consequently I see everything that's in basements, attics, and closets. Feel free to be callin me if you loose anything else, Helen."

"So Tom, have you discussed the box of Windley papers with anyone recently?" Helen asked.

"Carol Boxter mentioned your box to me, but no one else, lass. Why do you ask?

"Before we get into that, I have to ask you another question. Did you know Larry Windley?"

"I know *of* Larry Windley, but he was here before I moved to Hawaii. We have a lot to thank him for."

"How about Hans Albright? Do you know him?"

"No, sorry."

"Okay. Here's our little problem. Someone has broken into my office, my home, and Ben's van in the past week or so. Nothing was taken, but we've become convinced that they're after something in that box. So if anything unusual happens, like someone asks about the box, or you see someone casing the joint, could you let us know?"

"Casing the joint?"

"Excuse her Tom." Ben said. "She's become proficient in sleazy detective lingo."

Tom's eye twinkled. "Helen, you can count on me to be case'n all the joints for those dirty rats."

"Thanks, Tom."

"Home at last." Helen sighed. "It's sort of nice to have you and Windy staying here, Ben."

"Just sort of nice?"

"You know what I mean. I love having you here. Windy feels right at home too. Speaking of Windy, where are the furry kids? They're not in the bedroom or the closet. Did you try the laundry room?"

"I have looked everywhere. Are you sure you left them inside?"

"Positive. Check the washer and dryer while I look in all the kitchen cupboards. Those little devils! Where could they be?"

"Washer and dryer are empty. I know all of your windows have screens, so they couldn't have escaped that way. Ah! I know – the shower! They love to play in the shower."

"Ben, this is spooky. I just put out some fresh canned oysters. How could they resist a treat like that?"

"Canned oysters are not fresh. But that's beside the point." With that said, Ben reached for the switch that turns on the ceiling fans. As the blades started their slow wind up to full speed, Mambo flew north landing on the couch. Windy, with her landing gear up, slid to a smooth stop at the edge of the dining room table.

"Ben! What happened? Windy! Are you all right? Mambo, your tail looks like a giant bottle brush!"

"Looks like they're okay, Helen. Windy's shaking, but then I would be too if I just flew across the living room. These two goof balls were probably flattened out on top of the fan blades watching us humans search through every cupboard and closet, then when I suddenly turn on the fan, they blasted off."

"How did they get up there, Ben?"

"The only possible way that I can see is from the top of that kitchen cabinet. Unbelievable!"

It took Mambo and Windy a good ten minutes of intense cat ablutions before they were ready to dine on the canned oysters. By the time Helen and Ben settled down with a bottle of Merlot for the evening sunset watching ritual, the kitties were sprawled out on the sun-warmed patio, batting at each other in a lazy relaxed little boxing game.

"Lovely, huh!"

"Yeah."

"Helen, isn't Tom O'Connin a little old for restoration work? He must be in his eighties."

"Tom has a lot of help with the actual work, he mainly decides what needs to be done and then supervises while younger guys do the physical part. But he's fit for his age and he's a very talented restorer. He was responsible for a great deal of the fine restoration in San Francisco and Sacramento. We've been very fortunate to have him here in Lahaina. I think he intended to retire here, but just couldn't stay away from the old buildings."

"Helen, look at Mambo, he's sniffing your shoe like it's going to attack him."

Ben clapped his hands suddenly, causing Mambo to go straight up like a helicopter.

"That was a dirty trick, Ben. I think he's nervous because he smells d-o-g. Mambo hates them."

"You don't have to spell d-o-g – you could just refer to it as 9-0. Mambo would never catch on that you were discussing a dreaded canine."

Ben leaned over towards Mambo and said: "I'm sorry old boy, come here and forgive me." Mambo looked at Ben, sniffed the air and backed up two feet. Then, with Windy trotting behind him, they both disappeared into the dark bushes.

CHAPTER 9.

Tuesday, October 26th

"Pass the salt, please. Oh, and the pepper too." Nacho said, as he looked over the delicious spread of breakfast cuisine. "Thanks Keoni. We sure enjoyed your music in the park the other night."

"Mahalo, Nacho. The slack key concerts in the park are becoming a popular Sunday night event. We won't be playing next week because of Halloween, but I hope you guys will come back again in two weeks."

Justin pulled up a chair and joined his friends. "Good thing you guys came early, there's a cruise ship in; Pineapples is in for a busy day. How's the food?"

"Everyone nodded and said: "Great!"

After filling his plate with scrambled eggs, bacon and pancakes, Justin launched into his report: "I've been asking around about this guy named Perp. He's bad news, but not the worst news. By that I mean that he's never threatened anyone, used a weapon, or used any kind of physical violence. My nephew knows him from school. He thinks Perp is just running with a bad crowd and goes along with them to be popular. Seems he was beaten up a couple nights ago, and now he's in the hospital with multiple bruises and a concussion."

"Judging from the scratches on my van, Perp was fairly serious about getting inside. He may not be a violent person, but in my mind the destruction of personal property is serious."

"Yeah, I agree with you Ben. I was just passing along what I heard from others. So, what have you guys found out? Who knew about the Windley box?"

"Keoni answered Justin's question: "My brother Henry, Carol Boxter and Hillary Mason all knew about the box. Helen says her friend Hillary only mentioned it to one person, who did not pass it along, and Carol Boxter told no one except Tom O'Connin. As for my brother Henry, I told him that I'd kept the box for 30 years and how Helen had recently found it. A couple of nights later he was in the same bar as Hans and Holden Albright. They knew Windley back in the old days, so Henry told them about the box."

Helen gave her report: "Tom, the Restoration guy, knew about the box but he never talked about it. He's going to keep an eye out for anything suspicious at the Master's Reading Room or the Baldwin House, or any of the other historic sites."

Ben's cell phone suddenly went off. "Sorry guys, I meant to turn the thing off while we're eating. "Hello. - - Really? - Oh my God! - - Yeah, yeah. - - Okay - - Right. Thanks, Tom"

"Well," Helen said. "all I got from that conversation is that it was Tom with some shocking news."

"You asked him to case the joint and watch for unusual happenings, so he decided to call and let us know that he found a - - - excuse me, maybe I'd better wait until we've finished eating."

"A what?" they all shouted in unison.

"A bone – a human leg bone!"

After brunch Helen and Ben decided to take a leisurely drive to Kahului, where Maui County Hospital is located. They took the picturesque route through Wailuku, the lovely old town that is the seat of Maui County's government.

"I like driving through Wailuku," Helen said "with its modern buildings like the Maui County Courthouse mixed in with the old church, the Bailey House Museum, the tree-lined streets and the historic buildings along Main Street. As much as I love Lahaina, I have to admit that it's nice to be in a non-tourist town. It has a whole different feel to it. Remember when I was on jury duty and had to drive over here to the Courthouse every day for four weeks?"

"Yes, I do. There has never been a time when you were so quiet."

"What's that supposed to mean?"

"Nothing. I mean nothing. I just meant that as a juror, you were just following orders and not talking about the trial."

"It wasn't a bad experience at all. I learned so much about our legal system, and I enjoyed the early morning drive across the island."

As they turned right onto Main Street, Helen noticed that several of the old buildings were in the process of being restored. It was obvious that the community was serious about protecting its history.

"Let's park the van, Ben, and take a walk. We can start at the old church; there's an interesting cemetery there, and then we can work our way down through some of the shops."

An hour and a half later they pulled into the parking lot of the Maui County Hospital. They located Perp in room 203, which he shared with two older men who were watching a football game on TV.

"Perp? Hi, I'm Ben Anderson ... the guy with the van you tried to break into? No cause for alarm, I'm here on a friendly mission to gather some information. If I wasn't in a friendly frame of mind, I might be bringing you a bill for damages to my vehicle. But as I said, relax and let's chat."

Perp was far from relaxed. He was in pathetic condition, mostly covered with bandages like a mummy, with only a few patches of metallic magenta skin showing here and there. He nodded in a helpless and seemingly cooperative manner.

Ben continued: "Why my van, Perp? Were you looking for something particular?"

"Can't say." He mumbled through his swollen lips.

Helen patted his hand, and said: "You poor thing, I know it is hard for you to speak, so just nod if I'm right. Someone told you to break into the van?"

He nodded.

"This person wanted you to remove a box of papers?"

Again, Perp nodded.

"This person was your uncle, Hans Albright?"

This time he shook his head.

"Was this someone you know?"

An affirmative nod.

"A friend? - - No? Okay then, a relative?"

Reluctantly, Perp nodded yes."

"Okay, not your Uncle Hans, so maybe it was your Uncle Holden?" - - No? – What other relatives do you have? Sorry, I know your father is in jail."

"Let me try." said Ben. "Was it a man?"

Perp shook his head.

"A woman asked you to break into my van? - - Is she the person who beat you up?"

There was a long moment when Perp seemed to fall asleep. Then slowly, he nodded.

As they drove out of the hospital parking lot, Ben said: "I'm not ready to head home yet. How about you?"

"I have an idea." Helen responded eagerly. "Lets get some salads and head upcountry for a picnic."

Ben grinned and said: "Add a bucket of chicken and a six pack of cold beer, and it's a deal!"

On the western slope of Haleakala, up in Jacaranda country, Helen and Ben parked the van on the shoulder of the road and stood looking into what appeared to be an unused pasture. It was a lovely spot. The air smelled sweet and except for the trill of a chirping bird and the hush of a soft breeze, there was almost complete silence. Gathering up the bucket of chicken and the picnic basket that Ben always keeps in his van, they approached a formidable split-rail fence. Ben climbed over first, with the basket, then aided Helen, who was carrying the bucket of chicken, her purse, and binoculars.

Unrolling a couple of beach mats on the lush green grass of the pasture, Ben sat down, removed plastic plates and forks from the picnic basket and said: "Pass the chicken, please. I have to admit this was a good idea. I didn't realize I was so hungry until we spread out the food. Chicken goes really well with pasta salad."

"I know what you mean; the cool fresh air, and this fabulous view enhances the flavors."

With a drumstick in one hand and binoculars in the other, Helen pointed the chicken leg down the hill and asked: "What is that, anyway?"

Ben stared off in the distance towards the turquoise sea. "A boat? Maybe a barge?"

"No, I mean what is that growing over there, just over the hill?"

"Pot?"

"That's what I thought."

"Seems like sort of bad place to grow pot. I mean if we discovered it so easy, then why wouldn't the cops discover it?"

"Maybe they never come here for a picnic. Do you think we're on private property?"

"Sure, Helen. How could we be not on someone's property unless we were at a public park or on a beach?"

"Now I feel uneasy. What do you think we should do?

"I think we should continue with our picnic and forget we ever saw that field of whatever it is."

"I thought you said it was pot."

"My dear, I'm not sure I would know pot if I saw it. For all I know, it's some exotic herb."

"You mean like rosemary or oregano?"

"Yeah. Hand me a beer, please."

"Okay. What's that, Ben?"

"Huh? What? I don't see anything."

"I mean, what am I hearing?"

"Are you referring to that bleating noise?"

"Uh huh."

Ben looked around and said: "It's a sheep that's probably strayed from the flock. Look, it's just a little guy – probably only weighs 50 pounds."

"I think it's more like a 70 pound sheep. What if it has a whole gang of friends?"

"I believe that's called a flock . . . a flock of friends . . . or relatives.

Glancing at the wooly animal grazing peacefully with his back turned to them, Helen said: "It may be a black sheep."

"It's tan. I think one of its parents was a black sheep. It's probably just an adventurous sheep."

"You know what they say: Good sheep stay within their flock and do as the good shepherd wants."

"What about black sheep?"

Helen reached for a paper napkin, wiped the greasy chicken off her fingers, and said: "You mean like my Aunt Katillia?"

"Your alcoholic kleptomaniac aunt?"

"Yeah. I believe she qualifies as a black sheep. Do you ever feel like a sheep, Ben?"

"No. More like a springbok. How about you?"

"Me neither. I never wanted to be in a flock . . . it seems suffocating . . . too exclusive and similar."

"I know what you mean." Ben said, as he stood up and reached for Helen's hand, pulling her to her feet. "Okay here's the deal; you grab the bucket of chicken, the binoculars and your purse. I'll get the basket, the salad, and the rest of the stuff."

"Then what, Ben?"

"Then run like hell for the van."

"What are we running from?"

"Damned if I know. No time to find out – anything that snorts and has pounding hooves should be run away from, in my opinion!"

On the drive back to West Maui, Ben broke the long silence. "Well, that was exhilarating! I didn't know they snorted."

"You call that exhilarating? It was more like scary!"

"Did you get a look at what we were running from?"

"No, but it sounded like a 2,000 pound bull!"

"I agree . . . it even shook the ground!" Ben said. "I must say, I never knew you could run so fast - and the way you cleared that fence in one mighty leap - I'm quite impressed!"

Helen smiled, and they lapsed back into a comfortable silence for a while.

"Not to change the subject, but do you think we got the truth from Perp?"

"Yes, I think so. When I threatened to bill him for damages, it seemed to encourage him to cooperate. I believed him when he said it was a girl who ordered him to search my van. It must have been her who beat him up – maybe because he failed to get into the van. It must be humiliating to get beaten up by a female."

"She must be a frightening female! It's a shame he couldn't, or wouldn't tell us her name. Where to now?"

"Let's stop in Lahaina and see if ole Hans is at his store today."

"Good idea, I want to talk to him. I'm thinking about buying one of his hula girl lamps."

Standing behind the counter of Hula Hans Sandwich Island Treasures was a young female clerk. "Is Hans in?" Helen asked.

"No. It's his day off. He'll be back Monday. Can I help you?"

"Could I take a closer look at that hula girl lamp; the one on the top shelf?"

It required a stepladder to reach the heavy lamp. The young female clerk was upset that she had to drag out a ladder. This was blatantly obvious by the amount of sighing and mumbling of four letter words. After reaching the lamp she climbed down and, none to gently, banged it onto the glass counter.

The lamp, which was mostly bronze, was cast to look like the trunk of a palm tree. Leaning with her back against it was a ceramic hula dancer wearing a silky grass skirt, and holding a ukulele.

"Odd that she's pale and sort of blonde." Ben observed.

"I'm thinking that this lamp dates back to the 1920's when Caucasian women were the popular depiction of hula girls. They were created by advertisers from the mainland, and they appeared on cans of cookies, menus, sheet music and magazine covers." Turning to the clerk, Helen said: "Excuse me miss, but is the lamp an original?"

"Could be. I don't know."

"Thanks for your trouble," Helen said, "but I think I'll wait until I get more information about the authenticity of the lamp before I make a decision."

Out on the crowded sidewalk they found it was impossible to carry on a conversation, so they headed down the street to Kimo's deck for a cool drink.

Once the waitress took their orders, Helen and Ben both spoke at once: "Did you see the bandage on her wrist?"

"Oh, we're good! I mean really good! I tell you Helen; she's the one. She's tall, built like an athlete, and could easily have been mistaken for a guy the night I saw someone run across your patio. She must be the woman who got Perp to break into my van – the one who beat him up."

"Yes, I agree. Who is she? How can we find out?"

Ben leered – he had that really crazy look as he whipped out his cell phone and started to dial. The crazy look quickly morphed into a frustrated frown when he realized he didn't know the number.

"Let me look it up for you. Hula Hans? Be right back." Helen said.

Once again leering crazily, Ben dialed. "Hello you lucky winner! This is KRMP in Honolulu. Congratulations to you, the lady with the right phone number for the Pick of the Day Contest. Hold on to your hat . . . you have just won $500! Tell us your name, a little about yourself and how you're feeling right now. - - - Yes I suppose it is hard to believe - I can hardly believe it myself. - - Yes I realize you have customers you must deal with. Stay on the line for just a moment, Miss Lucille Wonnaku, and our secretary will get your address . . . the very address to which we will be sending your five hundred dollar check."

Ben handed the phone to Helen who, cool as a cucumber, said: "Miss Wonnaku, is that with a ku or a koo? - - And your address and phone number? - - Thank you Miss Wonnaku, and again, congratulations."

As soon as Helen clicked off the cell phone, Ben said: "So, where does she live?"

"She has a P.O. Box and an unlisted number."

"Oh, rats, I hate it when that happens."

Lucille Wonnaku hated being a clerk. She felt the world owed her a hell of a lot better life than that. Maybe winning this radio promo was a good sign. Five hundred bucks was better than a poke in the eye with a sharp stick! Maybe her luck was going to change. God knows, she had suffered enough lately: sliced by broken glass and nearly clawed by an attacking cat, or a deranged mongoose, it was hard to tell in the dark. Dealing with that little snot, Perp, was no picnic either. But at this moment, she felt as though her luck was picking up. Winning $500 seemed like a very good sign.

Once they were back home on Helen's Patio, watching the cats eat a bird, life felt more relaxed — more normal. "Sam's wedding is the 31st, isn't it?"

"Yes."

"The 31st is Halloween. I hope it's not a late evening wedding, I'd hate to miss the party."

Ben was, of course, referring to the amazing crowd of happy costumed revelers who gather in Lahaina every year to celebrate. The Halloween happening started years ago - it just happened - and each year since, more people appear. Thirty thousand showed up last year.

To accommodate the crowd, Front Street is closed to traffic. Then in the late afternoon a Keiki Parade kicks it off, with hundreds of cute costumed kids and their parents walking the parade route from the Jodo Mission to 505. When it darkens, the adults take over the town. Dressed as six packs, sharks, monsters, table settings, shower stalls, spotted cows, celebrities and other amazing things, they spend the evening strolling along Front Street and through Banyan Park to enjoy the music, food booths, and costume contest.

Also in town for the evening are eighty cops who mingle in amongst the crowd of revelers, keeping an eye out for trouble; but it's a mostly peaceful crowd doing what humans love to do most – have a good time!

"I'm not sure whether Sam's wedding will be in the evening or not. Things seem a little disorganized. The last I heard, her parents were out of jail on some sort of bond and she said they were going to take it easy and act like tourists, but somehow I don't think Sam believes them. She seems unhappy for someone who's about to get married. I think I'll give her a call."

Ben petted Mambo and Windy, who had finally forgiven him for turning on the fan and for consorting with a canine. "Here, use my phone then you won't have to get up and go in the house for yours."

"Thanks. - - Hi Sam, it's Helen, your maid of honor. How are the wedding plans coming along? - - Oh, really? - - - Yes, I know there is a world of difference, but - - - Sure, come on over."

"Sam's on her way over? How about I disappear for a while and let you two talk wedding."

When Sam arrived, Helen could see at a glance the tension and stress in her beautiful face. "Come sit down Sam, you look frazzled."

"You have no idea what it's like to try to please the Byrdes, who are, as you know, the most religious pious people on the planet, and at the same time try to fit my bizarre parents into this situation."

"I'm afraid you and Woody have extremely opposite parents. There is no way you can totally please either of these families, so I suggest you and Woody do exactly whatever it is *you* want to do."

"Well, Helen, we've sort of been trying to do just that. But Woody's father wants us to be married in his church, and my parents want us to be married while parasailing together. How odd is that?"

"What do you and Woody want?"

"We want to run away and elope!"

"Then do it. Head to Kauai, or wherever, and have a beautiful peaceful ceremony, without all the stress. Then when you come back we'll have a reception and invite the whole nutty bunch."

"Really Helen, do you think the Byrdes and my parents would ever forgive us?"

"Once they get over the shock I'm sure they will. They may be odd, but they love you and Woody."

CHAPTER 10.

Wednesday, October 27th

On Wednesday morning, as she unlocked the padlock on her office door, Helen noticed that the broken window had been repaired. After a quick glance from the veranda out across Front Street, she opened the door and was greeted by a frightening noise. A burglar alarm? Why hadn't someone told her about it? As she tried to figure out what to do, the beeping persisted in a deafening resonance which, she was reasonably sure, was only a prelude to the full alarm.

When this happened, Helen clamped her hands over her ears and ran out of the room. It was no better on the verandah where she stood with her hands over her ears for what seemed like an hour, but was actually only four minutes.

When the police arrived, she recognized the officer from that awful day when she and Mambo had been threatened by a knife-wielding murderer.

"Mrs. Grant! I responded as fast as I could. Got a problem, or are you just testing your new security system?"

Helen shouted over the extraordinary racket. "It's an accident. It would have been nice if someone had told me there was an alarm. Could you please show me how to shut the stupid thing off?"

"Certainly." He shouted back. "All you have to do is go to the box next to the closet, at the back of the room, and punch in your secret number. Then the beeping will stop. Be sure you memorize the four-digit code. Sorry you had to experience the full beep - let's hope it doesn't happen again."

"You call that beeping? It's more like blaring! It's enough to give a person a heart attack!"

"Well, Ma'am that's the idea. No intruder is going to hang around with all that clamor going on."

"So every time I enter the room I have to go through this stress? Swell! As usual, the innocent guy gets punished for what the guilty guy did!"

With her heartbeat back to normal, Helen turned her attention to the little orange notebook entitled *Gayle's Story*. It contained several hand drawn maps. Helen recognized one as the southern portion of the harbor area. On it was an X, marking a spot that now housed restrooms next to a small garden area. Another map showed an X in the Baldwin parking lot, midway between the house and Luakini Street.

Back in the 60's the Arbor Shops would have been in that location, but in the early 70's the shopping area burned down, nearly taking the Baldwin complex with it. Even today you can see the scars from the flames on the old Mango tree near the back of the house. Helen had seen some amazing pictures of that fire in the Maui News, along with a story explaining that it had been arson, with all of the shops a total loss.

Once again she read the lament on the first page of the notebook: *Almost gone, I leave only a dim memory of my former self. Will anyone come to my rescue, or will I crumble into oblivion? If only I could be rid of my terrible secret, I could die in peace.*

How dramatic, she thought, squinting at the tiny map. It was hard to make out, but she could see that an X was located between Luakini and Wainee streets, near Hale Aloha, which would have been in ruins 30 years ago. The once proud meeting house had been built after the 1853 small pox epidemic, when thousands of Hawaiians died on the island of Oahu. On Maui, the doctors, including Rev. Dr. Baldwin, vaccinated everyone, insisting that it must be done. Then they constructed a temporary village near Mala, where all visitors to Maui were held in quarantine. Thankfully it worked; there were only two small pox deaths in West Maui. In grateful thanks for their deliverance from the terrible disease, the Hawaiian residents of Lahaina built Hale Aloha.

The large thirty by sixty foot building belonged to Wainee Church and was used originally as a meeting place, then in later years as a chapel for English services and eventually as a school and community meeting place. After 1930 it began to deteriorate, until in 1940 it was declared unsafe. An attempt was made in 1947 to restore it, but failed due to a Kauʻaula wind that took the roof off, along with the steeple and the bell, which crashed to the ground. The same windstorm leveled Wainee Church, known as the Native Church, where both Rev. Richards and Rev. Baldwin preached to Hawaiians for over 40 years. Hale Aloha's bell has rested in the churchyard since 1951, and is still there today.

In 1973 restoration on Hale Aloha began; a major undertaking since the roof was gone and the stone walls were crumbling. The empty window frames looked like blank eye sockets staring out on the surrounding yard with its array of abandoned cars covered with vines and inhabited by rats.

Tom O'Connin and his crew managed to completely restore the old building to its original condition with the exception of the bell tower, which was finally added and dedicated in 1996. It's a perfect replica of the original tower, standing next to Hale Aloha like a lonely sentinel watching over the nearby cemetery. Perhaps one day the bell will be returned and Lahaina's residents will once again hear it chime.

Helen shut the notebook and put it in her purse, then headed out the door, taking time to memorize the code numbers and engage the alarm.

Tom O'Connin was under the Baldwin House porch, so Helen sat and waited with 9-0 until he crawled out covered with dust, dirt, and spider webs.

"Thank God there are no snakes in Hawaii." he said.

"Can you take a break, Tom? I have something to show you, and I need your expertise. How about I treat you and 9-0 to lunch at Pineapples."

Helen watched 9-0 curl up next to Tom.

"9-0 seems right at home here under the table."

"That's why the wee lad and I like to eat here on Pineapple's porch. No one seems to mind the dog a'tall. How can I be helpin' you, Helen?"

"Listen to this . . ." Helen read aloud the sad lament in the little orange notebook, then said: "Tom, this has to be referring to Hale Aloha before it was restored."

"Hale Aloha was one o' me biggest challenges. Twas a very sad mess indeed – and yes, I can see how it could spark a parson to write a sad epitaph, since it sure'n b'gory looked like a gonner. By the fate of the angels we had pictures of her and a copy of the plans to boot. So all the boys and me'self had to do, was to push up our sleeves and rebuild the entire building. The lads used as much of the original stone and wood as possible, and the dear old folks of Lahaina, who remembered Hale Aloha during better times, passed along their memories."

"About it's secret . . . did you find anything unusual there? Hear any legends or old stories about the place? Find anything unusual?"

"I remember one o' the men got really spooked about goin into the old ruins after hearin a tall tale. Twas concernin' a particular night, and dark as pitch it was too that night, when at the witchin' hour a blood curdling scream came from within the ruins. Legend has it that a wee dog sat there and howled for ten days straight after that. The police be searchin' the place for two days in and around the old building and amongst the old abandoned cars, but they found nothing. For many a year after that, no one went near the place."

"Tell me about the bone you found under the Baldwin porch. Was it from a recent death?"

"No, lassy, I don't think so. It looked pretty old to me, not ancient, mind you, but maybe 40 to 50 years. The crime lab is testin' it now. The nice tech lad that picked it up said it looked like it was from a female body."

"Have you ever found any other bones?"

"Oh sure, now and again they be poppin' up. Some are old as the hills, and we have 'em blessed and reburied, but others are more recent. I remember findin' parts of a hand over in the little garden by the harbor, near the new restrooms."

"Male or female?"

"They were thought to be female, as I recall."

Justin stuck his head out the door and waved a greeting.

"Come join us Justin, you know Tom O'Connin, don't you?"

"Sure. How are you Tom? We have your favorite Tonga pie today.

Can I interest you and Helen in a couple of slices?"

"Fruit salad for me, thanks." Helen said.

When he returned with their lunches, he pulled up a chair and joined them with a cup of French roast and two blueberry donuts. "What is that, Helen?"

"This is the mysterious notebook I found in the box. I think it's the object of the attempted burglaries."

Helen showed Justin the maps and the strange ode to Hale Aloha, and Tom brought him up to date on the legend of the howling dog and the old bones he had found.

"Hey guys, this is turning into a regular Halloween fright story. The only difference is that it's real. Do you think someone got murdered and chopped into pieces? Oops! Sorry, I forgot we're eating."

"No problem Justin, I have a strong stomach. Yes, I believe that is a possibility, and I also think it is possible that my office and home break-ins are connected to the murder."

"Holy Cow!" Nacho said, as he wheeled up to the table. "Did I hear right? It was a murderer that entered your house and your office? Well, this is going too far, Mrs. G., you have to protect yourself. You cannot be alone! You need protection."

"Don't worry, Nacho, Ben has moved in."

"No way! You guys did it? And you didn't invite me?"

"Relax, we have not done it. Ben and Windy are only staying with Mambo and me because it's so hot at his place and also because he's concerned about the break-ins."

Justin turned to Nacho and said: "This notebook is the key to everything . . . it's what the intruder is after. There's clues here, Nacho, clues to a big crime that happened a long time ago."

Toms' eyes were fixed on a spot in the center of the table. Looking up he said: "I have to be getting' back to me job. Thanks Helen, for the delicious lunch. You guys sure have given me a lot to be thinkin' about!"

After Tom and 9-0 left, Justin leaned over as close to Nacho and Helen as he could get and whispered: "Don't look around. I think the guy with the bandages, reading the paper at the next table, could be Perp."

Very casually Helen reached down for her purse and glanced back. "It's him alright. I wonder how much of our conversation he heard."

Wednesday evening:

"I'm making a curry feast."

"Sounds great Ben, can I help?"

"I can handle it, just sit and keep me company while I make my world-famous sauce. I guess it wouldn't hurt if you chopped a few green onions while you're waiting and put some peanuts and coconut in the sectioned thing. Oh, and you could peel and chop the hard boiled eggs while I get the lamb ready for the barbie?"

After porking out with two huge piles of fluffy rice covered with pieces of lamb, condiments and curry sauce, Helen was in a very mellow mood. I'm so full, I don't think I can get up for at least an hour."

"Then sit still while I throw the dishes in the machine and return with an espresso or two."

Over hot lattes they sat at the patio table, side by side, looking at the orange spiral notebook.

"So, Ben, what do you think?"

"I think that so far your conclusions are probably right. It looks like the X's are locations where body parts were buried. By the way, is this Larry's handwriting?"

"No. I'm familiar with his handwriting. This handwriting looks feminine to me. Maybe it belongs to Gayle . . . it is titled *Gayle's Story,* after all."

CHAPTER 11.

Thursday, October 28th

The morning air was fresh, and the sky glowed pink from Kahoolawe to Molokai.

"This is probably the most spectacular sunrise I have ever seen, Helen. Come out here and enjoy it. The coffee can wait."

After the last pink cloud faded to pale gray and the shiny pink waves returned to their normal aqua, Helen and Ben sat down to blueberry muffins and fresh brewed coffee.

"So, what did you think of the sunrise?"

"It was okay."

"Just okay? I thought it was splendid!"

"Well it was, until the part where Lanai turns pink."

"Yeah, I guess it was a little pale this morning. I think the cloud formations near the mountains have something to do with that – or possibly the amount of vog in the air."

"It's the clouds, I think. When they're not there, the sun peeks over the mountains and shines on Lanai, turning it that rosy color."

Ben leaned back in his chair and said: "Are you going to continue educating me about the Plantation Era?"

"I'm so glad you asked. Want me to read you a line or two from my story?"

"Sure do."

"Okay, it's still kind of rough, but here goes. It's a collection of human-interest vignettes from journals, newspapers, and from the recollections of long-time Lahaina residents.

Memories of the Plantation Era in Lahaina
1860-1960

1860: When the whaling ships stopped coming to Lahaina many businesses left town, shops, hotels, saloons and markets disappeared. Then, just at the right time, West Maui's first sugar mill began production. At first it was quite rustic, using three heavy wooden rollers that revolved together by the use of cogwheels, motivated by mules. In this way, the cane was pressed and the extracted "juice" was then boiled in tri-pots left here from the whaling ships.

In a newspaper article from 1874, concerning the temperance movement in Lahaina, it was reported that "plantation mules are in the habit of imbibing the fermented 'skimmings' thrown out from the mill. It is a common thing for them to be seen on Sundays in a 'beastly' state of inebriety."

In 1877 people in Lahaina were stunned to hear for the first time, a human voice transmitted over a phone line from Wailuku. That same year the first lumberyard opened across the street from the Baldwin home, where the library is located today.

It's hard to believe now, but back in 1878 Lahaina was becoming well known for its vineyards. The Malaga grapes afforded a "pure and healthy beverage to supplant the filthy compound known as Lahaina beer."

Immigrants from Japan, China, Portugal and Korea were being imported to work the fields, giving a revival to the businesses on Front Street.

In the center of town, Courthouse Park had a new look: a double chain fence, with the chains running through 6"x6" posts. It completely surrounded the park with a turnstile entrance at each of the four sides. The Banyan tree was very young then, and much smaller, having been planted only four years earlier. The new chain fence helped to protect the young tree from roaming cattle.

1897: Lahainaluna School was furnished with electric lights, powered by water. Haircuts were 10 cents. Men parted their hair in the middle, and wore celluloid collars on white silk shirts with blue or pink armbands, pig-top pants and long nightshirts.

Three times a week an inter-island steamer arrived in Lahaina, an event that never failed to excite the town. Most businesses closed so the proprietors could rush to the wharf. Here they joined a crowd of townspeople dressed in their Sunday best, and a line of hacks, horses and drivers. Some were waiting to see who would embark, some to welcome family members or friends, and others, to pick up their mail and supplies.

Chinese businessmen, identified by the long que (braid) down their back, operated many of the businesses on Front Street. These included several restaurants, groceries stores and laundry shops.

Native Hawaiians had kuleanas up in the valleys, where they were growing taro, sweet potatoes, vegetables, and bananas, and raising chickens, pigs and dogs.

Midnight horseback riding was a favorite pastime in those days. It was dangerous on dark nights, but everyone who owned a horse enjoyed riding in the light of the silvery moon.

On one Saturday night each month, the mill manager gave a dance for his workers. Waltzes, Two Step, Scottish, Virginia Reel, Polka and Masurca were played on an accordion by a white man named Johnsen, the only person in town who knew the music.

In 1898 there were only three Hawaiian grass houses remaining in Lahaina. The plantation workers lived on the plantation in separate camps for each ethnic group, with simple quarters and few comforts.

Occasionally one of the lunas treated the men poorly. It is reported that in 1898 a German luna drove the Japanese men like a herd of cattle down the steep road to the fields, to get an extra half hour of work from them. Sitting on his horse, he used his vicious dogs to hurry them along. Many of the workers were bitten, and before long the luna began to carry a revolver for protection. Although plantation life was rugged, with few comforts and hard work, the workers generally were treated well, and events like this were rare.

"Ben, you still awake?"

"Sure I'm awake. I find your story quite interesting."

"Want to hear more?"

"Uh huh."

Helen turned the page and read on:

The Turn of the Century

Arthur Wall was Lahaina's postmaster from 1898 to 1916. He was present on August 12, 1898, when Hawaii officially became a territory of the United States. On that poignant day, most of Lahaina's residents were gathered in front of the Courthouse near the flagpole. They stood at attention, softly signing the strains of Hawaii Pono'i, as Arthur lowered the Hawaiian Flag and raised the American flag. Following the ceremony there was a luau in the spacious courtyard, and in the evening, a dance was held on a circular platform constructed around and under the Banyan tree.

It had been nearly 60 years since Lahaina was the capitol of the Sandwich Islands, and 40 years since the whaling ships stopped coming. The turn of the century marked the 40th birthday of the Pioneer Mill; Lahaina was well into the Plantation Era.

Arthur Waal kept a journal while he was Postmaster, filled with vignettes and short stories with detailed descriptions. His writings have become a treasure to us today. He wrote: Lahaina had ten kerosene lamps, which were lit each evening at sundown by Charles Hoopii, Police Officer and Night Watchman in the sheriff's office. Four of the lampposts were located at the corners of the Courthouse square; four more along Main Street, (now called Front Street) at the corners of Prison, Dickenson, Lahainaluna and Papalaua Streets. The ninth was in front of the Lahaina Store and the tenth at the Wainee and Lahainaluna intersection. Occasionally they were extinguished by a kona wind.

There was no breakwater back in 1898; (that wasn't built until the 1950's) so there was a beach in front of the Courthouse. The wharf was about as primitive as in the old whaling days – one had to climb down the steamer side to small boats. It had been extended 50 feet in 1883, and in 1885 a regular lighthouse was erected.

On the Kaanapali side of the wharf, (Library Park) was the fish market. Moses Poepoe lived nearby, dealing in fish and poi and other Hawaiian edibles. Right around the bend in the road was the Japanese Shimura Hotel; Sing Kee restaurant and Bakery; Y. Sato fish market, and near the corner of Front Street was Goo Lip General Merchandise Store.

The Baldwin home was vacant, and had been for years. Inch thick dust covered the floors, but the grounds, with large breadfruit, mango and kiawe trees, were well attended. Stones from the ruins of Rev. Richards home next-door were being used for curbing along Main Street and to help fill in the drainage canal that would become Dickenson Street.

Hale Aloha was in bad shape and abandoned at the turn of the century, but Governor Hoapilii's home, built back in the 1830's, was well maintained and housed a family of Hawaiians. Also in good repair was the old adobe building near the royal taro patch, known as the house in which the preparation of the first Book of Law was made in 1844. This building was used later by Gilman & Co, a chandlery store supplying whalers, and then by the Pioneer Mill as a warehouse for sugar awaiting shipment by steamer to Honolulu. It was torn down in 1913 and replaced by Lahaina's first movie theater, next to the Pioneer Hotel.

"Ben, guess what I found in the July 8, 1905 Maui News?" Helen asked, and then continued without waiting for an answer; "An article about Arthur Waal that noted he was in San Francisco, where he purchased 135 bronze boxes for the Lahaina Post Office. The article went on to say that Lahaina had the best equipped third class office in the Islands."

Ben was smiling. "I'm always interested in hearing about the Courthouse. Every time I walk in there, I can almost feel the past."

"Sounds like you're catching history fever."

"If I am, I caught it from you, my dear. Is it fatal?"

"It's not fatal, but there is no known cure. Just rest, while I finish the turn of the century part of my story."

In 1901 Matt McCann's Saloon, Cigar Stand & Card Room was in business, along with two hotels: the Lahaina Hotel, and the brand new Pioneer Hotel, built by George Freeland. Among the businesses on Main (Front) Street were the Ka Maile Bar, owned by Judge Richardson; the Kalei Nani Saloon, owned by Kahauelelio; and a livery stable owned by Okamura. In 1901, Bismark Stables built a large livery stable in the rear of McCann's Saloon. People in Lahaina seldom walked if a hack could be had. Rego, the mail contractor, also had a stable and hack business. About this time the Saloon added a lavatory and bathroom, the water for which was pumped into a 1,000-gallon tank from a well on the premises, by a gasoline pump, which also supplied water to the road board for sprinkling streets.

The first motor cars had to bump along the rutty and often impassable roads; they caused quite a stir when they first arrived in Lahaina. It was noted that in 1904 "a GASOLINE OLD mobile came skinning through the streets of Lahaina . . ." Just a few months later Mr. Dow made it from Lahaina to Wailuku in one and a half hours, in his Ford Detroit motor car.

> *Lahaina organized a baseball team in 1905. At the opening of the league, the Pioneers downed the Ilimas, 9 to 5, and a good time was had by all at the first "wagonette" party.*
>
> *Jack London, former Queen Liliuokalani, and Teddy Roosevelt's daughter were among the prestigious people who visited Lahaina in the early 1900's. In 1908, five U.S. battleships of the 3rd Division anchored in the roadstead. Crews from all the ships were treated to a luau, set up on long tables around the Courthouse yard. That evening, a grand ball was held for the admiral and officers under the Banyan Tree, which was lighted for the first time with colored electric lights. (Power supplied by the Pioneer Mill.)*

"So that's about it for the turn of the century." Helen said. "Next is 1913-1915, but I'll save that for another time."

"I like the story so far. I never knew about the hacks and the . . . Oh, look, Helen, Windy wants out. I'm resting here in the hammock from my attack of history fever – could you get up and open the door for her?"

"Gladly, but one of these days soon I am going to give her cat-door-opening lessons."

Windy and Mambo hopped up on table and then onto the storage cabinet and stared down at Helen and Ben who were now engrossed in a more serious conversation.

From his reclining position in the hammock, Ben said: "After reading the little orange notebook last night, I'm wondering; what if the leg bone Tom found under the porch is from the same era as the hand bones, and what if they really are female bones? My God, what do we have here, a 35 year old chainsaw murder?"

"I think that's a little dramatic Ben, it could have been done with an ax. Coffee? Danish?"

"And an ax is not dramatic? Frankly I'm getting worried. Yes, both thanks"

"About what?"

"Well, for one thing, about Tom O'Connin. If Perp overheard you guys when you were having lunch on Pineapple's porch, then Tom is another person in danger. He knows about the bones, and he's old enough to have been here when the 'chainsaw' murder happened."

"He is old enough, but he said he came to Lahaina in 1975, nearly 10 years later. But then of course Perp may not know that. Okay, I'm phoning Tom right now."

Helen dialed and said: "Hi Tom. How are you? - - Fine? Oh that's great! - - Well, yes, actually I *was* calling to inquire about your health. Ben and I are worried about you being connected to this intruder mess. Yesterday this kid named Perp, who tried to break into Ben's van, was sitting at the next table while we were eating lunch. I didn't notice him until after you left and I'm not sure what he heard. - -Okay Tom. - - Pet 9-0 for me. – Bye."

"So, did he take you seriously?"

"I hope so. How about you climb out of the hammock, and we go check out your house? Sam's parents have been quiet and out of sight too long. I'm worried. Besides, I have to start planning Sam and Woody's reception. Maybe Flo will help."

Things appeared normal as Ben pulled his van into the driveway of his renovated cane house. A rental car was parked off to one side, and two other vehicles were pulled up on the lawn. "They must have company. I wonder if it's Sam and Woody."

"I don't see Woody's yellow Ford, or Sam's Mustang, either."

Flo Fields answered the door wearing a purple silk robe and carrying a crystal ball. She glared at Helen. "You sure have a knack for coming at the wrong time, honey, we're right in the middle of a reading."

"Reading?" Helen parroted.

"You know, lady, I'm beginning to think you're either stupid or grossly uninformed. A reading! Like as in Tarot Cards – fortune telling – clairvoyant stuff, you know! Either come in and be quiet, or leave."

Ben spoke up: "Since it's my house, I choose to come in. Wow, I haven't seen one of those since I was a kid. Look Helen, a shrunken head."

"Gak!"

Flo yelled at her husband: "Homer, get up off your butt and get some incense for these two." Homer, dressed only in his underwear, obeyed and then disappeared.

Sitting at Ben's pilgrim-style dining table were two couples holding sticks of burning incense. They seemed to be tourists, and were introduced as the Smallvales and the Middletons; names that seemed to suit them, Helen thought. To Ben they looked like nice, rather unassuming people who were holding incense sticks which were stinking up his house, causing him to wonder if the smell would ever leave.

Flo waited until everyone was seated, three on each bench, and then took her position at the head of the table. She swayed back and forth for a while, seeming to go into some sort of trance. It was very quiet until a low moaning sound came from the direction of the kitchen. Mrs. Smallvale shrieked, causing Ben to drop his stick of incense. "Oops, sorry," he apologized.

Flo continued in her trance-like state while the moaning grew louder. Then suddenly, bursting out of a cloud of smoke, appeared the form of a butterfly – or possibly a moth, it was hard to tell in the cloud of billowing gray fumes and sparks of fire.

"Okay, that does it!" Ben's voiced boomed out so loud that the startled group all got up at once, tipping over one of the benches.

"Out! All of you! Get out of my house!"

It only took seconds for the Smallvales and the Middletons to head out the door, with Flo in hot pursuit, shrieking something about them owing her $50 each. They ignored her as they hopped into their cars, slammed and locked the doors, and proceeded to dig deep ruts in Ben's lawn as they built up traction, finally speeding away.

Flo was steamed. "Really, Mr. Anderson, this is a crappy thing to do on the eve of my daughter's wedding. Does it make you feel like a big man to chase my clients away, and then throw us out in the street?"

Ben looked angry, as he said: "First of all, Flo, your daughter is eloping, as you know, so there is no wedding, and secondly I do not feel 'crappy' about throwing you or your 'clients' out, since you nearly burned my house down."

Helen was busy opening all the windows and making sure Homer was not on fire. His homemade wings were a little singed and smoldering slightly, so she took him outside and turned the hose on him. This brought a tirade of smutty words, which she ignored. Ordering him to stand in the driveway until he dried off, she headed back into the house where Ben was busy throwing clothes into suitcases. Flo sat watching him, smoking a cigarette and holding a glass of bourbon. "I never saw such uptight people," she said. "One minute you're Sam's friends and the next you're a couple of dreebs.

"I believe that's dweebs, not dreebs." Helen corrected.

"To my way of thinking," Flo spat out, "you're a couple of boring dreebs! It's no wonder Sam called off her wedding, she probably just wanted to get away from you two."

"I wonder where they'll go." Helen said, as Flo and Homer drove off in their rental car.

"Home to wherever they came from, I hope." Ben answered, as he righted the tipped over bench and started picking up the incense sticks. "As for where they go tonight, I couldn't care less. They'll be fine. Flo seems to be the world's champion scammer, I'm sure she'll think of some way to threaten some unlucky hotel with a lawsuit and end up in the penthouse suite. People like that get away with murder."

"I hope you're wrong about the murder part." Helen answered. "Are you still worried about Tom? I know I am. Now that Flo and Homer are gone let's invite Tom to stay here, where he'll be safe.

"Good idea, but first we need to calm down and collect our thoughts." With that said, Ben headed to the kitchen, wiped a long line of ants off the stove, and put some water on to boil. Fortunately the chocolate and marshmallows were in the refrigerator, safe from the pesky insects.

"Thanks Ben. Thanks for the comforting hot chocolate, for the tiny marshmallows, and for not telling me I'm crazy to worry about Tom."

"You're my best girl – my best friend, and the only truly sane person I know. Tom may well be in danger. He can move in here tomorrow and stay until we straighten this mess out."

"You mean until we solve a 35 year-old murder?"

"Yep. I'll phone Tom, then let's head for home and fix dinner."

After dinner, a delicious chicken Caesar Salad made with grilled chicken breasts coated with 12 secret spices, Helen sighed with contentment, and said: "Sunday is Halloween – what are we?"

"Two amateur detectives on the hunt for an ax-murderer."

"And what kind of costume does that inspire?"

"Well, let's see . . . a brown tweedy cape, strange cap with odd ear flaps, magnifying glass, and a large curved pipe with opium or something in it."

"Good Grief, Ben, you'd expire of heat exhaustion in a tweed cape."

"Oh, I wasn't thinking of me – I was thinking of you."

"Sometimes you are so weird. I know, how about we get some long twisted . . ."

"Hold that thought, my dear, while I get the phone. Hello!? - - Keoni, what's happening? - - What a great idea – that way you won't have to deal with all the .. . - - Yes, I am sure she will. - - Okay, we'll see you later."

"So?"

"So, Keoni said he and Lani would like to come here, park their truck, and walk into town with us Sunday night."

"Perfect! I don't know why I didn't think of that. That way they won't have to deal with all the traffic."

"They're coming as Sonny and Cher."

"This I gotta see, Keoni must weigh 225 lbs!"

"Okay, tell me more about this fantasy costume you have in mind." Ben said.

"I was picturing sort of a harem thing with little... What are you grinning about, Ben? You look evil. Did you already get costumes? . . . Say something!"

"Busted! Yes I did . . . and wait until you see them."

Ben rushed into the bedroom and rummaged around in the closet, causing Mambo and Windy to flatten out and travel in hunting mode to the doorway to see what they could see. Just as they arrived, the door slammed shut in their faces. Not willing to give it up, they sat down to wait.

"Ben, what's taking you so long?"

The bedroom door opened. Windy ran into the kitchen and flew to the top of the refrigerator. Mambo looked up, frozen in place. Only the tip of his tail twitched as the huge mouse-like thing stepped over him and walked into the living room. His green eyes turned black as they focused on the object, not in fear, but in awe.

"Bigfoot! You're a perfect Yeti – tall, lean, and hairy! But won't you suffocate in all that fur?"

"It's not real fur you know. And look, under the arms and in the crotch, and behind the knees, and around the neck – there are mesh air vents. I think I'll be okay - and if I glue some hair on my face, I won't need a mask."

"Puleeze don't tell me I'm going to be your bigfooted mate!"

"Sorry, they only had one bigfoot costume – you're going to be a Gray."

"An alien? Oh, I wish James were here. Where's my costume? Surely it's not in that little bag."

"Try it on, I can't wait! Your head is on the dresser."

When Helen finally emerged from the bedroom, Mambo ran to join Windy on top of the fridge, where both of them looked down on the strange scene below.

"Ben, I think the tights are the right size, but this shiny gray stretch top seems a little snug. Actually I think the mask will be bearable because it's so light - maybe it's made of some alien material. It has vents too, and I can see through the big slanted eyes."

"Never have I seen a sexier alien! You are the perfect height for a Gray – and those sneakers – what a nice touch! If I weren't in this fur suit, I think I'd get turned on."

"Take it off."

CHAPTER 12.

Saturday, October 30th

On Saturday morning when Ben saw the mess in Tom's apartment, he was stunned. "Tom, what happened? Your place is torn apart! I was afraid something like this would happen. Are you all right? Let's not worry about cleaning this up right now, I think we should get going. I'll feel much better when you and 9-0 are settled at my house."

It was very easy to convince Tom that he had to hide for a while.

"B'gory and all the saints, Ben, I never saw such a thing. Some bastard came in yesterday while I was at work, and tore the place apart and asunder. I tried to clean it me self, but me bones are just getting too old for this kind o'mess. Come 9-0, I've packed your dishes and your cushion, we're off to Benny's house – we'll have us a fine ole time."

Sitting at her desk in front of her laptop, completely absorbed in her writing, Helen was unaware that Ben had returned until he crept up behind her and whispered in her ear: "What could your face possibly look like, lovely lady? The backside of you is perfection. Your nape and shoulders are so smooth and tan, not to mention the curve of your . . ."

"My nape?" Helen interrupted. "You mean the back of my neck?"

"Of course I mean the back of your neck. What else could a nape be?"

"It's just that I don't want a nape. I hate that word."

"Okay, you no longer have a nape. You have a swan-like appendage on the opposite side of your throat, where your spine connects to your brain stem. How's that for romantic?"

"All right already, I have a nape! So, did you get Tom and 9-0 all settled into your house?"

"Yes. We were right to be concerned about Tom's safety. His place had been thoroughly searched and trashed. I was stunned when I saw it . . . gave me the creeps. Tom was pretty shaken up too; he and 9-0 were all packed and ready to head to my place. Once we got there 9-0 sniffed out every corner and acted right at home."

"Is Tom okay? I am so sorry he got involved in all this. Whoever is looking for the box must have thought Tom had it – or thought he had the notebook."

"I agree." Ben said. "What are you up to?"

"Still working on the Plantation Era story."

"Good, lets head out to the patio, get comfortable and you can read me the next chapter."

"Okay, I'll read the part about the time from 1913 to 1915. You ready?"

"I'm ready . . .shoot."

The Pioneer Theater was built in 1913, and what a thrill it was for the residents of Lahaina to be able to view the latest Hollywood movies! Across the street at the Courthouse, electric lamps were lighted for the first time, and south of town the Lahaina Armory building opened. The grand two story building was 100 feet by 60 feet, and sported a "capacious" drill hall, a stage on the main floor, and storerooms and ammunition rooms in the basement; all at a cost to the taxpayers of $10,000.

Across the street from Armory Park, where once the Royal Kamehameha's had lived on a small island in the sacred pond called Loko o Mokuhinia, trash was filling the stagnant remains. On orders from the Health Department, the old fishpond, along with all other ponds and the canal near the harbor, was filled with dirt. In former times mountain streams refreshed the ponds. But with the coming of sugarcane, the streams were diverted to irrigation ditches for the growing of crops. In 1914 the mill train brought fill dirt from Honokowai, traveling on temporary tracks laid through town. A steam plough spread the fill, and in 1918 the area became Malu'ulu o Lele County Park, sporting a ball field, and courts for basketball and tennis.

Duke Kahanamoku visited Lahaina in 1912, just after his record-breaking swim at the Olympics. The following year he choked an eleven-foot eel, that viciously bit off his index finger.

Two years later, in 1914, the Pioneer Mill built the grand two story building on Front Street, known as The Lahaina Store, where employees could buy everything from plantation beef to clothes, with credit numbers called bangos. It was an architectural marvel at that time, and sported one of the first elevators in the Islands. The grand opening was held at the 1915 Harvest Festival. That same year a huge luau was held under the Banyan tree for a visiting Congressional Party. The tree was decorated with a mass of colored lights, and hidden in its branches was the orchestra.

About this time plans were made to replace all the stores on the mauka (mountain) side of Front Street. The old shacks were to be removed, and the old fish market replaced with a new one. George Freeland, who built the Pioneer Hotel, was building a new garage, and L. Decoto, a new market.

"Then in 1919, disaster struck. But that's another story." Helen said, with a smile.

"Hey, you can't leave me hanging." Ben insisted. "What disaster?"

"Okay, here goes. It was:

The 1919 Fire

The big fire of 1919 destroyed all the wooden buildings along Front Street from Dickenson Street to the Lahaina Store, which was spared. Starting at Dickenson, those stores were: Yee Lip General Store, Sing Lung Fruit Store, Wa Sing Barber Shop, the Lahaina branch of Bank of Maui, and Len Wai Store, which suffered the biggest loss, $30,000. All of these buildings were totally destroyed along with the fish market across the street from the bank.

The buildings in what we call Library Park today were also destroyed; The Japanese Hotel owned by M. Shimura, Yet Lung General Store, the Goo Lip building, several small businesses, shacks and the fish market. Most of these had no insurance.

The Pioneer Hotel was spared, and even had customers who peacefully slept through the whole event. The Baldwin House was saved by Akoi, a young boy who climbed to the roof with a garden hose, shielding himself from the intense heat with a small table. He was able to keep the roof and cornices wet, and to watch for sparks and embers.

More than 30 separate buildings were destroyed by the fire, which started at 11:30 on Saturday night, January 4, 1919. Origin of the fire was set at the Sing Lung Co. fruit store. The Maui News reported that two weeks after the fire, Sheriff Crowell got a confession from two boys, members of a gang of bandits who had robbed several stores and were planning a bank heist. Malicious revenge towards the bank was thought to be the motive for the fire.

"That was interesting, Helen. Makes one realize how vulnerable a town full of old wooden buildings is. What's next?"

"A section called, *Before World War II,* but that will have to wait for another time. I'm hungry!"

CHAPTER 13.

Sunday Morning, October 31st - Halloween

"Let's head into town early, Ben, I want to see how Tom and 9-0 are doing."

"Good idea. Be sure to lock the place up tight, so Mambo and Windy will be safe, and let's head out."

After making sure that Tom and 9-0 had everything they needed and were comfortably settled into Ben's house, they all climbed into the van and headed to work. Ben dropped Tom, 9-0, and Helen off at the Baldwin House, then headed to the Visitor's Center for a busy Halloween day.

On the porch of the Courthouse he noticed three college-age boys in leiderhosen, knee socks, and Alpine hats, attempting to yodel at three tantalizing young girls in tight, skin colored body suits, decorated with a fig leaf or two. Behind the Visitor Center counter, Estelle, the new volunteer, had become an amazing Spanish lady with mantilla, black veil and a red rose in her hair. Estelle was no Marjorie Bayview, no one could replace Marjorie, but she was definitely developing her own style. Ben watched as she greeted a group of four customers who were all wearing puffed out pumpkin costumes and pillbox hats. They introduced themselves as Jackie O' lanterns.

Estelle responded: "Aloha nui loa, kanes and wahines, and Mele Halloweni."

Somehow her attempt at speaking the Hawaiian language was kind of sweet, rather than offensive. She did mean well, after all, and the visitor's loved it!

Just as Ben reached to turn on his computer, Keoni arrived with three young boys in tow. "Hi Ben, meet Groucho, Harpo and Chico."

"I can see by your large nose, moustache and glasses that you are Groucho." Ben said, as he shook hands with the boy, who tapped his cigar in a Groucho-like manner. Turning to a blond curly haired boy, who was beeping a very annoying horn, Ben said: "Harpo, I presume, and let's see . . . cone hat . . . Chico!" The boys liked the recognition, and smiled as he shook hands with each one.

"So, Keoni, what are you and the Marx Brothers up to?"

"We've come to town to help set up the stage for the costume contest. These are three of my best workers from Boy's Camp. It's hot work out there, so we stopped by to get a cold drink of water and say Hi."

As the boys ran off to the water cooler, Ben asked: "How's the camp doing Keoni? All I hear is praise from the community for the work you're doing with those boys."

"The kids are great. It only takes a month or two of paying attention to them and giving them something fulfilling to do with their time before they mellow out. I gotta tell you though, some of them are real hard cases when they first arrive. I've had to spend a few nights at the camp myself, just to be sure everyone is safe. When they begin to trust us, then I back off on the security. Once they meet all the animals, make friends, and get invested in growing some of the crops, they change. It's like some miracle."

"Congratulations. That's about the most worthwhile job I can think of. Is there anyway I can help?"

"Got about $15k? Our buildings desperately need repairs and we need a new 'fridge and a washer and dryer. We get some money from a county agency and donations from a few interested residents, but it barely covers salaries, food and other basics – nothing left for improvements."

"Could Helen and I come out some time and visit?"

"How about following me back this afternoon? You gotta get out of town before they close Front Street, anyway."

Traffic on the highway was heavy as Ben and Helen followed Keoni and the Marx Brothers to Boys Camp.

"I think they're turning off, Ben. I don't know how Keoni got so far ahead of us. He said the Camp is about a mile back from the road."

Keoni was waiting next to a small wooden shed with mesh sides, pointing at a parking place.

"Pull up here Ben, next to the chicken hale. We have about 30 hens, as you can see, most of them running loose. They supply our eggs for us. Watch out for the goat, Helen, he'll eat anything. I think he's eyeing your purse."

"Oh, isn't he cute. Just look at that face. Hey Charlie, let go of my purse! Whoa, I think he took a bite out of my checkbook."

"Here Helen, give the purse to me, I'll put it in the van."

With the goat following along, Keoni gave them the grand tour of Boys Camp. Spread out towards the hills were acres of crops: corn, tomatoes and a variety of squash, from zucchini to pumpkins. Five or six boys looked up from their weed pulling, smiled, and waved to Keoni.

"The boys eat about half of what they grow, the rest we sell to make a little money for movies and field trips."

"What's that over there?" Ben asked, pointing to an acre of plants where several boys were working, up to their knees in leaves.

"That's the lo`i – the taro patch. We have an irrigation system like the old Hawaiians used, built by the kids, who learned the ancient method of closing off the stream to flood different areas at different times. They love this project. Come on and I'll show you the bunkhouses and the main hall."

The bunkhouses consisted of two rectangular buildings, each housing 20 boys, ages 10 to 17 and two counselors who were part of the staff.

"Kimo!" Keoni called out to a jolly looking Hawaiian man with an ample gut, known in Hawaii as an opu nui. "Meet my friends, Ben and Helen."

Kimo greeted them with a shaka sign and invited them to come in and see the mess hall.

"What a comfortable place to eat," Helen said. "open sides, cool breeze and a lovely view of the hills and the lo`i. Oh, my gosh, you have horses!"

"We have three, and one on the way. They're our greatest extravagance; but as far as I'm concerned we get paid back double in pure joy for the boys. They love to ride. Most riding privileges have to be earned, and like the rest of the animals, the boys have to take care of them and clean up after them too. Teaches them responsibility."

"I see what you mean about needing a refrigerator." Ben said, as he stared at what was probably one of the earliest electric refrigerators ever made. "That thing must have come over on the Thaddeus with the missionaries."

Kimo cracked up over Ben's little joke, and said, as he wiped away his tears of laughter: "You want old? Come see da laundry facilities. I tink we inherit dem from King Kamehameha da Great." Dissolving into laughter again, Kimo headed towards a small outbuilding, giggling and mumbling something that set off yet more giggling.

"Jolly fellow, isn't he?" Helen said, as they followed along behind.

"Kimo? Yeah, he and his wife, Lelani, are the mother hens around here. They're totally devoted to the boys. They listen to their troubles, talk and laugh away their nightmares, and make them smile when they're trying so hard to be cool. Everybody loves Kimo and Lelani."

"Where do they live?"

"They live in a small hale in back of the kitchen area."

"How did you get involved in this, Keoni?"

"I was a teacher, Helen. Taught high school math for nearly 30 years. During all that time I saw troubled kids come and go. I tried to help them, and maybe in some small way I helped a few, but it takes a place like this to make a lasting change. So when I retired, I leased this property and started to build Boys Camp. Lotsa people helped; Lani, my kids, my brothers, and friends, too. It's been a labor of love."

"Do the kids here have drug problems?"

"No. They come from shattered homes where their parents have substance abuse problems, but we only take those boys who have escaped drug use. Dealing with addicts is a whole other scenario."

"Thanks for the tour Keoni. I think Helen and I better head back home and get ready for the annual celebration of ghouls and goblins. See you guys about 6:00 or so?"

"Helen, why are you wearing those neon green running shorts over your gray tights?" Ben asked.

"Tights look good on a 20 year old, but at my age I feel more comfortable with a little more modesty."

"If you say so, but frankly I think you look fetching in tights. Besides I've never seen a Gray with loud green shorts and sneakers."

"Stow it fur-face, I'm, wearing the shorts! I wasn't aware you had been seeing Grays."

Changing the subject, Ben looked at Mambo who was on top of the refrigerator with Windy, watching them with caution. "Hey guys, you don't have to be afraid of me," Ben said to the cats, then to Helen; "You know, Helen, Mambo looks like the perfect Halloween cat, black, sleek and mysterious. Windy on the other hand is too cute. She needs a disguise."

"As what, a dog?"

"Dog. That reminds me – someone has to check on Tom and 9-0. I tried phoning a few minutes ago, but no one answered."

"There's the phone now, maybe that's Tom checking in."

Helen answered: "Hello? - - Justin! How are things at Pineapples this spooky night?"

Ben stared at Helen who was filling the long silence with hand gestures to her throat, brow wiping, and heavy sighing. Finally, she said: "Oh Justin, this is so awful. I. . ." She burst into tears, and handed the phone to Ben.

"Justin? What the hell is going on? - - - Oh, my God!"

After Ben hung up the phone, he held Helen in his arms for a while, then said: "Helen, pull yourself together, we have to come up with some sort of plan."

Keoni and Lani arrived and were shocked to see Helen's teary face.

"What's wrong?" Lani asked.

"Sit down," Ben said, "and I'll try to explain."

Before he could start his explanation, Nacho phoned, saying that he was with Justin and so far things were sort of under control but they needed to know if they should call the cops or not. Ben said, Not.

Turning to Keoni and Lani, he swallowed and said: "Okay now, here goes. About a half hour ago, old Tom O'Connin came staggering in to Pineapples in bad shape – out of breath, and distraught."

"Wow, I know Tom. Knew his daughter too." Keoni said.

Ben continued; "So when Justin saw Tom, he sat him down at one of the tables at Pineapples, got him a drink of water and tried to calm him down. Apparently Tom was nearly incoherent, repeating over and over that someone had taken 9-0 and was holding him hostage. Then he . . . Tom . . . he died."

Everyone held their breath, while the awful news sunk in. Helen went into another spasm of tears.

Ben broke the silence: "I am sure there's a lot more to this. Tom's apartment was trashed a couple days ago, so he was staying at my place. We think all the break-ins are connected to a 35-year-old murder. Look, I realize that all of this is speculation, but the fact of the matter is that someone took 9-0, and in the process, Tom died. I vote that we not tell the police just yet, maybe if we put our heads together we can come up with a plan to save 9-0 and catch a possible killer."

Keoni and Lani said they would help in any way they could. Ben, who had his arm tightly around Helen's shoulder, said to her: "Let's go, Hon - you can feel sad later. We have work to do; so get your head, lace up your sneakers and let's head to Pineapples.

Taking the back streets through town, Ben pulled his van into Pineapple's parking lot on Luakini Street. Justin waved them in to the back. "I am so glad you guys are here. We need to do something."

Helen, who was now more composed, said: "We will, Justin. We're perfectly capable of coming up with a plan to get 9-0 back. Where is Tom?"

"Please don't gag, but he's in the freezer. I know it's sort of not proper, but I had to do something with him – I mean, he looked sort of dead sitting there in the restaurant and I was afraid someone would notice and freak out."

"You did the right thing Justin." Ben said. "Where is Nacho?"

"Right here, my man," Nacho said, as he entered the backroom from the restaurant. "I've been watching and waiting to see if anyone was following Tom. No one was. Come on, let's head to the back table and have a little conference. Shit! You guys look like you escaped from Disneyland!"

Once seated, everyone leaned in close, and in a soft voice, so as not to be overheard, Justin said: "I'll try to remember all the details of Tom's last . . er, I mean the time when Tom arrived here, until the time of his, uhm, demise. He said he walked as fast as he could all the way from Ben's house. He had tried to phone you guys but got no answer."

"We must have been at Boys Camp. My cell was in the van. How did Tom find out that 9-0 was kidnapped and not just missing?"

Justin answered: "Oh, yeah, he said he got a note – someone tossed it through the window, your window I guess, Ben - tied to a rock. It nearly scared him to . . . uh . . . I think Tom died of a heart attack, or maybe a stroke."

"The note." Helen said: "Did Tom have it with him?"

"I never saw it, Mrs. G." Justin said. "But I guess he could have it on him."

Nacho looked at the strange group gathered at the table with him, and said: "Okay Cher, you and the cool alien are out – this is no job for women. A 200-pound Sonny and a 6 foot . . . exactly what are you, Ben?"

"Bigfoot."

"Oh right, I should have known. Like I was saying, a 200-pound Sonny and a 6-foot bigfoot are already attracting way too much attention, so I think it wise if Justin is the one that heads into the back room to search for the ransom note. I'd do it myself, but I don't think I can navigate my wheels in the freezer."

Justin sighed, and stood up. "Hoo boy, I really hate this, but I have to do it, so here goes."

With that, Justin disappeared into the back room.

While they waited, Ben explained that he was going to the head, and because of the complicated back zipper in his fur suit he might not be back for a while. "Keoni, can I borrow that belt you're wearing? I don't have pockets, and I need some place to clip my cell phone."

"Lani, your hair is dangling in your coffee."

"Oh, thanks Helen, I've haven't had hair hanging down to my waist since I was a teenager; it was long and straight then too, but not orange."

Justin and Ben arrived back about the same time - Ben looking hot and flustered, Justin looking chalk white, and Nacho looking grim.

Nacho spoke first: "Is that the note you got there, Justin? I hope to hell it's a clue to the deranged shit-head that did this to old Tom."

With shaking hands, Justin unfolded the typewritten note. It read: <u>S. door C House 8pm tonight</u> <u>with notebook and $5,000 or mutt dies. Come alone.</u>

There was silence as the note was passed around.

"Okay," Ben said. "Let's hear some ideas."

Tentatively, Nacho led off: "The note says for Tom to be at the south door of the Courthouse at 8 o'clock; so someone could be disguised as Tom?"

Justin put in his two cents worth: "What if we surround the area around the south door and observe people until we see someone staring at the door?"

"How about looking for someone with a small brown dog on a leash?" Keoni said.

Lani looked thoughtful. "The person who took 9-0 and wrote this ransom note probably knows exactly what Tom looks like. There's a lamp post near the south doorway, so I don't think any one of us would resemble Tom enough to pull this off; even Helen, who is the closest one to his size."

"Yeah, Tom is small in stature, but . . ."

Nacho leaned in close and whispered: "Tom has to be Tom! Now wait . . . don't get all riled up here. Yes, Tom is dead, but he loved 9-0 more than anything, so he would probably want to take part in a plan to save him."

"Jeez, Nacho, this sounds like something from a bad movie. How the hell do we get a dead body from here to the Courthouse without anyone noticing?"

"Think about it, Ben – it's Halloween! Half the population out there looks dead. There are thousands of people, so it's not likely anyone would notice – maybe they'd just think he had too much to drink."

Justin nodded and said: "Nacho, maybe you could head upstairs to the courtroom; the second floor is a great place to observe the whole area. You could keep in touch with the rest of us by phone."

"That works. If you could position yourself on top of the old Fort wall, you'd have a nice view of the surrounding area, including Canal Street. We'll need someone on Wharf Street and someone milling around in the crowd under the Banyan tree, near the stage."

Lani raised her hand and volunteered to be the Banyan spy. Ben looked worried. "I'm leery of the girls being out there alone. Lani may be safe because she hasn't been involved in any of this, but Helen's not – her office and house have been broken into by someone . . . probably the same person who has 9-0."

"Don't worry Ben, no one will recognize me with my alien head on."

"I'll be perfectly safe, don't worry about me." said Lani.

"Okay then," Ben said, "that leaves Helen behind a car on Wharf Street, Lani under the tree, and Keoni and me as free agents to go wherever our expertise is needed."

"What about the police?" Keoni asked.

Nacho looked at Justin, who looked at Helen, who looked at Ben. Ben said: "If we tell the cops, they'll take Tom. They might even freak out and close down the Park while they hunt for the suspect. With thousands of people in town this would be a major problem for them, so the way I see it, we would be doing the police a favor to wait until Halloween is over before we talk to them."

"Justin, are you free to leave Pineapples for a couple hours?"

"No problem, we have a big crew on tonight. I think we had better get going so we can get Tom positioned, or propped up or whatever, at the south entrance before the suspect gets to the area. The sun's gone down. It's nearly 6:30, so let's polish up our plan."

CHAPTER 14.

Halloween evening . . .

Thirty minutes later a report came in to Police headquarters from Officer Jannola, a six-year veteran of Halloween nights in Lahaina. "Chief Johnstone, I think we have a potential drunk situation on our hands, approaching Library Park - - No, not violent, but unable to walk on his own. - - Well, there's a 6 foot rat wearing a white belt, and a 200 lb. hippie guy, holding him up. - - Yes sir, two, both female. One tall, with a long red wig, and a small Gray in gym shorts and tennis shoes. - - Yes sir, a Gray . . . an alien, sir. - - Whatever you say Chief. I'll continue to monitor the situation."

Supporting Tom between them, Ben and Keoni headed past the site of *Kamehameha's Brick House and across Library Park towards the Pioneer Inn, with Lani and Helen close behind.

"Tom sure is heavy for a little guy." Keoni said. "Watch out for that six pack of Coors, Ben."

Ben turned to glance at the three couples dressed as beer bottles, encased in a cardboard pack. "I see 'em. Don't look back, Keoni, but I think there's a cop on our tail. Let's head for that bench on the P.I. porch."

Once Tom was seated on the bench in front of the Pioneer Inn, Keoni pulled Tom's hat down so it covered more of his face."

"You better sit next to him Keoni, he's leaning to one side."

As Helen and Lani approached, Ben pulled them into the hotel lobby. "Come on you guys, into the courtyard."

"What's the problem, Ben?"

"It's really hard to talk to you when I can't see your eyes. Where are they?"

"Look right here." Helen said, pointing to the large inner part of the bulging black plastic eyeballs.

"Oh yeah, that's better. The problem is, we have a cop tailing us. You two will have to come up with a diversion to distract him while Keoni and Tom and I disappear into the crowd."

"Leave it to us, Ben, we'll think of something."

When Ben returned to the porch, Keoni and Tom were in a 'conversation' with Homer, one of the local

*See Maps

fishermen, who seemed to know Tom. "Tommy my friend, you sure took your fill tonight – you're not lookin' so good. I don't think I ever saw him so out of it, Keoni."

Keoni pulled Tom back into a straight sitting position, put his arm around his shoulder, and said: "Don't worry, Homer, I'll take good care of Tom. In fact he'll be getting a well deserved rest just as soon as we find 9-0."

"Surely 9-0 isn't running loose!" Homer exclaimed. "We've a leash law now, you know. Well, if I catch sight of the little pooch, I'll leave a message here with the hotel clerk. Good luck, Tommy."

As soon as Homer wandered off, Ben said: "My God, Keoni, why did you mention 9-0?"

"Didn't see any harm in it. I thought that maybe Homer had seen him tonight. Thank God it's totally dark now. Are we ready to head out?"

"Wait just a minute or two, I think our tail is about to be distracted."

Helen, with her head firmly in place, and Lani, wearing a sequined orange mask, covering two thirds of her face, approached the policeman who was eyeing the three men on the hotel bench.

"Officer! Oh, officer – please stop him!" Lani shrieked.

"Stop who, ma'am?"

Lani's massive feather fan was fluttering wildly, and she was making noises like she might faint at any moment.

"Steady ma'am – just tell me what's wrong."

Helen pointed her arm and forefinger directly at the wharf, and said: "A nude male dancer! There's a crowd of cheering onlookers, and there's even a guy playing a guitar to his bumps and grinds. Over there . . . right there at the end of the pier! Some people seem shocked by the nudity, but others are fascinated. Frankly I think it is obscene!"

"Your name and address ma'am?"

"Oh, I uh – I'm from Kansas. Dorothy's the name, Dorothy Oz…borne. Cher here is my Auntie Em – Emily Ozborne."

Lani's scream was so sudden and so loud that Helen jumped and dropped her cell phone. Pointing to Library Park, Lani shouted: "Look Officer- there he goes!"

Officer Gullabol turned towards the park where a crowd was gathering to hear the live music. Thinking he saw the backside of the non-existent nude dancer, the officer suddenly sprinted into the park, giving Cher and the alien a chance to head the opposite direction, where they melted into the crowd.

"Ben, I think it's going to be impossible to prop Tom into a sitting position on those steps. He'll fall over to one side or the other and probably topple off the stairs entirely."

"I know, Keoni; let's see if we can borrow Nacho's wheels."

With their arms around Tom's shoulders, Ben and Keoni carried him so his feet were barely off the ground and headed into the Courthouse.

"Man, I must be hallucinating!" Nacho said as they entered the courtroom. "Jeez, even in New Orleans during the Mardi Gras, I never saw anything that looks like you two. Yes Ben, you could have passed as Bigfoot, until you put on that hippie belt - and as for you Keoni, those classy plaid hip huggers are heading south, if you don't watch it you're going to have a butt crack showing. I think I'm embarrassed to admit I know you guys."

"Are you through, Nacho? Or do you have something else insulting to say to Keoni and me?" They set Tom in a corner and took a couple of cold beers from Nacho's cooler.

"Nacho, you have no idea how hard it is to get around carrying a dead body."

Nacho looked out the window with vacant eyes, and said: "I carried my dying buddy five miles through a steaming jungle in 'Nam – don't tell me what I don't know!"

"Hey! Hey you two, calm down." Keoni said. "We're all a little stressed out over this situation. Let's just remember what it is that we're doing, and get on with it."

Nacho looked over at Ben, and his eyes focused. "Ben my friend, I am so sorry. I just went off on you, and you did not deserve it."

"It's okay Nacho – I made a thoughtless remark." Ben offered his hand, and Nacho took it in both of his. Clearing his throat a little, he said: "Well, okay then, what can I do for you two?"

"Loan us your wheels for about an hour?"

Standing near the stage, Lani said: "Helen, I'm going to mingle here under the Banyan tree so I can observe people as they pass by. At the same time I can get clear glimpses of the south entrance, and the area around it."

"Okay, Lani, see you later. I'm on my way over to that Mustang convertible on Wharf Street. If you need me, I'll be lurking behind it."

Where were Ben and Keoni? Helen wondered. *Tom isn't positioned on the steps.* Just the thought of Tom made her tear up. *Oh dear God,* she prayed; *Please forgive all of us for what we are doing tonight. We really believe it's the best thing to do at this time. And Tom, if you can hear me, please understand.*

When she looked up from her little prayer, Tom was seated in Nacho's wheelchair at the foot of the south entrance stairs, hat pulled down over his forehead, his head bowed, and hands folded in his lap. He was alone.

Luakini Street was almost empty of people, and calm, compared to the outrageous mob of revelers on Front Street. Vehicles were parked along both sides of the narrow road, so she felt very lucky when a car pulled out of a parking spot near the Baldwin House. After maneuvering her large van into the empty space, the tall woman dressed in black swore silently to herself and climbed out. Addressing a small dog in the back of the van, she yelled: "Shut up! Sit, you stupid beast."

Slamming and locking the door, she donned a black motorcycle helmet and headed in the direction of Banyan Park. It was 7:35, maybe a few minutes early, but it was always good to be on the safe side. There would be time to check out the crowd, to be sure the old geezer was alone. Five thousand dollars and the notebook – this was going to be easier than she had thought.

Helen, crouched behind a green Mustang watching the Courthouse entrance, was totally unaware of the dark furry thing that was approaching behind her.

"Good grief, Ben! Are you trying to give me a heart attack? It's bad enough that we're engaged in this bizarre adventure without suddenly being hugged by a Sasquatch! What's up? Seen anything?"

"I see poor old Tom, and it makes my heart ache. I do not, however, see anyone watching him, nor do I see a dog that looks like 9-0."

"Should I stay here, do you think? Or should I move in closer."

"My dear, in that getup you are quite noticeable, even on this weird night, and there's no place to hide between here and the steps anyway, so I think you should remain in this advantageous spot."

"Well, that was wordy – a simple 'stay here' would have sufficed."

"I never realized how picky aliens are." Ben said. "Cute, though! I just want you to be safe - we have no idea where this person will be coming from. Trust me, you are doing an important job here. I'm heading back to the Ali`i room to join Keoni. See you later."

Ambling down Luakini Street, Perp spotted her oversized van. Being naturally curious, he peeked in the window and nearly had a seizure when a yapping dog leaped at him. The dog was frantic, clawing with his little paws on the glass and barking at the top of his lungs.

"Shit, you nearly scared the crap out of me. Can you breathe in there?"

Perp's natural love of animals caused him to be concerned about the condition of a dog trapped in a vehicle for too long without water. *It's like her to do something stupid like that*, he thought. He tried to see if there was a water dish, but found the van too dark. So, without a thought to the consequences, he broke the window with a rock and reached in to rescue the poor little pup. Cuddling him in his arms, they headed off towards Burger King.

No one paid any attention to the leather clad, helmeted woman walking down Canal Street. As she approached the old Fort wall, she pressed herself up next to it, nearly disappearing in it's dark shadow. Above her, on the top of the old wall, Justin watched the crowd of sharks, witches, jesters, piglets, Lego's, Mickey and Minnie, and even a peanut butter and jelly sandwich; all of them behaving in a normal festive manner. No one gave a glance at the old man in the wheelchair.

He dialed Nacho; "Agent Justin reporting in, sir."

"Sir? Hey, I like that! It fits! This *is* Command Central, after all, and the troops should show respect. What's up Agent Justin?"

"That your wheelchair, Nacho?"

"Yeah, it got confiscated. What can you see from up there on the wall?"

"No suspects yet, but I can spot agent Gray, to my left and Cher to my right. Sonny and the giant ape are nowhere in sight. How about you . . . see anything suspicious?"

"Hey, man, I think I do! Just below you and to your right, hidden in the dark, is a very still form. I'll keep a steady eye on it."

"Ben are you sure it's okay for us to be in this room? What is this place?" Keoni asked.

"It's called the Ali`i Room. Lahaina's kids put together all this information about the Hawaiian monarchy - the pictures and stories - visitors love learning about the Kings and Queens."

Looking out through the glass-paneled door of the Ali`i room, they could see the back of the wheelchair and could dimly make out Justin standing on the Fort wall, talking on his cell phone.

Ben said: "Keep a watch out, Keoni, I'm going to head to the other side of the building and see what's happening over there."

On the north side of the Courthouse, he could hear "Jawaiian" music floating from the direction of Library Park. Several small tents near the wharf were selling local food, and lots of happy ghouls were milling around eating and enjoying the music. Standing off to one side was a police officer talking on his phone.

"Officer Jannola reporting another unusual occurrence, Sir. About twenty minutes ago, Officer Gullabol chased a naked man through Library Park. - - No sir, the suspect was not apprehended. The unusual part is that even though there were two witnesses who reported the antics of this naked man, no one in the Park could remember seeing him. - - Yes. Sir, they were two females from Kansas, sir. An alien in bright green shorts and a tall Cher with a feather fan. - - Yes, sir, I know it sounds like the same two that were sighted with the intoxicated gentleman, but it hardly seems likely . . . . - - Yes sir, I'll keep my eyes open."

Perp had managed to calm the little dog, who he had named Freddie, by singing him a soothing tune and softly petting his neck and rubbing his ears. Burger King kindly gave him a cup of water for the panting pooch and a length of heavy string to use as a leash.

"So, Freddie, let's go check out the action under the Banyan tree."

As Perp and the small dog strolled down Canal Street towards the old Fort wall, enjoying the festivities, Justin spotted them. Quickly he dialed Nacho: "On Canal Street . . . a dog that fits 9-0's description is with a kid who has him on a leash. Can you see them?"

"Yeah, man, I can see them. The guy seems oblivious to Tom, but I'll tell the rest of the agents to be on the alert."

"Nanu nanu." Helen answered her phone.

"That you Mrs. G.? Nacho here. Check out the mauka side of the Fort wall . . . a dark form is lurking there *and* we've got a dog sighting."

"Ben? Nacho here. Where are you?"

"On my way to the Alii Room."

"Good. There's been a dog sighting just mauka of the Fort wall."

All of the agents turned their attention to Canal Street, with the exception of Lani who was busy observing the crowd of people seated in front of the stage. At the same time, unaware that she was being watched, the leather-clad woman stepped out from the shadows and slowly approached the old man in the wheel chair. He hadn't moved since she first saw him; he appeared to be dozing.

Leaning over the wheelchair, she said: "Where's the notebook, old man? - Hello! Wake up! Did you bring the money?" Just as she reached out to grab him, 9-0 broke loose from the leash and raced passed the Fort wall towards her, at full speed.

"Ben!" Nacho yelled into the phone. "Are you watching all this?"

"Yes Nacho, Keoni and I are very near the door. Phone Helen and Justin, tell them to hold off for a few minutes – let's see what this black clad person is up to."

Hearing the barking dog, she turned and was shocked to see the mutt racing towards her. Hadn't she locked him safely in the van? Frozen in place, she stared at the confused dog as he stopped next to the wheelchair and looked from her to Tom. Cautiously he put his front paws on Tom's knees and began to whine and make little yipping noises. Gently he hopped up onto his lap and licked his face. Then suddenly he became very still, cocked his head and stared at his motionless friend. No one moved; Helen, Nacho, Ben, Keoni and the leather-clad person, all watched as the little dog slowly turned back towards the black figure. Then, from deep within his chest came a low growl, his upper lip curled back, showing a row of sharp teeth - suddenly 9-0 wasn't cute anymore.

Justin, who had been silently climbing down from the Fort wall, neared the stairs just as 9-0 leaped and sunk his teeth into her leg. In extreme pain she tried to shake him off, causing the maddened dog to bite deeper into her flesh.

She was screaming and grabbing at 9-0 when something incredibly heavy hit her in the back, knocking her to the ground. In her bleary haze of pain she looked up, just as an enormous gorilla placed his foot firmly in the center of her back.

"Keoni, try to grab 9-0 without getting chewed up. Nice tackle, Justin!"

"Thanks Ben. People are staring. I'm going to get Tom out of here. I'll take him upstairs, and call the police."

Perp was filled with fear. He could see that she was involved in something really bad. Freddie was being held in a tight grip by a large Hawaiian hippie with a dark drooping moustache, and was barking his head off. He had to go to him and try to calm him. He straightened his shoulders, and walked towards the hippie and the dog, past a large bear and a cool alien, and a police officer who was talking on a cell phone.

"Hello Chief? - - Officer Jannola, sir. - - No sir. This time we have a suspected dog-napper and a dead body. - - Yes, sir, that's right. - - Apparently of natural causes, sir. - - Yes, sir, that's correct; their names *are* Anderson and Grant. How did you know?"

"Was that Chief Johnstone you were speaking to?" Ben asked the officer.

"Yes, Mr. Anderson, it was. He seemed to already know it was you and the alien who were involved here. He'll be wanting to talk to you in the morning."

Perp approached Keoni, who was still struggling to hold onto 9-0, and said: "I'm good with animals. Can I try to calm him?"

"Sure, son, if you think you can, but let me tell you he's a strong little guy. I think I'll keep a grip on him, but feel free to talk to him, or pet him."

In minutes, 9-0 responded to Perp's soft voice and soothing petting. Helen and Lani, who had given their names to Officer Jannola, were seriously trying to disappear before Officer Gullabol recognized them as the Ozbornes from Kansas. "Let's stand behind Keoni, that way we won't be leaving the scene, we'll just be out of sight."

"See that kid, Lani? I think it's the same one that tried to break into Ben's van - the one who got beat up and ended up in the hospital - the one Ben and I visited a few days ago."

Approaching the boy, Helen said: "Perp, is that you?"

"Yes, ma'am. Sorry, I don't recognize you. I guess you could be a man – it's hard to tell with that amazing alien head. I was just trying to calm Freddie. I love dogs."

Keoni shifted 9-0 so his paws were on his shoulder. Perp continued to stroke his back. "I found Freddie locked in a van without any water, so I rescued him, but just as we got here he broke loose."

"His name is 9-0." said Helen.

"Neat name! - - - Nine-oh. Suits him better than Freddie."

"What's your name, son?" Keoni asked.

"It's Michael, but everyone calls me Perp."

"Everyone but me, I'm going to call you Michael. So, Michael, do you think your parents would let you keep 9-0 for the night? You seem to be the only one he responds to."

"Well, I really don't have any parents right now. My Mom died a year ago and my Dad's in prison for eight more years, six, with good behavior. I've been sleeping at my uncle's house or staying with some kids I know who have a tree house."

Justin pushed the wheelchair onto the elevator and waited for the door to close. As the elevator chugged up to the courtroom, he felt a sudden and overwhelming sadness that the little old man in the wheelchair was gone.

"Here's your wheels, Nacho. I'll lay Tom on the floor until the coroner gets here. The cops out there?"

"Yeah," said Nacho as he easily moved from the chair he had been using, back into his wheelchair, "they've been questioning everyone and giving first aid to the skinny Darth Vader. Seems to be a woman."

"You still got a beer in the cooler?" Justin asked.

"By the time the medical examiner removed Tom's body, and the leather covered woman had been bandaged and hauled off in a squad car, and after everyone had been questioned, the whole tired crew headed to Pineapples. It was after midnight, the town was emptying out and the restaurant was closed for the night. Justin turned on a few dim lights and set out a bowl of fresh pineapple and some chicken, but no one was very hungry. Mostly they talked about Tom and how they hoped he was looking down and approving.

Taking a sip from a glass of ice water, Helen said sadly: "The only thing that I think Tom would not have liked about this evening, was that heart-breaking moment when 9-0 discovered he was dead."

"Ben put his arm around her and said: "Maybe 9-0 needed to know – otherwise he would always be searching for Tom. I think he'll be okay tonight with Perp and Keoni; they're staying at Boys Camp where 9-0 will have lots of loving attention."

"I think I'll head home." Nacho said. "But soon, very soon, we'll have to have a meeting. This is far from over."

CHAPTER 15.

Monday, November 1st

"Helen, take a look at this." Ben said, pointing to his rib cage, his arms, and his neck. "It's probably from sweating all evening in that Sasquatch suit."

"It's heat rash, I think. Stay put, I'll get some corn starch."

"Jeez, I'm itchy and you want to make a basting sauce?"

"When my kids were babies, that's what I put on their rashes. It worked every time.

"Oh."

Once Helen had powdered Ben in every single place where the angry rash had popped up, he began to feel better.

"Thanks, my love, you always know what's best. Although I do feel a little cheated. I mean, a rash of this magnitude certainly deserves something more dignified than cornstarch, don't you think?"

"No. Leave your shirt off for a while so the air can get to it."

Helen got up in response to a knock at the front door. "Justin! Nacho! Come on in. Ben's out on the patio."

"Oh my God!" Nacho exclaimed. "What are you now, Frosty the Snowman? No, that's not right, you're the ghost of Christmas past."

Justin, stifling a grin, said: "You look sort of pale, white man, and itchy!"

"Are you through? Can we get down to business? We are, after all, adults. I'm sure we can handle a little powdered medication."

"It's cornstarch." Helen said.

"Ah, cornstarch – yes, I am very familiar with its thickening properties, which create a smooth and glistening sauce. Be careful, my man, that you do not get wet and become glue."

"Okay, Nacho, you have had your fun. Justin, do you want to add anything? If not, then I'll put my shirt on and call this meeting to order."

"I just want to say, Ben, that Nacho may have a point – in this heat, the combination of sweat and cornstarch could indeed . . ."

Helen took this moment to interrupt with the news that Chief Johnstone was on his way over.

Settled at Helen's patio table with iced tea and cookies, Chief Johnstone sat with his arms folded, scowling at Nacho, Justin, Helen and Ben.

"What's up Chief?" Justin asked in a cheery voice.

"What's up? What's up? Why don't you tell *me* what's up. I knew you guys had been too quiet for too long. I should have known you would come up with some crazy new adventure . . . but a dead man and a kidnapped dog? Talk!"

"Yes, Sir." Ben said meekly. "Let me start by explaining that we were minding our own business when suddenly there were two break-ins and one attempted break-in on our persons. Then old Tom O'Connin's apartment was trashed and his dog, 9-0 was kidnapped."

"Dog-napped." Justin corrected.

"Yes, I got that part from Officer Jannolas's report," said the Chief. "Which also mentioned a ransom note. Continue."

"Right. Then, would you believe Tom died at Pineapples?

Justin broke in; "Yes, sir. You see, Tom was frantic about the dog-napping of 9-0, so he walked and ran as fast as he could all the way from Ben's house, where he was staying, to Pineapples. That's about a mile. He got over-heated and very upset. He was in his eighties, you know. I think he had a stroke or a heart attack. He had tried to phone Helen and Ben, but couldn't reach them. So, anyway, after Tom arrived at the restaurant, he keeled over dead."

"That's it?" Chief Johnstone said.

"Not exactly, sir." Nacho said. "You see, Justin and I called Ben and Helen and they came to Pineapples right away with Keoni Sanford and his wife, Lani. By that time Tom was in the freezer, and . . "

"Excuse me? You put Tom in the freezer?"

"Yes, sir. Then Justin had to go in there and get the ransom note. I have it here, sir."

Chief Johnstone carefully read the note. "Notebook? What notebook?"

Helen answered: "That would be a notebook I found in a box of Larry Windley's papers. It appears to belong to a girl named Gayle and dates back to the 1960's. I haven't figured out what it means, if anything."

"I see." said Chief Johnstone. "It says here, in this note, that Tom was supposed to bring $5,000 in ransom money. When you read this note, did you have any idea who wrote it?"

"No!" they all answered in unison. Ben continued: "We decided on a plan to take Tom to the Courthouse steps, just as the ransom note instructed, and try to trap the dog-napper. So Keoni and I put our arms around Tom's shoulders and walked over there with him, and then we sat him in Nacho's wheelchair by the south entrance. Then we stationed ourselves in strategic places: Justin on the old Fort wall, Helen behind a car, Lani under the Banyan, and Keoni and I in the Ali`i room, inside the Courthouse. Nacho was coordinating it by cell phone from the courtroom upstairs. Well sure enough, the dog-napper arrived in a black leather suit and Darth Vader helmet and walked right up to Tom. That's when 9-0 broke loose and attacked her. The rest you know about. We're anxious to find out who the dog-napper is. Do you know her name?"

"Before I get into that, I want to know if Helen is any relation to an alien named Dorothy Ozborne of Kansas, who reported a nude dancer at the wharf."

Helen looked sheepish. "Sorry about that, Chief, but Ben needed a diversion so that Officer Gullabol wouldn't notice that Tom was deceased. It was sort of harmless, don't you think?"

"You don't want to know what I think. Why didn't you call the police in the first place? What ever possessed you to carry a dead body all over town? Don't you think that's disrespectful, to say the least?"

Everyone looked sort of embarrassed, while a few moments of silence ensued. Then, in her soft rational voice, Helen calmly explained: "Chief, we were all very fond of Tom. He was a wonderful, kind man – talented at restoration – a plus to society. Among his other fine qualities, he loved animals; particularly 9-0 who was the son of 8-0. So, when we came to grips with the fact that Tom had died and that there was nothing we could do to bring him back, we figured the next best thing was to get 9-0 back alive and well. That's what Tom would have wanted us to do. We didn't think he would mind being a part of our plan."

Chief Johnstone replied: "Okay so far, but why not call in the authorities? Why do you always have to take it upon yourselves to bring some nut to justice? Don't you know that it could be dangerous, not to mention illegal?"

"Well really Chief, if you have to ask a stupid question like that, you really don't know us very well." Helen snapped. "I'm not saying that the police would have bungled the job – I am just saying that as ordinary people, we could set this trap for the dog-napper and have a fighting chance that it would work. And another thing, we thought the police had enough to deal with on Halloween. We were just trying to do you a favor."

Everyone held his breath, and looked at Chief Johnstone with apprehension.

"Helen, I know you guys mean well, but the police have the means to detect fingerprints, DNA, and other hi-tech forensic methods of solving crimes that you do not have access to."

Nacho took a sip of iced tea, and calmly said: "Well, Chief, you gotta admit the plan worked - it was a success, and it didn't take days or weeks - and no one got hurt in the process, except for that bitch in black, that is."

"Chief," Justin said, "you're the best cop I have ever known. You are fair, level headed and you have a sense of humor."

"That's hitting below the belt, Justin. I mean, flattery is the surest way to get what you want."

Ben spoke up: "He's right Chief; you can think of it as just flattery if you want, but we really do admire you."

"I give up! You are the nuttiest bunch of people I have ever known. However, I have to say that in some bizarre way, you do get results. I cannot officially condone what you have done, but I can let you off with a warning: *Do not do this again!* Oh, and please don't do me any more favors."

"You didn't tell us her name." Helen said.

"Your Darth Vader is named Lucille Wonnaku."

After Chief Johnstone left, everyone gave a big sigh of relief.

"That was close," Justin said. "I thought for sure he was going to charge us with something. *Is* it illegal to walk around with a dead body?"

Later, as Helen and Ben carried the glasses, plates and iced tea pitcher to the kitchen, Ben said: "You recognized the name of Lucille Wonnaku, didn't you?"

"Hans's clerk? The one who won $500 and has a P.O. address and an unlisted phone number? Sure did."

"Bet she owns a pair of black leather pants with a hole about the size of Mambo's bite. Speaking of Mambo, where are the kitties?" Ben asked. "Not like them to miss a good meeting."

"Look up."

There they were, on top of the refrigerator, like two sphinxes side by side. "Hey you two, Halloween is over. Bigfoot and the alien are back in their boxes ready to be returned, so you can come down now and be sociable."

"You can't reason with a cat, Ben. Let's head to Kahukui, return the costumes, and then, on the way back, stop off at Boys Camp and check on 9-0. Maybe if we leave Mambo and Windy alone, they'll come down from their perch and relax."

As Helen and Ben turned off the highway and down the road towards Boys Camp, Perp was standing at the corral fence watching the horses, his eyes filled with awe. "Wow, Mr. Sanford, this place is so cool. I never saw so many great animals. Who takes care of them? How many are there? How many goats do you have? Do all these boys really live here?"

"Whoa, Michael, one question at a time. Yes the boys live here, we have about ten goats, three horses, eleven cats, not to mention a flock of chickens, a couple of ducks, and now, one dog. 9-0 seems to be doing okay . . . maybe a little quiet, but I notice that at times he gets distracted by a goat and has to bark and try to play with him. He won't succeed though; the goats will only tolerate him - but the boys . . . they're going to love him a lot."

"Thanks, Mr. Sanford, for bringing me here. I would have felt awful leaving Fred . . . I mean, 9-0, last night. That was so sad when he saw his dead master. I'm not sure I will ever forgive her for all the bad things she has done."

"When you say 'her' Michael, you mean the woman in black leather who was arrested last night, don't you? How do you know her?"

She's my cousin, Lucille. She's always trying to make me do things for her. I got in big trouble about a week ago when she told me to break into Mr. Anderson's van. The cop that caught me, let me off with a warning but later she beat me up bad. I never told anyone because I'm embarrassed that a girl did it."

Keoni looked up as Ben and Helen parked the van, and walked over to join them at the horse corral.

"Hi guys! How's 9-0 doing?"

"He's doing pretty good, Ben. Kimo says: 'He stay come going all da time!' Right now he's imitating a New Zealand sheep-herding dog. Trying to herd goats is impossible, but he doesn't know that. Maybe he's just trying to make friends with them."

Perp looked uncomfortable as he said: "Mr. Anderson, now that I can talk, I want to tell you that I'm really sorry about trying to break into your van."

"Ben smiled and said: "That's in the past, Perp. I'm glad to see your wounds are healing."

"Thanks. I thought your Chubaka the Wookie costume was awesome!"

Helen laughed out loud at this one. Ben frowned and said: "Bigfoot - I was Bigfoot! But never mind about that, what I want to know is how you came to have 9-0 on a leash last night."

Well you see, my cousin has this huge van, and on Halloween night I saw it parked. I looked in the window and saw this poor little dog shut in there without water or air, so I broke him out."

"Michael was just telling me all about his cousin, Lucille." Keoni said.

"If Hans is your uncle, then your cousin Lucille, is his daughter?" asked Helen.

"No, she's Uncle Holden's granddaughter. Uncle Holden is Uncle Hans's brother. Mr. Sanford, is it okay if I go find 9-0 now?"

"Sure. Maybe he's hungry. Ask Kimo to fix some food and water for him."

Perp headed off towards the kitchen, calling 9-0, who left his goat herding to come running. Helen, Ben and Keoni watched and smiled at the sight of a boy and his dog.

"We've heard that Perp, or Michael, as you call him, is not such a bad kid, just hanging around the wrong friends."

"He's fine, Ben. He just needs what all these boys need. His mother is dead and his father is in jail, so he just hangs out here and there, with no permanent home. I'm hoping he'll be able to stay here. Doesn't sound like his uncles or cousin would care. I'll have a talk with his Uncle Hans, and see what he says."

"Keoni, last night I thought you mentioned that you knew Tom's daughter."

"Yeah Ben, I wanted to tell you about that but in all the excitement I forgot. She lived here back in the 60's – all of us knew her. She was so cute and lots of fun. Her name was Bonnie. She was from San Francisco. I remember her talking about her Dad, who was into restoring old buildings. Windley asked Tom to come to Lahaina to do some restoration here, but at that time he was busy in the Bay area.

"So, where is Bonnie now?" Helen asked.

"She left Lahaina suddenly back in 1967, about the same time that Gayle disappeared. Everyone was puzzled as to why she left without saying goodbye."

"So, when Tom arrived in Lahaina, and you met him, did you ever ask him about Bonnie?"

"Yes, I did. I think it was around 1975 when Tom came here, and I when I asked him about Bonnie, he was very closed mouthed about her for some reason. He was always polite, but never divulged much info about her except that she was married and lived in New York."

"I wonder if she'll come here to make burial arrangements and deal with Tom's estate?"

Ben grabbed Helen's arm and said: "Let's head to my house and repair the broken window. Then we can return Tom's belongings to his apartment. If the police are there, maybe we'll be able to find out something interesting. See you later, Keoni."

"Just look at your house, Ben! Broken window, ruts in the lawn and ants in the kitchen!"

"Don't worry, all these things can be fixed. First I'll measure the window, then phone the glass place while you water my herbs, okay?"

Helen was unwinding the hose when she noticed a perfect footprint in the herb garden just a stone's throw, so to speak, from the kitchen window. Stepping carefully around it, she made a mental note to tell Chief Johnstone.

After packing up Tom's meager belongings, they headed to his apartment about a mile north on Front Street, where they found Chief Johnstone blocking the doorway.

"Well, imagine meeting you two here." he said, as he watched them approach.

"Morning Chief, we were just returning some of Tom's belongings."

"Thanks. I'd invite you in, but we're not quite through with our technical police investigation yet."

"Oh," Helen said, "we're not here to investigate, or to interfere in any way. We just wanted to give you a piece of information; there's a perfect footprint in Ben's garden, right near the kitchen window - the one the ransom note was tossed through. Tom was staying at Ben's house, you know, since his apartment was ransacked. Ben and I thought he would be safer there but obviously Lucille Wonnaku found him anyway. She must have thought it would be easy to get money from old Tom if she took his dog. Does she have a hole in her pants?"

"You're actually very humorous, Helen, but it won't work. You think I am going to tell you everything we know . . . everything that our investigation turns up. Well, think again. The police are fully equipped to handle this case without help from you and your amateur buddies."

Ben looked shocked. "Chief, I thought you liked us. I thought you even admired our style of detective work."

"I told you that I think, in some bizarre way, you get results. And of course I like you – all of you. It's just that sometimes you drive me nuts!"

"I totally understand, Chief. We'll be on our way now so as to get out of your hair. Actually Helen and I have some research to do on the notebook. Bye!"

"Hold it! Don't take another step. Note book? The one mentioned in the ransom note? We need to talk."

CHAPTER 16.

Tuesday, November 2nd

Justin set a plate of assorted donuts holes and a fresh pot of coffee on the table in the back corner of Pineapples, then pulled up a chair and sat down to join Helen, Ben and Nacho. "I've got about a hundred questions."

"I think we all do, Justin – shoot!"

"First off, how did this Wonnaku person know that Tom was staying at Ben's house? Okay, she's a dog-napper but why did she want the notebook? How did she know about it? Why did she think Tom had it?

Nacho spoke first. "I think she tailed Tom to Ben's house. He would have been so easy to follow. He had nothing to hide so he was open and unassuming. As for how she knew about the notebook; beats me!"

"Mrs. G., I think Perp is afraid of Lucille Wonnaku. Maybe she was holding something over his head. Or else he's just plain stupid!"

Ben spoke up: "Perp's not stupid, or even bad, just easily intimidated and easily influenced, I'd say. I go along with the theory that his cousin Lucille was threatening him with something, possibly a beating. I think that's how she got him to break into my van. But we're missing something important - there's a 30-year-old connection that we're overlooking."

Justin looked concerned. "What about the cops? Are we going to continue to be involved in this, knowing how Chief Johnstone feels about our amateur status?"

"That never stopped us before." Nacho said, as he reached for another chocolate donut hole.

Ben loaded up on donut holes too, choosing the remaining two coconut/macadamias, and pouring a fresh cup of coffee.

"Helen and I talked to the Chief about the notebook this afternoon. I'll bring you guys up to date on that in a minute, but first let me finish what I was saying about a 30-year-old connection. Hans Albright and his brothers, Holden and Morton, all lived in Lahaina when the alleged 'ax' murder happened. Recently Hans found out about the box from Keoni's brother, who happened to mention it to him in a bar one night. I think Hans told his brother, Holden about it. Then one of them got Lucille to do the break-ins. Does this make any sense?"

"In a way." Helen said. "Of all the Albright brothers, it seems to me that it's Holden who's behind the break-ins . . . him and his stupid granddaughter, Lucille. I knew when I saw her bandaged wrist in the store that day, before we found out she was related to the Albrights, that she was the one in my bedroom that night . . . the one who Mambo attacked . . . the one who . . ."

Justin finished the sentence. "The one who has a hole in her leather pants!"

Helen continued: "Today Chief Johnstone confirmed that the piece Mambo grabbed, neatly fits a newly patched hole in Lucille's pants. She's been charged with breaking and entering - three counts - as well as extortion, dog-napping and some other thing like coercion. However, they did not find her fingerprints in either my office, or my home."

Nacho looked puzzled. "So, what about this infamous notebook, Mrs. G.? What clues to the past does it hold? Is Windley involved in all this?"

"No, Windley was never involved in this, that I can see, except that he somehow ended up with the notebook, maybe for safekeeping. I strongly suspect he never read it. The notebook appears to have been written by a female."

Nacho interrupted: "When Tom phoned during our brunch last week, to say he found a human bone, do you suppose it was from the ax murder victim?"

"Possibly, Nacho. He said the bone was being tested, but that it appeared to be female and looked as though it had been there for about 40 years. But wait till you hear this; Tom found what was determined to be female hand bones at one of the map sites marked with an X. That was several years ago, and he reported them to the police at the time."

"Where were the hand bones?" Justin asked.

"Near the Harbor by the little garden. I think at the time, Tom was helping the archaeologists who were checking out the site in preparation for building the restrooms, and in the process the bones got unearthed. These bones were approximately the same age as the one he just found."

"Does this mean that we are surmising that one of the Albrights' is a murderer?"

Ben looked thoughtful. "That's a pregnant question, Nacho. I wouldn't go that far, but I will say it's possible, or maybe they're protecting someone."

"Profound, man. Is there any thing more in the notebook?"

Helen answered: "The lament and maps with X's are most of it. Chief Johnstone is insisting that I hand it over to the police tomorrow, but before I do that, trust me I will scan every page and print out copies. The Chief is a very nice man who means well, but lately he seems to be suffering from lack of imagination."

"I leave for Aspen in ten days. That means we have less than two weeks to solve this murder." Justin announced.

"No problem." said Nacho. "The only reason we haven't solved it before, is simply that we did not know about it. All we have to do now is find out who was murdered, when they were murdered, why they were murdered, and by whom. A piece of cake!"

"Ben, could you drop me off at Mrs. Sylva's? I know it's getting late, but I need to ask her a few questions."

"Sure can. While you're there I'll go home and let the furry kids out for some fresh air, get dinner started and come back and pick you up in less than an hour."

Mrs. Sylva was enjoying the early evening, sitting on the front porch of her Front Street home, in her comfortable rocker. "Hi, Helen – so good to see you."

"Hi, my friend. I hope I'm not interrupting dinner or anything."

"No, we already ate. Come sit. What's up?"

Helen sat on the bench by the porch railing and checked out the colorful crowd of people passing by on the sidewalk, then answered Mrs. Sylva's question. "Two things are on my mind. The first thing is; I'm writing a story about Front Street businesses and life in general, during the Plantation Era. I would love to hear about some of your memories during the thirties and forties."

"Those days were very different from now . . . good days, though. One big difference, the road to the otherside wasn't very good, so I guess you could say we were isolated. There was no highway until 1959.

It was okay, we had most everything we needed right here, and hardly anyone had a car anyway. Inter-island packets brought us supplies and mail and visitors now and then. Boat day was so exciting. I guess it was our contact with the world.

I was a kid in the thirties and a teenager in the forties. Most everyone worked for the Mill, and even though we all came from different places like Japan, Portugal, China, Korea, and the Philippines, we mostly got along fine. No one locked their doors, which was handy for ice and grocery deliveries."

"What were some of the events and special times that you remember?"

"Well, let's see . . . the U.S. fleet came to anchor in the Roads quite often; one time there was over a hundred ships out there! People came all the way from Wailuku to see all the ships lit up at night. We had luaus, ball games and dances for the sailors – they came ashore 10,000 at a time."

Mrs. Sylva smiled as her memories continued. "Oh yeah, there was that time when the potato chip machine caught on fire at the Lahaina Bakery. That's when bread was only 10 cents a loaf. On weekends there were dances and plays at the Armory, and in later years the Midnight Inn and Banyan Inn were popular nightspots. I remember the movie *Devil at 4 O'clock* was filmed here, although it was supposed to be in Tahiti, so the Pioneer Inn had French signs hanging in front and on the walls. Then they painted the outside walls of the Courthouse with black jagged lines from the ground up, to make it look like it cracked during the big earthquake."

"Weren't Spencer Tracy and Frank Sinatra in that movie?"

"Yeah, I think so." Then, grinning, Mrs. Sylva added; "For pure excitement, though, you couldn't beat a midnight car trip up north to Kahana to see the Night Blooming Cereus."

"What was it like at Christmas time?" Helen asked.

"I remember the Mill had a huge Norfolk pine tree in the park next to the Mill office and one year it was at King Kam School. After we decorated it, there was Japanese and Hawaiian dancing and packages of candy and nuts for the keiki. Santa always came to the Banyan Tree with treats, and there were colored lights strung over Front Street, from light pole to light pole, except during the war when all the lights were kapu because of the blackout. You said there was two things you wanted to ask me – what's the second thing?"

"The second thing concerns an alleged crime that was committed thirty years ago. What can you tell me about Hale Aloha, back then?

"Let's see, that would be in the sixties when my kids were young teenagers. Oh yeah, I remember telling them: 'Stay away from Hale Aloha.' I was always scared they they'd get hurt playing around the old abandoned cars. It's off the main road too, sorta spooky and isolated. There's an old story about screams coming from there at midnight . . . a woman's screams. My neighbors say a dog howled for weeks after that. I never heard it - just heard the dog next door - he howled every time there was a full moon. It's true about the screams though, I know lotsa people who heard them."

"Did you know Larry Windley?"

"No. Heard *of* him, but we never met."

"How about the Albright brothers?"

"Yeah, I know something about them. I went to school with the oldest one, Holden, and I've met Hans, the one that owns Hula Hans, but I don't know him very well. Morton, the third one, he's in jail. He has a son called Perp. They're a worthless lot. Hans is the only one I'd give two cents for."

How about Holden's granddaughter, Lucille? Have you ever run into her?"

"I only know gossip about her, Helen. She moved here from the Big Island about six months ago, and she's rotten as the rest of the bunch. Not a nice thing to say, but that's what I heard."

"Did you know a girl named Gayle, who lived here thirty years ago?"

"No. Sorry, Helen."

Did you know any of the Albright brother's girlfriends back then?"

"Only Hans. He had a steady girl in high school, and ended up marrying her. But as for the other two, no. I only know that Morton, the one in jail, he's always been a troublemaker. I think he's in for armed robbery. Holden was a handful back then, too."

"You knew Tom O'Connin, didn't you?"

"Yes, both my husband and I liked Tom very much. We're sorry to hear about his death. Do you know when his memorial is?"

"Chief Johnstone said it would be Thursday at the Columbarium, at 11:00 A.M."

"Tom has a daughter named Bonnie, you know. She's some kinda financial expert in New York City. He was very proud of her. You said you were investigating an old crime, Helen. What kinda crime?"

"We're not sure, but we think a woman was murdered, then dismembered; and her bones scattered in various places around town."

"Now I'm sorry I asked! Maybe that's the screams people heard that night, coming from the ruins of Hale Aloha."

"Maybe, but we have to stick to the facts, and right now I'm just gathering information. Can I count on you to keep this quiet for a while? We don't want to let the cat out of the bag, so to speak, and we don't want you to be in any danger."

"Don't worry about me, Helen. Mum's the word. But you gotta promise to keep me in the loop. Oh, and if you want, I'll ask round and find someone who actually heard those screams."

"Thanks. And don't worry, I promise to keep you in the loop." Helen said, giving her friend a hug.

After dinner, Helen and Ben sat at the dining room table staring at the notebook.

"Ben, I just know that *Gayle's Story* is not written *by* her, it's *about* her . . . it's clues about her murder."

"I agree. It never really says that someone was murdered, and yet that's the feeling I get from all these odd bits of information. Did you notice that part about the MRR being broken into? Didn't Windley live in the Master's Reading Room back then?"

"Yes, he did live there for a while, but we don't know exactly when the notebook was written - we just know it was in this box for 30 years."

Whoever wrote it had information, so why didn't they turn it over to the police? I get the feeling that the writer of the notebook knew who the killer was but didn't have enough proof, and that's why she jotted down all this information. Also I think she was afraid that the killer knew that she knew, or that she suspected he was the killer."

Ben looked dazed. "I don't understand your last sentence. All this thinking has made me fuzzy. Let's call it a night, my dear. It's probably too late to phone Keoni. I'll call him first thing tomorrow. I have a couple questions for him."

CHAPTER 17.

Wednesday, November 3rd

"It's the phone for you, Helen." Ben shouted from the patio. Helen picked it up in the kitchen where she had been scrambling eggs and making cinnamon toast for breakfast.

"Mrs. Grant?"

"Yes, speaking."

"My name is Bonnie O'Connin Hartfield. Tom O'Connin's daughter."

"Oh, Bonnie, I am glad you phoned. I'm so sad about your father's death. He was such a wonderful man. Are you here on Maui? Can I help you with anything?"

"I just arrived and I'm still at the airport. The only reason I'm here is to make arrangements for my father's memorial service and to take care of a few legal matters. I would never have come back except that Dad wanted to be interred in Lahaina, rather than San Francisco. He liked you very much, too, Mrs. Grant. He told me how nice you had been to him and 9-0. So I'm going to go way out on a limb and ask for your help."

"Certainly, Bonnie, go ahead. And please call me Helen."

"The last time I talked to Dad, he told me about the break-ins and about a notebook. He said you asked him questions about it and said it had information about an old murder. When I spoke with Chief Johnstone, he told me about the ransom note for 9-0. He said it demanded $5,000 and a notebook. He said you have the notebook. Is this correct?"

"Yes, it is, Bonnie. My friends and I have become quite entangled in all this. I think you and I should meet and talk in person. Perhaps at my house?"

"Thanks Helen, that would be great. Would four o'clock this afternoon be okay?"

"Four o'clock is fine. Let me give you instructions to get to my house."

Bonnie O'Connin-Hartfield is a petite 5'2" weighing in at 110 lbs, which is what she weighed when she was 19 years old. Even after the birth of her two children, she got back in shape and back to her job as a financial advisor for the second largest brokerage firm in New York in record time. Bonnie has always been driven to succeed, even back in 1965 when she came to Hawaii at the age of twenty, seeking her first adventure.

This morning as she drove from the airport towards Lahaina in her rental car, she was overwhelmed by how much Maui had changed. There was more traffic, more people, more tourists and Mainland discount stores and new shopping malls.

Nearing Lahaina, her feelings of sadness, anxiety, and fear began to peak. She turned off the highway at the south end of town and headed north on Front Street, admiring the row of beautiful waterfront residences. On the beach, only a few feet from where Larry and Keoni used to live, stood a five-story hotel and a quaint New England-style shopping area. Back in the old days that beach had seemed so remote and peaceful.

As Bonnie approached the heart of town, the sight of the huge Banyan tree made her feel welcome. It looked the same - still amazing, still filled with myna birds, and still guarding the stately old Courthouse. Turning down Hotel Street, she parked the car and strolled over to take a look at the tiny harbor. It was bursting at the seams with an amazing collection of catamarans, sailboats, fishing boats, and even an inter-island ferry. Along the shoreline there were ticket and information booths for fishing charters, dinner cruises, parasailing and snorkeling. Already her memories of 30 years ago were beginning to dim.

The pier had been upgraded, too, with the addition of a small building, probably for the Harbormaster. On the north side of the pier, Lahaina's whale ship, the *Carthaginian*, creaked and groaned as it moved with the tide. Bonnie recalled reading that the original *Carthaginian*, purchased after the filming of the movie Hawaii, had hit the reef and sunk in full view of the town, twenty some years ago.

Leaving her car near the harbor, she adjusted her dark glasses, pulled her baseball cap down over her forehead and walked up Hotel Street past the Pioneer Inn, across Front Street and into the yard of the Baldwin House and the Master's Reading Room. Memories flooded back as she stood gazing at the old buildings. With tears in her eyes, she thought how sad it was that her father and Larry were not here to greet her.

"Hi Keoni. - - Yes, it's Ben. I'm phoning from Helen's patio. - - No they're sitting down near the surf making sure it rolls in. They may be hypnotized. - - Helen? She's glazed over in front of her laptop, and is not on this planet. - - Yes, I have a purpose in phoning and, if you stop asking me questions for a minute, I'll get to the point. Last night we studied the notebook and we have some questions for you. How well did Larry Windley know Gayle and Bonnie? - - Uh huh, uh huh. - - Was Bonnie a girlfriend?"

Helen slid the screen door open and stepped out on the patio, signaling Ben that she wanted to talk to Keoni when he was through.

"Uh huh. Yeah, I see. - - Okay, that's a good idea. Helen's signaling me that she wants to talk. See you later."

"Hi Keoni. How's Lani and Sara? - - Is Lani always baking? - - Well, we certainly enjoyed her pies and the coconut cookies too! - - Yes, I do have a question for you. Back in the old days did you hear the scream that allegedly came from the ruins of Hale Aloha? - - Uh huh. How well did you know Holden and Morton Albright? - - Oh. Okay then, I'll wait. Aloha."

"Did Keoni tell you he was on his way over?"

"Yeah. What did you learn from him?" Helen asked.

"I learned that Larry knew Gayle for a short time, and that he admired her expertise about history but was not romantically involved with her, and that Bonnie was very precocious and cute but not Larry's type either. She did however have a wild crush on him. She followed him around and even made a pest of herself at times."

"All I learned is that Keoni did *not* hear the screams at the time they happened and that he and Lani are on their way over."

Bonnie walked to the Episcopal church to confer with the minister and make the final arrangements for her father's memorial service. Then she headed to Tom's apartment where she found a complete mess. It looked as though the place had been ransacked, and there was evidence of a police investigation as well. She rapidly sorted through his clothes, packing all papers, family pictures and a few mementos into cardboard boxes, which she loaded into her car. She then phoned the Salvation Army and told them they could come and take everything that was left; then she headed to her hotel.

When Keoni and Lani arrived at Helen's door, they were carrying half of a dark chocolate double layered cake, frosted with cream cheese, and a quart of vanilla frozen yogurt. Helen brewed up some coffee and they all settled around the patio table to enjoy the treat.

"Lani, this is to die for!" Helen exclaimed. Ben, with his mouth full, just nodded.

Lani smiled modestly, saying: "Isn't it nice that the gray humid weather is finally gone? It seems like Halloween is the turning point when the humid weather leaves and our wonderful winter begins to arrive. Does that mean you're going to be moving back to your house, Ben?"

Caught off guard, Ben answered: "Wow, Lani, I don't think so. I'm not ready for that. Windy and I are ensconced very happily right here. I guess I'll wait until Thanksgiving or until Helen kicks us out, whichever comes first."

"Speaking for myself," Helen said, "I would miss Windy. She's a cat-in-training and really should spend more time with Mambo. They're so cute together."

"Please notice that she did not even mention my name." Ben said.

"How did you two meet?" Keoni asked.

"It was fate," Ben answered. "or perhaps a matter of luck, that I came along in time to rescue Helen."

"Rescue me?"

"Who's telling this story, you or me?" Ben asked, then continued before Helen could answer. "It happened about a week after I first arrived in Maui and was just getting settled into my new job as Regional Manager of the Maui Visitor Centers. I thought it would be a good idea if I knew a little history about the Courthouse, so I proceeded to ride my newly purchased bicycle over to the Research and Preservation Society to see what I could find out. Just as I was approaching the office, Helen was leaving, carrying a huge pile of books. She must have tripped over the doorsill because she and her books tilted and fell to the ground. Being a naturally gallant type, I helped her up, picked up the books and carried them up to her office. Well, one thing led to another until later we found ourselves having a romantic interlude at Kimo's.

"Isn't it odd," Helen said, "how two people who have experienced the same moment in time, can see it so differently? Want my version?"

No one spoke, so she continued: "I did indeed have an armload of books as I headed out of the office door that fateful day, but I did *not* trip over the doorsill. Instead, an out of control bicycle ran me down. It sped out of nowhere and flew apart, sending the rider and me sprawling onto the cement. Yes, it was an accident; but it may have been triggered by the rider, who was driving like a maniac."

"Maniac? Is that what you think? You know full well that I stopped at least four inches from the doorway. I was not driving recklessly or in any way acting like a maniac!"

"You have to admit, Ben, that the bike itself was a disaster waiting to happen. As I recall, the handlebars fell off and one of the wheels went careening into the bushes."

Lani and Keoni were patiently waiting for the story to end. "Jeez," Keoni sighed, "I'm almost sorry I asked how you two met. Do you guys have an ending for this saga?"

"I will tell the end of the story." Helen said. "As Ben said, one thing led to another. The first thing was a trip to the Lahaina Clinic where we both got treated for cement burns and a badly bruised elbow . . . mine! Secondly, as we hobbled our way back into town from the clinic, both of us began to feel weak and shaky, so we stopped at a waterfront restaurant to have a non-alcoholic beverage and a snack to raise our blood sugar. How romantic is that?"

"Ben smiled. "Ah, yes, I remember that evening as though it were yesterday. There I sat in pain, feeling faint and weak, unaware that it was love, not cement burns that was causing my distress."

Keoni, shaking his head and grinning, said: "Okay you two, cut the comedy routine and let's get down to business. Helen, you asked me if I knew the other Albright brothers, Holden and Morton. Unfortunately, I did. What a bunch of useless, no good, stupid, deranged, brutal . . ."

"Please Keoni, you are being redundant." Lani interrupted. "I too knew them. They were sort of worthless except for Hans, who got married to his longtime girlfriend right after high school. He and she would have been better off if they'd moved to another island. They've spent way too much time bailing the brothers out of trouble; Morton; with the law, and Holden; with women."

"Lani's right. Holden was an abusive jerk who allegedly raped several girls. Rumors, of course, no girl ever pressed charges, but the rumors were very strong. Morton's problem was that he loved guns. He was always shooting at rats or tin cans. When he got married and had Perp, or Michael, as I prefer to call him, we didn't hear much about ole Morton for a few years until the dumb shit robbed a gas station at gunpoint. While he was waving the gun around, it went off, shooting one of the gas pumps. He and the gas station attendant freaked out, fearing that the pump would explode. They both ran down the street yelling: "Fire!" When Morton was apprehended he still had the gun and the $1,500 in cash he had stolen. It wasn't his first arrest, so they threw the book at him."

"A sad tale for sure," Helen said, "especially for Perp. His mother died recently and I feel sorry for him."

"It's always the kids who suffer most." Keoni said.

Lani interrupted to ask: "Has anyone found out if Tom's daughter is coming for the funeral?"

"Bonnie phoned me from the airport this morning," Helen answered. "Said she's here to arrange for the memorial service and asked me about the notebook. She's stopping by here at four this afternoon."

Keoni frowned. "Why is it I get this uneasy feeling when I hear Bonnie's name? She was harmless enough back in the 60's. She seemed to be a good friend of Gayles. I have the feeling she may be the key to all this mystery."

"Don't worry," Helen said, "I'll pump her for information. I have become quite proficient in the art of interrogating a person without them realizing what's happening."

Ben made a sniffing coughing kind of noise.

"And what is that supposed to mean, Ben?"

"Nothing. Just clearing the ole nasal passages."

Grabbing a stack of plates, mugs, silverware, and the coffeepot, Ben and Keoni slid the screen door open and started into the house. Taking advantage of the open door, Windy shot out like a cannonball.

"Guess Lani and I should get going into town and get the shopping done." Keoni said, as he slid the screen door shut. "I want to talk to Hans about letting Michael stay permanently at Boys Camp. Then I'll head out there to see how 9-0's doing."

Lani, who was carrying a broom out to the patio, opened the screen door and Windy ran back in before she had a chance slide it closed.

"Just lean the broom in the corner, Lani, I'll do the honors later." Helen said, as she slid the door open in time for Windy to speed past in blur of cat fur. "Before you guys take off, I was wondering if you would consider helping help me plan the food for Sam's reception. She and Woody Byrde eloped to Kauai and I'm in charge of planning the reception when they get back. I'm happy to do it, but it's a bit overwhelming. There's so much to do, and I really need your input, Lani. I've reserved the Moir Mansion for Saturday evening, and would you believe I was lucky enough to get Mr. Ron to help with the theme and decorations?"

Ben opened the screen door and Windy dashed in. "Dammit, Windy you're driving me nuts! I wish you'd learn to use the cat door. What's Mysteron? Some kind of new-age fortuneteller? Why don't you just ask Flo and Homer?"

It's Mister Ron, Ben." Lani corrected. "He's the latest rage around here for creating unique parties. They say no one ever forgets his unusual flower arrangements, his decorations, or his birds."

"Ignore Ben, Lani, he knows full well it's not Mysteron. That's just his odd humor. You have heard of Ron, haven't you Ben?"

"Hell yes! Birds, you say?"

"Yes. He's famous for climaxing the evening with a flurry of doves, or sometimes just putting little birds in cages on each table. I heard that one time he even had parrots singing the Hawaiian Wedding Song."

"Guck!"

"Ben, you're making me nervous." Helen frowned. "Mr. Ron will be here tomorrow morning for coffee and a planning session. Please try to be polite and not say anything offensive."

Ben 'zipped and locked' his lips, looking at Helen with an innocent smile that said, 'trust me.'

"Your halo is slipping slightly to the left." Lani remarked.

Quickly Ben 'adjusted' it, while continuing to look angelic.

Lani turned to Helen. "Helen, I'd be happy to help you with the food for Sam and Woody's reception. I'll gather some ideas and give you a call later."

"Mahalo for helping me out, Lani, and for bringing the best chocolate cake I ever tasted."

"Indeed!" Ben added.

CHAPTER 18.

Later Wednesday . . .

Mambo and Windy were in the middle of their afternoon siesta, curled up in a shady spot on top of the storage shed, when Bonnie O'Connin Hartfield arrived. They didn't bother to get up.

"Sit here, Bonnie. I'll bring some iced tea. Are you hungry?"

"Not hungry, but plenty thirsty, thanks Mrs. Grant"

"It's Helen, remember? Ben's at the Visitor Information Center right now, but he said he would like to meet you and promised barbecued flank steak and fried pasta if you stay to dinner."

"Yes, I would really enjoy that." Bonnie said, as she visibly relaxed. "My, it's lovely here. I've missed Hawaii."

Helen set down a tray of iced tea and sliced lemons. "Why did you stay away for so long? I would think with your father living here, you would have been a frequent visitor."

Several moments passed in silence while Bonnie seemed to be lost in thought. Finally Helen interrupted. "Would you like to tell me about it? Maybe it will help if I told you that I believe you wrote the orange notebook. I believe that it's information or clues about Gayle's death."

"What makes you think that?'

"Several things; For one, you left Hawaii about the same time Gayle disappeared. You left without letting anyone know where you were going. If it hadn't been for your father coming here to do restoration work, you would have succeeded in disappearing completely. Secondly; I have the notebook and I've read it; the handwriting seems to be that of a woman. Adding this up, it seems to me that you wrote it thirty years ago and then disappeared, possibly because you were afraid. Just how well did you know Gayle?"

"You're very good at figuring things out, Helen. Gayle was my friend and my roommate. We were quite close. She was a couple of years older, but I worried about her. She was intelligent and studious on the one hand, and so stupidly daring on the other. I warned her about the company she was keeping, but she always thought she could handle any situation. Then, one night, she went out with a man named Holden Albright and she never came back. I knew she had been raped and killed by him, so in a panic I left Hawaii and never let anyone know where I went. I asked my Dad to please never talk about me or tell anyone where I was living."

"So you knew that Gayle was murdered?"

"Yes, and I'm afraid that the slime bag who killed her, figured out that I know."

"What happened to her body?"

"It's a long story, Helen, and I think I hear a male voice. Sounds like your friend Ben just got home. I'll continue later."

"I'm home!" Ben yelled from the kitchen, as he started putting the groceries away. A few minutes later he headed out to the patio with an iced bottle of Chardonnay and three glasses.

"Bonnie, I presume, nice to meet you. Sorry it's under such sad circumstances."

He popped the cork and turned to open the door for Windy. "Helen, we have to teach Windy how to use the cat door. Why she can't learn do use it is beyond me. She apes everything else Mambo does, but totally backs off from the little swinging door."

"She's a cat, Ben. Maybe she just likes having the power to make us get up and wait on her."

"I don't think Windy has a devious bone in her furry little body – but rather, I think she is afraid of the cat door. After all, remember how frightened she was of you when you were an alien?"

"Me? It was your fur suit that freaked her out! It took her two days to come down from on top of the refrigerator."

Bonnie stared at Helen and Ben with a puzzled frown. Mambo and Windy, who were tired of looking back and forth from Helen to Ben like a boring tennis match, turned and with their tails straight up, walked in single file off the patio and down to the waters edge, where they sat side by side staring at the surf.

"So, are you guys hungry?" Ben asked. "If so, I think I'll get dinner started."

"Good idea. Bonnie and I will set the table."

Sunset, which happened in the middle of dinner, was peach, silver, turquoise and gold, as usual, but left an afterglow of lavender that was quite amazing.

"Do you think this glow is due to volcanic ash, Ben?"

"No, it's due to the good food and wine."

"I know you guys are mellowed out," Bonnie said, "but there's more. I'd like to finish telling you about Gayle and the time we spent in Lahaina."

"Please go ahead, Bonnie." Helen said, as Ben started clearing the table.

"On the plane flying over this morning, my thoughts were whirling like a kaleidoscope of flashing pictures, so I just let the images run back to that time in 1965. I was twenty years old and thought I had the world by the tail. There I was in Hawaii and doing research work for the nicest guy in the world; no matter that he hardly knew I existed. I thought I could change that by becoming his most amazing researcher. After I had been here for a while, Larry sent Gayle and me to Oahu for a month to do research at various repositories. We jotted down everything we could find about Lahaina's history, as per his instructions. Then, after working all day, Gayle and I would head to Waikiki for a swim and have dinner at one of the upbeat bars. Life was good."

Helen waited while Bonnie gazed out at the waves, deep in thought.

Suddenly she continued. "Then my mind skipped to a day not long after Gayle and I returned to Lahaina from that trip to Oahu. I remember running down Front Street calling her name: '*Gayle! Hey wait up!*' She turned and waved as she recognized me. I thought she looked like a goddess. She was tall and walked like a queen. That day her hair was sending out tiny gold flashes of sunlight and I remember thinking that freckles on tan skin looked good on her. She stopped just short of being beautiful - it was hard to figure out why. Maybe it was her high IQ or her attitude, which was aloof and standoffish, especially if she didn't know you well. I asked her:

"How come you're in such a hurry? Have time for a coke?"

"I'd love that Bonnie, but I'm in the middle of something very exciting, historically speaking."

"Come on, Gayle, take a minute to relax and tell me about this exciting historical thing."

"Well, okay, but just for one tiny minute."

"The story Gayle told me was indeed fascinating; and her tiny minute became a full hour."

"Are you telling me that you may have found a painting of Princess Pualei? My God, that is news! No one living today has any idea what she looked like. She's always described as smiling and beautiful, but it's believed that no pictures of her exist."

"That's right. For some reason there are no sketches or paintings of her – except the one I'm on the trail of."

"How did you get on the trail of it?"

"When I was typing the information we collected for Larry I carefully read every word, and soon I got caught up in a very interesting story. In several of the Government memos I noticed a reference to a portrait painter who visited the palace in 1839. That palace would have been Hale Piula, here in Lahaina, on the beach where Armory Park is now. King Kamehameha III built Hale Piula right across from his residence on Moku`ula. It was large; two stories with a veranda and lots of windows that reflected the sun, which gave it it's nickname of Crystal Palace. Even though the Crystal Palace was not in use for long, it did have several notable portraits hanging in its halls, and I believe during the visit of this artist, he painted a portrait of Princess Pualei."

"How can you be sure of this?"

"I found a memo saying that the Princess was becoming impatient with the long sittings. Then in a later memo I read that 'she' did not like the painting and ordered it destroyed. It did not say who 'she' was,

but because of the time frame, I surmised it was referring to Princess Pualei."

"So the alleged portrait was destroyed?"

"No, the canvas was re-used – a common practice for artists at the time."

"How do you know that?"

"I don't know for sure, but figure it's a good possibility. So I went to the archives myself and I followed every reference about that portrait painter. He was a Frenchman, very popular with the King and his crowd, who was invited to all sorts of social events. I noted the names of other portraits he painted while he was in Hawaii; there were five of them. I located four of the portraits, all in Oahu now in the Royal Hawaiian Museum. So I phoned the museum and asked them if they knew where the fifth portrait was. They said they thought the Higgins family of Maui owned it. Sure enough, a member of the Higgins family does own it. Would you believe it is right here in Lahaina?

"Wow! Where?"

"Hans Albright and his wife got it as a wedding gift from her parents, Mr. and Mrs. Alfred Higgins, and I believe that beneath that painting, is a portrait of the Princess."

"No way! Who's in the portrait that's painted on top?"

"A popular Englishman who was in tight with the King. He's not well known to the average reader of history, but in the archives there are records of him advising on military matters."

Ben got up, glanced at Helen, and walked down to the water's edge to light a couple of tiki torches. She gave him a slight shrug and a let's-see-what-happens look.

Still lost in her memories, Bonnie's kaleidoscope turned to a day when she and Larry were in the MRR talking about the restoration of the Baldwin House. "I was a rapt listener because everything Larry said was important to me and I wanted him to notice that . . . to notice me. He asked me what happened to Gayle's face. He said: *She's in terrible shape – looks like someone beat her up.* Before I could tell him what happened to Gayle's face, this friend of his, Keoni Sanford showed up wanting to know the same thing. He was very worried about Gayle, and said in an angry voice: *It's one of those damned Albrights. I warned her not to get involved with them.*

Suddenly, without warning, Bonnie burst into tears causing Ben to rush to her aid with a paper napkin. Blowing her nose and wiping away her tears, she said: "I knew so much back then and I never dealt with it. Gayle was murdered! I know this because I saw it happen."

"Oh, my God!" Helen and Ben said in unison.

"After Gayle got beat up, she said she was going to tell Holden to buzz off. I begged her to be careful, to take Keoni or some other large guy with her when she confronted Holden, but she was determined she could take care of him by herself."

"Was Holden harassing her?" Helen asked. "Stalking her?"

"Both. But Gayle wanted the painting. She wanted it so bad that she took too many chances with Holden. She decided that before she told him to buzz off, she would ask him to steal the painting from his brother, and in return she would give him some sexual favors."

"The woman must have been nuts!" said Ben.

"Anyway, Holden stole the painting and gave it to Gayle. Then a couple days later, he came to collect the sexual favors. So when he came to pick her up, I followed them. He took her to Hale Aloha, which was a great make-out haven. I hid inside the old ruin of a building and peeked out through a window frame. They were talking. Arguing. Then I saw him hit her very hard. Not with is hand, but with a stick, or club. She fell to the ground. I turned to jelly. I could not move. I was frozen with fear, thinking he could hear my heart beating. I dropped to the ground and tried to become invisible. After a while I heard a noisy vehicle pull up and a door slam. I could hear Holden and another man arguing, then I heard the car or truck door open and shut again. Then I heard chopping."

At this point Helen got up, went in the house and returned with the bottle of cognac that she had been saving for Ben's birthday. She poured three glasses and said, with a sigh: "Continue, Bonnie."

"I just laid there, too scared to even take one little peek. I put my hands over my ears because what I thought was happening was too awful. Finally they left and I just stood there, sick to my stomach. I was so totally panicked that I just ran for home, cutting through the back of the Baldwin House by the Arbor Shops. When I got to the front I heard noises, so I waited in the shadows until I saw two men walk towards harbor carrying a shovel."

"Who were they?" Asked Ben.

"Holden, and I think the other one was Morton."

"Why didn't you go to the police?"

"I was terrified. Scared to the very core of my bones. I knew that somehow I would end up like Gayle if I turned them in."

"So, you left town?"

"Yes."

"In my panic I knew I had to leave everything connected to Gayle's death, behind. I needed to make myself free of all of it so I could be safe. I wrote the things in the notebook, hoping that someone would eventually figure out that Holden killed Gayle. I know this doesn't make much sense, but I was totally freaked out and scared to death.

"How did you find out about the . . . er . . . ah . . . locations?" Ben stammered.

"The next day in a sort of casual way, I mentioned that Gayle lost her favorite hair clasp when she was with Holden, and I asked if anyone had seen them the previous evening. One of the guys that had been night fishing said he saw Holden digging in the dirt at the little park by the harbor – probably for worms."

Ben stood and stretched. "Excuse me Bonnie, but as fascinating as all this is, I am about ready to drop. Please excuse me, ladies."

"I'm sorry, Ben. It *is* getting late." Bonnie apologized. "I guess I just got to reliving my past and lost track of time. I'll be heading to my hotel now. Thanks for listening to my story, and thanks for the delicious dinner."

After Bonnie left, Ben extinguished the torches and put the patio back in order while Helen filled the dishwasher. "You certainly put a sudden end to the evening, Ben. What did you think of Bonnie's story?"

"I think it's b.s! Pure b.s.

As they turned out the lights, Mambo and Windy made a dash for the bed. "I'm heading over to Hana early tomorrow for my monthly revue of the Visitor Center. Damn shame I have to miss your meeting with Mr.Ron."

"Will you be spending the night in Hana?"

"Yeah, but don't worry, I'll be back in time for Tom's memorial service."

CHAPTER 19.

Thursday, November, 4th

Early Thursday morning, Helen was at her computer in the Master's Reading Room getting caught up on some work. At the same moment, Ben was turning his van onto the access road to the Maui Prison. Having never been to the prison before, it took a few tries before he found the Admissions Office.

Approaching the stern looking female clerk, he introduced himself. "Ben Anderson. I phoned late yesterday to arrange visiting time with Morton Albright."

"Down this way, Mr. Anderson. You have exactly half an hour. There will be a guard in the room with you at all times."

The visiting room was bare, only a long table and two chairs. Ben sat waiting, hearing footsteps and jingling keys, and the echo of a security door sliding open. After a few minutes, a prison guard escorted Morton Albright into the room. The guard took his position by the door. Morton sat in the other chair, and barked: "Who are you? What do you want?"

Ben thought he looked like Hans, only paler. Avoiding an introduction, he said: "I want the truth, Morton. In 1967 a girl named Gayle Reeves disappeared, apparently a murder victim. Due to facts that have recently come to light, you and your brother Holden are the number one suspects in that murder."

"Look, mister, I have no idea what you're talking about. Me and Holden never killed no body."

"We only have a half hour, Morton. I'm the guy you want to confide in. I'm the guy who may be able to save your neck. I'm the guy . . ."

"Okay, I get your drift. Why, after all these years has all this come up?"

"Gayle's 'disappearance' came up because a notebook containing compelling information, recently surfaced. Also, someone with personal information about her is in town. Looks like you're about to be nailed for murder one."

"Jeez you sound like a lawyer. A sleazy lawyer!"

"What I am, is your salvation. Talk to me Morton, tell me what you know about Gayle Reeves."

Finally out on bail, Lucille Wonnaku limped from her grandfather's car toward the house. During her few days in jail, her mind had gone over and over the events of the past few weeks. Twelve stitches on her wrist from the damned broken window and five more on her leg from dog teeth! And on top of all that, she was rotting in a jail cell. Her plan to get $5,000 ransom for the dog had blown up . . . what a night that was! The old man was dead. Shit, he'd been dead the whole time she was talking to him at the Courthouse! Someone had set a trap for her that night. Who? She was angry about loosing the ransom money. Even the $500 she won on that radio program hadn't showed up. Last but not least, there was Perp. He was gone! Disappeared, the little rat, just when she needed his help.

Holding the sketch she found in Windley's box, Helen re-read the note on the back: *Have you seen this locket before? May have belonged to a princess. I need to know ASAP.*

She reached for the phone and made a long distance phone call to Oahu.

"Good Morning, Royal Hawaiian Museum." a pleasant voice answered. "May I help you?"

"Good morning. I'm Helen Grant, Historian at the Research and Preservation Society in Lahaina. I need some information about a missing locket that may have belonged to one of the Ali`i."

Helen waited while she was connected to the head archivist, Miss Hunter.

"This may be a waste of time, Miss Hunter, but I was wondering if you know anything about a locket with three rubies and seven diamonds set into sterling filigree in an oval shape. The locket may be about two inches long and one inch wide. The chain is rather heavy and ornate and looks Spanish, as does the locket."

"Let me take a look in the catalogue to make sure, but I believe that's the locket that British Commodore Worthington presented to Princess Pualei, in 1839."

Helen heard the sound of pages being turned. "Here it is! Yes, it fits your description. Why do you ask? Have you seen it? Do you have a picture of it?"

"I haven't actually seen it, but I have a sketch and a short written description that I found in a box of old papers that had been stored for 30 years."

There was a slight pause, then Miss Hunter said: "I'll send a copy of the color photo to you, if you like. The *Aloha Locket*, as it is known, has been missing for about 30 years . . . strange coincidence!"

"Miss Hunter, when you say the locket is 'missing,' what do you mean? Was it stolen?"

"I don't think so. Originally it was here at the museum in the storage wing where we keep all artifacts that are not currently on display. It's a massive collection and objects are carefully catalogued. Rarely do things come up missing, but in this case it seems to have. It doesn't mean it was stolen, but more likely that it was mislabeled and stored in the wrong place."

"Who has access to the artifacts?"

"Only accredited employees of the museum and, at times, volunteers from the University who are history majors or those studying to be curators or archivists. They can accumulate credits by volunteering to help catalog our vast collection."

"Just one more question. Does the museum keep records of the students who worked there through the years?"

"I imagine so, Mrs. Grant, but you would have to speak to the records department."

"Thanks Miss Hunter, you've been very helpful."

"You are so welcome. Please keep me informed; this is an important and valuable artifact, and it would be wonderful to locate it."

Helen's meeting with Mr. Ron was scheduled for 11 o'clock, so she headed home in time to hose down the patio and fix a pot of coffee. As she was arranging a tray with coffee mugs and cookies, she heard a male voice at the front door:

"Yoo hoo, anyone home?"

"Oh, Mister Ron, I didn't hear you drive up. Come in."

"Your door was open, and I've been warmly welcomed by your committee of two; they're darlings! The big black one and I have already bonded."

"Mambo's the black cat, and his little shadow, the sandy tiger striped kitty is named Windy. They know which people are welcome here. Believe me, if you weren't welcome, Mambo would have bitten a hole in you pants! Come out on the patio and make yourself comfortable. I can't wait to hear what plans you have for the wedding reception."

While the morning was still cool, Nacho and Justin decided to meander on foot and in wheelchair, down Luakini Street to do some sleuthing. As they neared the little road that leads to Hale Aloha, Nacho glanced up and remarked: "It's bigger than I pictured. Taller and longer - big windows, too. Cool bell tower!"

They stood taking in the building and its surroundings, which include a cemetery on the mountain side and a parking area on the makai side.

"Why does it look so forlorn? Maybe it's the location next to the cemetery."

"Yeah, I feel it too." Justin said. "It's out of the way here, stuck between Luakini and Wainee streets. The story we heard about screams and the howling dog is probably what makes it feel forlorn. The dismembered body scenario doesn't help either."

"Man it's broad daylight, and somehow we have managed to spook ourselves. What's that?" Nacho said, pointing to a small building set about 15 feet away.

"I think that's a new restroom building for the people who lease Hale Aloha. Probably built because the old building doesn't have one; they didn't have inside plumbing back in those days, you know."

"Think anyone died here, Justin? I mean it is sorta remote, but a screaming murder? Tell me again why we're here?"

"Because scoping out the scene of the alleged crime is something sleuths do."

"Okay, let's picture this place as it was 30 years ago. Mrs. G. said it was crumbling away, walls falling down, only window frames left, overgrown with weeds, and lots of abandoned cars around. The cemetery was here at that time of course, but I wonder if all these houses were. If it was so darn creepy thirty years ago, why would any woman come here?

"Logical, Nacho. Now we're getting somewhere."

"Maybe she was brought here tied up and gagged?"

"Then how did she manage those blood curdling screams? Justin said, with a flourish.

"Right! And another thing," said Nacho, "if she screamed her head off, wouldn't the attacker leave? I mean wouldn't all that screaming attract attention, possibly causing someone to come and investigate or to phone the cops?"

"So if you were going to kill someone and then chop them up, where would you do it?" Justin asked.

"I wouldn't do it here, that's for sure. This place is slightly remote, but still close enough to houses for the residents to hear screams, howls, and other noises. Besides, only in gothic stories does someone die in an old crumbling abandoned building and have a dog howl for a week afterwards."

"So, what do you think happened?" Justin asked.

"I deduce that if Gayle was here, she came willingly, for some reason we do not yet know. Then, I think things may have gotten out of control. If she was killed by one of the Albrights, it must have been in a sudden act of violence . . . not premeditated."

"A violent act, like rape?" Justin asked.

"A possibility. If so, that would point to the Albright with the bad reputation with women . . . Holden!"

"There could have been other reasons to kill her."

"Reasons, such as?" Nacho asked.

"Such as to keep her from talking; or for revenge; or money . . . reasons like that."

"Hard to believe that a couple of dim bulbs like Morton and Holden were into anything heavier than small town, small time crimes. Also it's hard to believe that an educated, brilliant history student like Gayle Reeves would have anything to do with those two . . . unless she wanted something from them."

After the planning session with Mr. Ron, Helen spent the rest of the day straightening up the house, changing sheets and doing laundry - nice normal routines that felt comforting after the strange events of the past few weeks.

With Ben still in Hana, she sat alone on the patio, relaxed in the warmth of the late afternoon sun, nibbling on raw carrots and broccoli. As the sun slid lower towards Lanai, all thoughts of murder, notebooks, break-ins, and Tom's death, disappeared. She dozed. Mambo and Windy headed towards the bushes for a night prowl. Then sudden loud banging at the front door startled them. All three heads turned in unison.

Helen checked the peek hole before opening the door to Justin and Nacho who were smiling and holding a large tub of chocolate ribbon ice cream and a jar of butterscotch syrup.

"Hope we're not interrupting, Mrs. G. Where's Ben?"

"Hi Guys. Ben's over in Hana for the night. Come on in and tell me why you're here, while I forget about my low cal evening and grab a jar of maraschino cherries and some whipped cream."

Helen got spoons and bowls and led the way to the patio where they dug into rivers of chocolate and mountains of vanilla ice cream, topped with butterscotch and whipped cream and crowned with a cherry.

"I haven't had an ice-cream sundae for at least ten years." Helen said. "This is so decadent. I knew there was a reason why I had raw veggies for dinner."

Between bites, Justin and Nacho filled her in on their scene-of-the-crime sleuthing.

"Interesting deductions, you two, but wait till you hear Bonnie's story! She was here yesterday and admitted to writing the notebook. She said she was a close friend and roommate of Gayle's. She also said she witnessed the murder and the dismemberment, saying it was Holden who did it, aided by his brother, Morton. Said she was so scared that she left town and never came back."

"Holy Cow! So that's why her father never talked much about her?"

"Yeah."

Nacho continued: "If she and Gayle were such good friends, and especially if she witnessed this gruesome murder, wouldn't you think that Bonnie would want to tell the police everything? I don't get it!"

"You're not alone; listen to this, my friends . . . Ben has a gut feeling that Bonnie's story is pure b.s. and I am inclined to agree with him."

CHAPTER 20.

Friday, November 5th

Helen woke at dawn, ready to fast walk all the way to work. Ice cream and butterscotch-guilt is a great motivator. Once at her desk in the Master's Reading Room, she tried to figure out where to insert information about the mosquito-fogging truck into the Plantation story. Was it really DDT that they sprayed throughout the town? Then there was the Peanut Man with a pole across his shoulders, selling bags of peanuts, seeds and manapua and 'powerful pig, dim sum', or simply meat in a wrapper. People said he carried a stash of gold coins with him. Certainly these were interesting stories, as were the gambling-judge vignettes and the Madam-of-Front-Street tales. There was so much more to do before the Plantation Era story was finished.

It was nearly 10:30 . . . just as she was beginning to worry that Ben wouldn't get back from Hana in time for Tom's memorial service, he arrived with two incredibly beautiful leis dangling over his arm. Standing in the doorway he looked at Helen for a moment, not saying a word.

"Ben, what's wrong? It's not like you to be silent."

"Nothing's wrong. Everything's right. Sometimes I look at you and I honestly can't think of anything romantic or funny to say. You just take my breath away."

Helen smiled. "No one ever said that to me before."

The sentimental moment eased away as Ben checked his watch and said: "Let's go. We'll make it just in time."

The memorial was a celebration of Tom O'Connin's life. Many of Lahaina's residents came to pay their respects, drape their leis over his urn, and tell stories about their friendship with Tom and his dogs; from 5-0 to 9-0. Mr. and Mrs. Sylva were there, along with Chief Johnstone, the employees of RAPS, Nacho, Justin, Justin's family, Keoni and Lani, Bete and Dr. George and many more friends.

"There's Hillary – and look who's holding her hand." Helen observed.

"Joe, you old renegade, how are you?" Ben asked. "Hi Hillary. I heard that you've been keeping company with this character."

Hillary laughed and turned to Joe. "Renegade? So, my friend, what secrets are you keeping from me?"

Joe put up his hands in surrender and said, with a grin: "I give up. It may take a while Hillary, but I will tell you all my secrets. Better I tell you than have my old buddy Ben blurt out the story."

"Where's Bonnie?" Ben asked, " I haven't seen her since we got here."

Keoni and Lani wandered over to join them. "Looking for Bonnie? Pastor Jameson is quite worried about her - she never showed up today."

"Ben, we're nearly out of cat food and there's nothing much for our dinner either."

"Here's a plan." Ben said. "We feed the kids the last of the kibbles and some canned tuna, then you and I have an elegant dinner at a lovely seaside restaurant."

"That sounds like magic, Ben. We haven't spent enough time doing those special little things together, lately. How about I'O^s?"

I'O sits next to it's sister restaurant, Pacific'O, on the beach at 505 Front Street. Tonight, as their charming British waiter, Chris, approached their seaside table, Hawaiian music from the nearby luau drifted by, mingling with the sound of the softly lapping waves.

After Chris described the fresh fish of the day, and answered their questions about the menu, they ordered their entrees and a coconut shrimp appetizer.

"Ben, this was an awesome idea. I love it here. I hope we haven't ordered more than we can eat."

"Don't worry we'll dine for hours, slowly savoring each bite, and then when we're ready to burst we'll have Chris put what's left in a kitty bag for Mambo and Windy. Now, tell me about your day."

"Today I did some investigating and found out that Gayle Reeves worked in the archives department at the Royal Hawaiian Museum when she was at the University of Hawaii, back in the 60's. The Head Archivist, Miss Hunter, told me that at that time, a valuable locket disappeared - a locket that fits the description of the one in the mysterious note. It could have been mislabeled and put in the wrong place in archival storage for thirty years, but I suspect it was stolen by Gayle."

"Excellent work! I'm impressed with your investigating, and with your lovely eyes, and your sweet smelling hair, and . . . .Good God! I think I'm beginning to vibrate!"

"Ben, snap out of it – it's your cell phone!"

"Of course it is . . . I knew that. Excuse me while I take this call."

Helen sipped her wine, and gazed at the stars until he returned. "What's wrong, Ben?"

"Hold on to your hat, my dear – Holden Albright is dead! His body was found on the cement walkway, eight floors below Bonnie O'Connin's hotel room."

"I can't believe it! What does this mean? Is it murder? Where is Bonnie?"

"Nobody knows where she is right now. I guess you've figured out that was Chief Johnstone on the phone just now. He suspects foul play, and thought we'd want to know about Bonnie's disappearance. He wanted to know if we had seen her today. Apparently we were the only people she talked to besides Pastor Jameson, since she arrived in Hawaii."

"What does Chef Johnstone think happened?"

"Didn't say. Here comes Chris with our entrees. I hope I'm not asking too much of you, but let's try to transport ourselves back to before the phone call, and try not to worry about this mess right now."

"*Tiger by the Tail* for you, Mrs. Grant. You can relax, I've arranged for one delicate tiger prawn topped with just a touch of lilikoi sauce for Mambo, thus leaving you free to enjoy every bite of your dinner."

Turning to Ben, Chris set down before him a piping hot plate of *Lamb 'Pa'*, saying: "Your tenderloin of lamb on wasabe and chive mashed potato. I deleted the black bean sauce for Windy's little snack."

"Thanks, Chris. You always make the evening a special adventure. Beats me how you can stay so serious when you talk about cat snacks."

As she took the first bite of her delicious dinner, Helen said: "As I recall, you were just going to tell me about your trip to Hana."

"Yes, well I have a confession to make. There's more to my trip than checking the Hana Visitor Center. I made a pit stop at Maui Prison."

"Morton! You went to see Morton?"

"Yep. And believe me he's a real stupid and destructive man, filled with hateful grudges. I rue the day he ever gets released from prison."

Chris replenished their wine glasses, and silently left.

"Did you find out anything from Morton?"

"Yes. The dumber they are, the more they talk. I led him to think that enough evidence had surfaced lately to link him to the murder of Gayle Reeves. Somehow he came to the conclusion that I was a sleazy lawyer and I did nothing to disillusion him about that. I also 'forgot' to mention my name, and he did not ask. He said he and Holden never killed anyone, and he wanted to know why Gayle's name had come up at this time."

"Did you tell him?"

"Yes, I told him about the notebook surfacing after 30 years which, by the way, he seemed to be totally unaware of and I said that someone was in town who had evidence about Gayle's murder."

"You didn't mention Bonnie's name?"

"No, I didn't say anything because Morton went into a rage about Holden. He said the rat-faced jerk probably found the locket and was keeping it from him."

"Whoa, Ben! The locket? The locket that I suspect Gayle stole from the museum?"

"Must be. Morton got so riled, the guard came over to see if I was okay, then told Morton to quiet down or he would send him back to his cell. So he got quieter, which was almost worse. He rambled on, mumbling and getting himself worked up into a quiet rage. He said, and I quote: *Holden's an ass. Always getting himself in with the wrong woman. She was a bitch; her and that little blonde slut friend of hers. Both of them acted like they was too good for him. Holden wanted Gayle bad, but he kept his distance cause Sanford was always around somewhere and he was too big to tangle with. Then the dumb blonde bitch told one of her boy friends, Vodka Dan, about the locket. Vodka Dan told Holden, and Holden started to drool. He broke into the place where Gayle worked and then searched her room, but he never found it. He couldn't even beat the information out of her. At least that's what he said.*"

Chris cleared away the dinner plates, and brought fresh brewed Kona coffee. Helen was deep in thought, and barely noticed. She said to Ben:

"Morton told you that Holden beat up Gayle in an attempt to find out where the locket was, right?"

"Right."

"But he didn't say that Holden killed her?"

"No, he didn't say that."

CHAPTER 21.

Saturday, November 6th

The morning after Holden's death, Helen received a phone call from Bonnie. It was short and sweet. In a shaky voice, Bonnie said: "Don't think bad of me. I'll contact you soon." Helen reported the phone call to Chief Johnstone, who said Bonnie was a murder suspect. As much as Helen wanted to work on solving this mess, she had to put it aside because Sam and Woody's wedding reception had developed a major problem.

At first, the plans had gone swimmingly; she and Lani had gotten all the food preparations under control,

Mr. Ron was ready and the final shopping list was complete. Then suddenly this morning, at the last minute, Helen received a catastrophic phone call.

"Ben, you will not believe what just happened! There were two bookings made for the Moir House on the same evening. The records show that I was the second one to make a reservation for tonight, so we lost it. They said they were so sorry about the mix up and any inconvenience it might cause me. Well, that does not even begin to cut it. I am so pissed! I am irate! I am incensed! I am going to explode!"

"What good would exploding do?" Ben asked calmly. "Let me tell you what you would do if you weren't imparting this splendid tirade. First, you would get your list of guests and their phone numbers. Then you would ask a few close friends to help you phone every one of them, and inform them that the reception will be *here* this evening, instead of at the Moir mansion."

"Here! Here? Are you insane, Ben? Sixty people, here? You mean at my house? This evening?"

"Yes."

"What are you doing?"

"I'm phoning *'We'll Do The Dirty Work For You,'* they can clean the house and patio while you and I make a run to Kahului. Now get your cell phone and call a few close friends with those phone numbers, then call Lani and let her know about the change. Then notify Mr. Ron and his birds."

Helen looked worried. "What about Mambo and Windy? They'll freak out if strangers come in the house while we're gone. Mambo might even pull one of his sneak attacks on the cleaning lady! And I refuse to leave them outside."

"We'll leave them in the master bathroom with a note on the door that says: **Stay out - - Killer cats!** It will only be for a few hours and I'm sure they'll survive. As for having a crowd of people here, the kitties love a party and will only add to the festivities."

"If you say so, Ben, but I have a funny feeling about all this."

"Nerves, my dear, just a case of nerves."

Following a whirlwind shopping spree at three different malls in Kahului, the van was loaded with party supplies and they were ready to head back across the island to Lahaina. Halfway there, Helen looked out of the van window at the old pali trail and said: "How could three tiki torches and fifteen stackable plastic chairs come to $265.00? How could a few groceries and a couple of cases of champagne, purchased at a wholesale outlet, come to $500.00?"

"Surely Sam and her parents are going to pick up most of the cost." Ben replied.

"Well if they are, they never said anything to me. I could go into bankruptcy!"

"Okay now, lets calm down and just get through this day. We'll worry about that problem later."

"Gak! What is that smell?" Helen said as she opened her front door.

"Disinfectant, I think. It's really overpowering, isn't it? I'll turn on the fans and open the doors. You let the cats out of the bathroom; they're probably hungry."

Mambo and Windy stood in the bathroom doorway, sniffing the air and sneezing. Helen was glad to see they were safe and well. Mambo was first to step out of the bathroom and into the bedroom. Windy followed, dragging a long piece of toilet paper, part of a completely unrolled pile of tissue covering the bathroom floor. She dragged it behind, flicking her hind leg now and then, while aping what Mambo was doing. They both sauntered across the living room in slow motion towards their food dishes.

"Quite a sight watching two cats move simultaneously in slow motion." Ben said, as he stepped on the trail of toilet paper. "Kind of reminds me of a cartoon."

"Well at least they're okay and the place is clean, even if it does smell like disinfectant." observed Helen, running finger along the top of the dining room table. "Let's unload the van."

"I'll put the champagne on ice in the coolers. The back of the carport seems like a good place for them. Then I'll take the new chairs out on the patio. Want them out on the lawn? How about having the new tiki torches lined along the edge of the patio? Is that Flo and Homer, snorkeling out near the reef?"

"Tell me you made that up, Ben – the part about Flo and Homer snorkeling out by the reef."

"I'm pretty sure it's them. Who else has red hair that bright, but Flo? I wonder if they know you live here. God help us if they come walking up the beach in snorkel masks and swim fins."

Helen started to giggle at the thought of those two walking up the beach, looking like creatures from the deep. The giggles quickly turned to laughter. Soon she was doubled over and out of control. Eventually, after dissolving into tears, she sat down to pet Mambo and regain her natural self-control.

"That was really quite charming." Ben smiled. "Usually it's me who looses it. I liked it a lot."

"It wasn't for your benefit, but it's always nice to know I've made you happy. Somehow I feel so much better. What say we open a bottle of champagne and celebrate."

"Why are you two sitting on the grass with bare feet, drinking a bottle of wine, two hours before the big reception?" asked Keoni.

Ben waved and said: "Pull up a bottle and join the party."

Keoni yelled: "Lani . . . come out here. Bring a bottle of champagne and two more glasses."

"Knock, knock . . . anyone home?"

"Jeez, that's Mr. Ron. What will he think?" Helen said as she scrambled to her feet. "We're out on the lawn, Ron."

"How special! I see you're relaxed and ready for me to take over. Don't fuss, just continue to do what it is you were doing, while I work my magic." Mr. Ron disappeared in the direction of the kitchen.

Helen sat back down on the lawn. "Is everything in control, or completely out of control?"

Lani answered: "I vote for completely *in* control. The food we planned is ready, Helen. I put most of it in the refrigerator, and the rest in coolers, on ice. Your house is clean, I can tell by the smell. The chairs on the lawn and the tiki torches look perfect, and Mr. Ron is here. All we really have left to do is get dressed and greet everyone."

"You're right, Lani. Where do you suppose Mr. Ron put the birds?"

Turning towards the large mango tree next to the house, Ben said: "I hear noises coming from that direction, so I suppose he's putting them in the shade of the tree – hopefully in cages. What birds, exactly?"

"It's a surprise. At the end of his parties, Ron entertains the guests with his trained birds. He's famous for that,"

"Okay."

CHAPTER 22.

Saturday evening . . .

As zero hour neared, Lani and Keoni went home to shower and dress.

Gazing into the closet, Ben asked Helen: "Which shirt do you think I should wear?"

"How about the navy blue one with the little white flowers, like Magnum's?"

"Okay. That'll go with my white slacks and my navy blue baseball cap."

"Cute. Now zip up my dress, and tell me everything is under control."

"Helen, I'm beginning to think this party is going to be memorable," said Ben as he zipped. "one that Sam and Woody will always remember. You look lovely in that color of blue, my dear."

"My dress is green, a shade of sea green, and thanks. You look pretty darn good yourself. I hope you're right about Sam and Woody having a memorable reception. They should be here any minute now. Where are Mambo and Windy? I haven't seen them for a while."

"They're fine, relax. I'm going to check out the coolers to be sure the ice is holding out."

Helen found Mr. Ron fussing over the dining room table. Protea flowers and lovely ferns were laid end to end down the center of the table, which was covered with a starched white linen tablecloth. In the center of the coffee table sat a dramatic arrangement of Bird of Paradise and Red Ginger. "The house looks lovely Mr. Ron. I like the special little nut dishes made out of coconuts, and the champagne glasses tied with purple and moss green satin ribbon."

Mr. Ron beamed. "I think you will also approve of the cake, Helen. It's a three tiered creation, which is being kept cool in Brian's air-conditioned van. He will drop it off about 8:15. Now quickly, come out on the patio and see how it looks, before the guests arrive."

"Oh, Ron, it's lovely. How did you get those paper lanterns strung from tree to tree? And the twinkle lights all over the bushes and along the fence – even coiled around the palm trees. It looks so magical!"

Ben slid the screen door open, joining Helen and Ron on the patio.

"Ron, this is my friend, Ben. Ben meet the famous Mr. Ron"

Ben smiled and held out his hand. "Nice to meet you Ron. I've heard a lot about you and your birds. I have to say, the place really looks great."

"You're a dear to say so, Ben. My crew did all this while you and Helen were dressing - they always work miracles. Next, they will be your waiters for the evening, except for Clive, who will be parking the cars."

"Thanks for taking all the stress from my shoulders, Ron."

"Helen, dear, that's my job."

Near Helen's carport, Mambo and Windy sat close together in the twilight shadows watching a yellow '36 Ford pull in behind Ben's van. No one noticed them sitting there and no one noticed them when they stretched and strolled leisurely towards the old mango tree next to the house.

"Helen, this is lovely." Sam exclaimed.

Woody gave Helen a hug and said: "Sure is, Mrs. Grant. I don't know how Sam and I can ever thank you. I see *my* parents are here, and even Grandmother, but I don't see *your* parents, Sam, are they coming?"

Helen answered. "Hillary phoned them this morning at their hotel. They were out, so she left a message."

"Hey, this is my one and only wedding reception, and I am not going to spoil it by worrying about Mom and Dad. If they show up, fine – if they don't . . . . Oh my God, Woody, what is that?" Sam said, pointing towards the beach.

Walking up the beach came two humans, one of who resembled King Neptune and the other, a mermaid. As they neared the patio, the piercing voice of the mature mermaid, who was carrying a plate of food, rang out like the bells of doom; "To our daughter and her husband, we bring gifts from the sea."

Just then Nacho and Justin arrived. "Hey Sam," Nacho said, with a big grin. "Congratulations on the recent nuptials."

Justin shook hands with Woody. "What's wrong, Woody? You look like you've seen a ghost."

Flo set a platter of assorted seafood nested in something green and slimy and garnished with tubular black and white striped things onto the patio table. Then flipping the long green hair of her wig off the plate and over her shoulder, she hoisted up her spandex tube top and turned towards the gaping guests - most of who were staring, and wondering if Mr. Ron had lost it. This nautical theme was definitely not his usual style.

Flo continued to rant in her shrill monotone voice, saying that she was willing to forgive Sam for eloping with what's-his-name and for being a runaway daughter. At the same time Homer set a large boom box on the patio and proceeded to plug it in to the outlet near the door.

Helen glanced over at Sam and saw in her eyes a mixture of panic and anger. Big tears were about to roll down her beautiful cheeks. A great feeling of love suddenly welled up in Helen's heart, and she knew she had to stop these fools from ruining Sam and Woody's evening.

As the boom box blasted out a nautical jig, Homer and Flo clasped hands as though they were preparing to dance . . . or chant. No one got a chance to find out because just then, Mr. Ron appeared.

With a dramatic flourish, he swept the screen door open and glanced at Helen, and she at him. With their minds attuned to one another, they went into action. Ron unplugged the boom box, grabbed it and the tray of seafood and disappeared into the house while Helen, aided by Ben, escorted a very angry Flo and a slightly drunk Homer towards the front door. Woody tossed Ben his car keys.

"Take the yellow Ford Ben, I'm parked behind you."

With Flo and Homer stuffed in the back seat, Ben put Woody's '36 Ford in gear and headed into town.

While Ben was gone, the party shifted into full swing. Keoni's friends from the Library Park concert played Hawaiian music out on the lawn. The waiters moved silently among the guests with trays of champagne and other assorted wines. People mingled in small groups, some standing down at the edge of the surf under the stars and the silvery half-moon, some dancing on the patio.

The delicious array of food set out on the dining room table was drawing attention. People wandered in and out of the house, plates piled high with delicious teriyaki chicken wings, fried rice, island-style ribs, poke, salmon, assorted fresh vegetables, a variety of sauces, and other island taste treats from Lani's kitchen.

Lani and Keoni sat on the patio with the newlyweds amongst the lanterns and twinkle lights. "Sam, I am so sorry about what happened."

"Thanks Lani, but you don't have to feel bad about it. It's better that my parents aren't here. Sometime soon I'll go to Nevada and visit them, but right now I just don't want them involved in my life."

"Where are you two going to live?" asked Keoni. "Here in Lahaina, or Upcountry?"

"We've agreed to live in Lahaina. I plan to relocate my custom car business here. Sam has her job at the hotel in Kaanapali, and frankly I think it best that we both break a few ties with our families."

Lani laughed. "I wish you two the best, whatever you do. I hope you'll drop by sometime and visit us in Olowalu."

At 8:15 Brian carefully backed his beeping, air-conditioned van as close as possible to Helen's front door. Then he and Mr. Ron, with one of the waiters to guide them, carried the lovely three-tiered wedding cake out to the patio table. Everyone gathered around for the cake-cutting ritual, no one noticing the rustling noises by the old mango tree near the side of the house.

"Ben! You made it back just in time. Here, have a piece of this heavenly cake."

"Thanks my dear. Everything okay?"

"Sure, why wouldn't it be?"

Woody's parents, Rev. and Mrs. Byrde, and his grandmother, Beverly Valdera, were just preparing to leave for their home in Kula when Mr. Ron announced that it was time for his big surprise, so they decided to stay. Everyone grabbed a chair or sat on the lawn, waiting in anticipation for the evening's climactic event.

As they waited patiently for the show to start, two adorable cats appeared on the patio, kind of like they were the star performers. Everyone applauded as they posed like twin statues of Egyptian royalty before their subjects.

"Ben, why does Mambo have a feather stuck on his paw?"

Ben gasped: "Oh, God! Please don't tell me Windy just burped."

As his panic continued to grow, Mr. Ron and Brian appeared carrying a small stage with a with a red velvet curtain, just like the old Rivoli Theatre used to have, Helen thought.

As the velvet curtains parted, the strains of Tiny Bubbles, played on ukuleles, floated from some unknown source. The sight was inspiring to Mambo. He instantly slouched into hunting mode with Windy following suit, her little chin vibrating and her teeth making clicking noises.

Whispering a nearly silent, "Oh Shit!" Ben quickly dashed to the patio, scooped both cats into his arms and headed to the master bathroom.

When he returned to sit by Helen on the lawn, he found her staring at the sight on the stage. Three myna birds, dressed in white collars, black bow ties and little tux shirt fronts that reached to their claws, stood lined up on a horizontal pole. Two of them were side by side, followed by an ominous space, and then a third bird.

"Helen," Ben whispered in her ear, "Why is there a space? Is there a bird missing? I think there are supposed to be four birds."

Before Helen could answer, they began to sing in their loud creaky Myna bird voices, each bird singing one word at a time. It went something like this:

Bird #1: Tiny
Bird #2: Bubbles
 - -
Bird #4: the

"Not too bad, considering bird #3 is missing." Ben whispered to Helen, who gave him a glazed look.

The second chorus was done with special lyrics, especially for Sam and Woody.

Bird #1: Sam
Bird #2: and
 - -
Bird #4: You're

Bird #1: so
Bird #2: fine,
  - -
Bird #4: be
Bird #1: happy
Bird #2: and
  - -
Bird #4: divine.

It was apparent by the loud burst of applause that most everyone was fascinated to watch trained Myna birds sing a song. For those guests who regarded singing birds differently, it is notable to mention that not a single one of them was insensitive enough to laugh outright. No one wanted to hurt Mr. Ron's feelings. Chief Johnstone was among those who had to swallow his laughter, along with Nacho, Joe and Keoni."

Helen glanced up at Ron, who stood with his hands clasped at his chest proudly gazing, with tears in his eyes, at his prize birds.

The unexpected climax came when two huge macaws swooped in and landed on Ron and Brian's shoulders in perfect unison. This was followed by a lovely rendition of the *Hawaiian Wedding Song* played live, by Keoni's friends from Library Park. Everyone, including Sam and Woody, the guests, Mr. Ron, Brian, Clive, the waiters and the assorted birds, sang along. It was the perfect way to end Sam and Woody's memorable evening.

Keoni, Lani and Chief Johnstone stayed to help clean up. While they were busy washing dishes and chattering away about the events of the evening, Mr. Ron's crew packed up the trays, platters, silverware and other equipment. Ben helped Ron carry the stage out to Brian's van, where the two macaws and three Myna birds were back in their cages, waiting to head home.

"Ron, there are no words to say how sorry I am about Bird #3. I feel like it's my fault for not watching the cats more closely. Is there any way I can try to make it up to you? Can I compensate you in some monetary way, perhaps?"

Thanks for offering, Ben, but nothing could ever replace Pedro; he was my finest vocalist. His death was not your fault, or the fault of the cats. I love all animals and I understand their primal urges. Mambo and Windy could no more control themselves than my lovely birds could if they saw a delicious lizard or perhaps a gourmet insect. Please don't let this tragedy spoil your memories of the evening."

"Ron, you're a gentleman and a scholar." Ben said, shaking his hand. "Thanks so much."

Back in the kitchen most of the mess was under control. Mambo and Windy were sprawled out on the kitchen floor, but no one seemed to mind. Chief Johnstone, who was feeling no pain after consuming numerous glasses of champagne and several cans of beer, said: "I would like to congratulate Ben and Helen for getting through a party without a major crime event.

Maybe you guys are finally over your. . . Jeez, Ben, was that a car crash?"

Everyone raced out the front door in reaction to the sound of metal crunching and glass shattering.

"Smoldering volcanoes! Look at my car!"

Standing beside the stove in police car, was Bonnie O'Connin Hartfield. "I'm sorry. I am so damn sorry. Helen? Where are you?"

"I'm right here, Bonnie. Why don't you come into the house."

"I have someone with me." Bonnie said, as she opened the passenger door of her rental car. Out stepped a tall, 50'ish strawberry blond. She appeared to be completely bewildered.

Keoni pushed his way forward until he was face to face with the woman. "Gayle? Gayle Reeves?"

Stunned into silence, they stood in the middle of the street, and stared at Keoni and Gayle. "You're alive?" he said. "Oh my God! Where have you been?" We thought you were murdered!"

Gayle looked down at the pavement, seeming to be deaf. Finally Chief Johnstone said: "Come inside everyone. I know it's late, but I have a few questions." He walked off mumbling something like: "I knew it! Inviting a dead person! I knew they'd come up with something nutty!"

Ben took Helen's hand and as they headed towards the house, he said: "I think we better make some coffee."

CHAPTER 23.

Sunday, November 7th

Let's not answer one more phone call, Ben. It's 7 A.M. and already it's been ringing non-stop. I think I slept a total of three hours last night, and I'm exhausted. Where's my coffee mug? The one with the plaid gecko?"

"I'll get it. I think it got put in the wrong cupboard last night when people were cleaning up the kitchen. Climb into the hammock and take a catnap while I find your favorite mug and whip up a light breakfast. Orange juice or tomato? Rye or whole wheat? Scrambled or boiled?"

"Tomato, rye, boiled, and marmalade. Thanks, Ben."

"No problem."

Helen carefully backed her butt onto the hammock and laid back in total comfort, instantly dozing off.

Ten minutes into her catnap, crucial hammock-balance shifted and she tumbled out onto the lawn. Mambo came over to rub against her leg as she attempted a graceful recovery. Windy stared at her until a mealy bug walked by, then stared at the mealy bug until Mambo walked by on his way to the beach. Like a shadow, she followed him.

"Nice recovery." Ben said as he set the breakfast tray on the patio table. Come, sit. Chairs are much safer than . . . "

"I don't care to discuss it, Ben. Could we talk about last night instead?"

"Where do you want to start? With Flo and King Neptune? The Myna Bird Murder? Or perhaps, the Grand Finale?"

The finale. For weeks now, we've been trying to figure out who killed Gayle Reeves and chopped her up – and then we find out she has been alive all along."

"You sound disappointed."

"No, I don't feel disappointed, but maybe a little foolish. I thought we had become great detectives, but great detectives don't try to solve murders that haven't happened."

"Personally, I believe we were well on the way to un-solving a non-murder." Ben said.

"Huh?"

"You got to admit, my dear, that Gayle's is an interesting story. Hold it, I think someone's at the door."

"At this hour?"

"Nacho? Justin? I didn't think you two were ever up this early."

"Only when we hear rumors that Gayle Reeves lives!" Said Nacho. "We tried to phone you guys, but the line was busy for an hour. So here we are. What's happening?"

Ben led the way to the patio, where Helen was pouring coffee into her plaid gecko mug. She said: "Hi Nacho, Justin, I had a feeling it might be you. Well gang, we blew it! Our 30 year old murder victim is not only alive and in one piece, but to top it off, she just killed Holden Albright!"

Justin sat across the patio table from Helen, while Nacho pulled his wheelchair up next to Ben. "Say what?"

Ben answered: "Last night Bonnie came here. For some reason, probably her emotional state, she ploughed her car into Chief Johnstone's squad car. He was a little tipsy and had been planning to hitch a ride home with Keoni and Lani, but believe me, he sobered up fast after Bonnie crashed the party with Gayle in tow."

"Get on with it, man." Nacho said, as he helped himself to toast and coffee.

Ben continued: It seems that much of what Bonnie told Helen and me the other day really was b.s.

However, part is true. For instance, thirty years ago, Gayle Reeves *was* a brilliant young woman with a promising future. She was studious and hard working and had a passion for history – especially Hawaiian history. Then one day she stole a beautiful and valuable locket from the Royal Hawaiian Museum. Later, when she lived in Lahaina and Bonnie was her roommate, Bonnie found it hidden in Gayle's drawer."

Justin interrupted: "Who was telling this story last night, Bonnie or Gayle?"

"Oh, sorry Justin, it was Bonnie. Gayle was just sitting there with a fixed stare, not saying a word."

"What's Gayle like? What does she look like?" asked Justin

"She seemed bewildered and confused – hardly said a word - just sat staring at the floor. As for how she looks . . ."

"I can describe her." Helen said. "Gayle is in her 50's, but she has no lines on her face. It's blank. There are no signs of having lived a life; no laugh lines, no crow's feet, not even a gray hair amongst the reddish blonde ones. Her features are perfect, somewhat like a doll's face. All of us, Chief Johnstone, Keoni and Lani and Ben and I, were mesmerized."

Nacho growled: "Me, I'm *not* mesmerized. On the contrary, I'm going to explode if you guys don't finish telling the story!"

"Sure thing, Nacho." Ben said. "Where was I? Oh, yeah, Gayle was upset that Bonnie found the locket. She swore Bonnie to secrecy, but like most secrets, it wasn't kept. Eventually word got to Holden and

Morton Albright. Being a couple of stupid opportunists, who were always looking for a few easy bucks, they decided to take the locket from Gayle. They had no idea it was historically valuable, probably thought it was worth a few hundred dollars. Anyway, Holden, who was in lust with Gayle, got her alone and tried charm her into showing it to him. When this didn't work, he beat her up, but she managed to break free and run for it. After that, she gave the locket to Bonnie, and asked her to put it in a safe deposit box. Bonnie did this, and then cautioned Gayle not to go out alone. Keoni, Windley and others, were also worried about Gayle. They suspected that Holden was the one who beat her up so they tried to keep a protective eye on her, but, despite this, a week later Holden raped Gayle, nearly killing her."

"Near Hale Aloha?" asked Justin.

"Not sure where the rape occurred, but that's where Bonnie found her. Gayle was in bad shape, but somehow Bonnie got her back to their rooming house. She phoned Gayle's father in New York, then nursed Gayle's wounds as best she could while she waited for Mr. Reeves to fly to Hawaii. It was then that she began to notice that Gayle had other wounds – deep emotional wounds. When Gayle's father arrived, he immediately packed her stuff and took her home to New York. Bonnie, who was very frightened of Holden, went with them on the same plane, relieved to be out of Lahaina."

"What about the notebook?" asked Justin.

Helen answered: "After the rape, while Bonnie was waiting for Mr. Reeves to arrive, she concocted the lament and fake maps. She wanted to leave clues making it look like Holden murdered Gayle and dismembered her body. Bonnie already found out from some locals that there were bones near the little park by the harbor, so she made it seem like they were Gayle's bones. Then she drew the little maps and put an X here and there to indicate where Gayle's bones were buried. Before Bonnie left for New York she put the orange notebook in Larry Windley's desk. He was either was too busy to read it, or to figure it out, or he forgot it was there. Then, when he went out sailing and never came back, it got packed away in the box, along with his other papers. Through the years Bonnie must have wondered what happened to it. Maybe she thought it got tossed out. It was only just before Tom died, that she knew it had surfaced. When she came to my house the other day and tried to convince me that Holden killed Gayle, she still wanted him to be arrested and charged with her murder."

"Awesome, considering Gayle is still alive!" said Justin.

"The locket . . . what happened to it?"

"That's quite interesting, Nacho. Bonnie took it with her to New York. She kept it, thinking that when Gayle recovered she would give it back to her. But Gayle was in and out of mental hospitals with a fairly blank mind, for the next twenty-five years, suffering one breakdown after another. She was finally released about five years ago, and has been living with her father since. She never asked Bonnie about the locket, so it stayed in a safe deposit box.

Through the years, Bonnie became close to Gayle's father. She was like a daughter to him, and he thought of her children as his grandkids. She was closer to him than to her own father."

"So you're saying that Gayle spent half of her life in a mental institution?" Nacho asked.

"Yeah."

"I have several questions, but the most urgent one is, why did Gayle show up here?"

"Revenge." Helen answered. "To all appearances her mind had cleared after twenty-five years, but deep inside, undetected, a malignant hate had grown. So when Bonnie left for her father's funeral, Gayle followed. She used Bonnie's itinerary . . . the same airlines and same hotel. She would never have attempted to plan a trip like this by herself. She arrived the day of Tom's memorial service, Thursday, November 4th."

"I'm sorry, but all this sounds odd to me." said Nacho. "I still don't see why Bonnie didn't give information to the police 30 years ago. She could have mailed the information from New York, if she was afraid of Holden."

Helen continued: "You're right, she could have found a way around it, but there's another reason. Holden stole a painting from his brother. He stole it because Gayle asked him to, promising him sexual favors in return. Huge mistake! She used Holden to do her dirty work, and then when he came to collect, she balked."

"My God, how could Gayle be that stupid? She knew he was a violent scum bag."

"I know, Nacho, I feel the same way. My guess is that as an avid historian, she developed a personal bond with Princess Pualei that warped her good sense. I think she coveted the locket because it belonged to the Princess, not because of its monetary value – the same reason she wanted the painting of her. Gayle was obsessed. As soon as Holden delivered the stolen painting to her, she took it out of the frame and rolled it into a tube, wrapped it in protective canvas and hid it."

"Where?" asked Nacho and Justin in unison.

"Nobody knows, and she's not talking.

"Oh my God!" Ben shouted. "That's why the Windley box was the target of the break-ins! Lucille was after the painting! Not the notebook! She didn't find out about the notebook until that day when Tom, Justin and Helen were eating lunch on Pineapples porch. Perp overheard the conversation and must have told Cousin Lucille what he heard. Then she and Grandpa Holden figured out that the notebook might have clues to where the painting was hidden."

"Let me get this straight," Justin said. "When Holden heard about the Windley box surfacing, he got his nutty granddaughter to break into Helen's office and her house and your van, searching for the painting? Maybe the locket too? *Not* the notebook? Then later Lucille found out about the notebook and because it might have clues to a hidden painting, she took 9-0 and asked for it and $5,000?"

"Right."

They all sat quietly for a few moments. Then Nacho said: "So Gayle killed Holden!"

"Yes." Ben said. "She planned it well in advance, arriving in Maui the morning of the memorial service which, by the way, is the reason Bonnie wasn't there. When Gayle got to the hotel she phoned Holden and invited him to Bonnie's room. Bonnie says she pleaded with Gayle not to invite him over, saying that it was a dangerous idea. But there was no stopping her from facing the man she had hated all those years. Bonnie says she had no idea Gayle was planning to kill Holden. Said she was caught off guard when Gayle suddenly pushed him over the lanai railing. The hotel room was on the eighth floor, so he died instantly when he hit the cement sidewalk below."

Justin interrupted: "How could she manage to push Holden over the railing? Wouldn't he put up a struggle? Wasn't he stronger than her? I mean she doesn't sound like the most physically fit person on the planet."

"I think I might be able to answer that." Nacho said. "Holden basically took her life from her when he raped her. For thirty years she spent every minute hating him and wanting revenge. I think all that hate gave her the strength to shove the creep over the edge. Either that, or Bonnie helped her."

"Did Gayle actually admit she killed Holden?"

"Yes, she did, Justin. At first, while Bonnie was talking, Gayle was silent, then suddenly she whispered:

It's over – it's finally over. . . the filthy bastard is dead!
Chief Johnstone reminded her about her rights to legal
representation, but she continued to stare at the floor,
whispering: *I killed him at last.*"

Everyone sat for a moment, letting all the new
information sink in. Finally Nacho asked: "So, does
anyone have any idea where the painting could be
hidden?"

CHAPTER 24.

Sunday afternoon . . .

Lucille was lost and sad. Someone had killed her Grandpa Holden, the only one in the family who understood her. Her parents on the Big Island were always fighting and always drinking; either too drunk or too angry to notice her. A few months ago she left and came to Maui, but now it seemed like her life was even worse than it was before.

Hans and his wife acted like they had done her some big favor by letting her work in that junky shop. As for Uncle Morton, she hadn't seen him since she was about eleven and could hardly remember him at all.

His son, Perp, was a little weasel. Where the hell was he, anyway? Probably hiding somewhere with that damned dog. How she would love to find that stupid mutt and fire a bullet through it's head.

Lucille would have done anything for Grandpa Holden, and now he was gone forever. Well there was one thing she could do for him – she could keep looking for what he wanted. Okay, so it wasn't in the Master's Reading Room, or in the cottage on the beach, or even in the van. It had to be somewhere! She jammed her bandaged leg into her tight leather pants. The dog bite was throbbing and the stitches in her arm itched, she was hot and sweaty, but grimly determined.

At three o'clock that afternoon Helen awoke from a long nap feeling rested. She showered, slipped on a pink cotton sundress and wandered out on the patio to let the sun and breeze dry her hair. Ben was gone; a note on the table said he would be back around five. So much had happened the last few days. She had to wonder what would happen to Gayle now. Would she be charged with murder? Declared insane? Maybe let off due to extenuating circumstances? There were so many questions.

The phone rang. Mambo and Windy twitched their ears. Helen answered: "Hello? - - Bonnie! What's happening? Where are you? Where's Gayle?"

"Gayle has been charged with second degree murder and is in the hospital undergoing some tests. She's not feeling well and so far they can't figure out why. Her father's arranging for a big-time attorney from Oahu to defend her – maybe try to get her off due to her mental condition. As for me, I am heading to your place with a gift for you."

When Bonnie arrived, Helen saw that she had a paper sack in her hand.

"Oh good, you brought some pastries."

"Not hardly, Helen. Take a look at this."

Bonnie removed a black velvet jewelry box and opened it, exposing diamonds and rubies to the sunlight. Prism-like sparkling lights flashed in all directions. Mambo and Windy chased the magical rainbows like they were butterflies.

"Oh, Bonnie, the locket! It's beautiful! May I hold it?"

"Not only can you hold it, I am leaving it with you to do whatever you think is best. I only ask one thing; if you should decide to return it to the museum, please don't tell them that Gayle took it. She was a good person who sort of got caught up in the romantic side of history. She has had such a dreadful life. Please don't add this disgrace to her already grim existence."

"I think that could be arranged." Helen said. "Has Gayle seen it since she gave it to you 30 years ago?"

"No. She hasn't mentioned it in all that time, and I don't think showing it to her now is a good idea. She seems to be slipping away again into her own little world."

"Did Gayle ever give you any idea where she hid the painting?"

"This is really weird Helen, but I remember on the flight to New York, after she was raped, she said that no one would never think of looking in such a logical place. I asked where that place was, of course, but she never said any more about it."

"What are your plans now, Bonnie?"

"As soon as I give my deposition, I plan to fly back home to New York. I have to be in court on Thursday in Wailuku, and hopefully I can leave for the airport the following day. So I'll say goodbye now."

Helen could hardly wait for Ben to get home – she was dying to show him the locket. As soon as he opened the patio door, carrying two large sacks of Chinese take out, she opened the black velvet box. The last rays of the setting sun gave light and life to the precious stones, causing Ben to gasp.

"The *Aloha Locket*, I presume. It's lovely . . . very exotic and Spanish looking. I take it Bonnie dropped it off?"

As Helen related the afternoon visit with Bonnie, Ben struggled to get his chopsticks in a finger-twisting position that would allow him to pick up big things, like shrimp and peapods, from the carton of Chinese takeout. Mambo sat poised to grab anything that might end up on the floor.

"Nothing's ever over till it's over, is it? More rice?" He said.

"What does that mean, Ben? Yes, I would like more rice – it goes perfectly with the broccoli and beef "

It means that it's not over until we find the painting. Where do we start looking for it?"

"Pass the soy sauce, please. Thanks."

"That sketch of the locket you found in Windley's box . . . why do you suppose it was there?" Ben asked.

"It was Bonnie's handwriting, so I surmise that after Gayle gave her the locket and told her to put in a safe deposit box, Bonnie got curious about it's history and made a sketch of it. She must have given it to Windley, who was a good person to ask about historical matters, since he was knowledgeable in that area."

"Okay. Now refresh me on this; did Bonnie know about the stolen painting back in 1967?"

"Yes, but she had no idea where Gayle hid it."

"Back to my original question: Where do we start to look for the painting?"

"The only clues we have are that it's rolled up and wrapped in something protective, and that it's hidden in a logical place that no one would think of looking."

"Like?" Ben asked.

"My mind is a blank, I can't think of any *logical* place where a rolled up painting could have been hidden for 30 years without eventually being discovered. Of course she could have buried it, in which case we would have to dig up half the town to find it. Or maybe she left it with someone in Lahaina who has it in their attic and has forgotten all about it."

"Tell you what, my dear, let's go have a chat with Hans. It was after all, his painting originally. Maybe he knows something helpful."

The evening was cool and clear when Ben and Helen parked the van near the harbor. Hand in hand they strolled up Canal Street, past King Kamehameha III School.

"Isn't this where the whaling boats came in to get supplies?" Ben asked.

Helen, who can never pass up chance to paint a historical picture, described the Government Market place that was built over the canal. "Of course all the tropical foliage they used to build it, dried out and it wasn't long before it burned down." Pointing towards Front Street, she continued: "See there, Ben? That's where the Bridge of Sighs was, right over the canal. It led to Rotten Row where the saloons and bars were located."

Turning left, they walked past the Banyan tree, the Pioneer Inn, and the Library, ending up at Han's shop, near the seawall. He was standing behind the counter waiting on a customer, but he glanced up, indicating to Ben that he would be right with them. As soon as the customer left, he put the 'Closed' sign in the window and invited them out on his seaside deck behind the store.

"Please sit down. I have some things I want to say. First of all, I hope you don't think I was involved in any of the sick things that my brother did 30 years ago or any of the stupid things he and Lucille did recently. He's been a trouble maker all his life, and all I ever wanted was for him to shape up."

Helen spoke up: "We know about Holden and Morton and the troubles they got into, and we know that you were not involved. We're here to see what you know about the painting that was stolen from you and your wife 30 years ago."

"Oh, that thing? It was a wedding gift from my wife's family. Frankly I never liked it, so when it was stolen I was sort of glad I didn't have to look at that Englishman's face any more. My wife's family was upset when they heard about the theft, even reported it to the police, but after a few months even they forgot about it. I never knew it was Holden who stole it until yesterday, when Chief Johnstone told me. I had no reason to think it was Holden. What would he want with an old painting?"

"You have any idea where it might be hidden?" Ben asked.

"I have no idea, but I ought to warn you that Holden's granddaughter, Lucille, is following in his footsteps. She's looking for the painting too and will stop at nothing to find it."

"We've run into Lucille before." Helen said, remembering back to Halloween night when 9-0 attacked the black clad idiot. "She's responsible for the break-ins and for what happened to Tom O'Connin. Frankly Hans, I would like to see her locked up for a long time!"

"So would I, Helen. Maybe with her and Morton in jail, and Holden dead, I can finally have some peace and quiet in my life. By the way, what's the big deal with this painting any way?"

"We're not sure, Hans. Helen and I and some of our friends are trying to find out more about it, and it's connection to the past. If we find out anything important, we'll let you know."

CHAPTER 25.

Monday, November 8th

"Ben, I think we're being followed by a large van."
Helen said.

"Are you sure?"

"It's been with us since we left the bank, it was
there when we went to the grocery store, and I saw it
just now as we left the drug store."

"Okay, that does it! No doubt it's Lucille who's
following us. Let's stop and see Justin, I have an idea."

It was just past lunchtime; Pineapples was not crowded as they entered and were greeted by Justin. "Hey, you two, what's up?"

"Hi Justin. Can you join us? Where's Nacho?"

"He's at work but he'll be by shortly for a coffee break. Don't look now, but I think Lucille Wonnaku just came in."

"That's the plan, my boy. She is following us and I want her to think that we've found the painting. This time we'll be ready for her and we'll catch her in the act of breaking in. I want her locked up for a long, long time and this is one way to do it."

"Does entrapment come to mind?" Justin asked.

"Only if entrapment can be proven, and in this case, how? Besides, Helen and I may actually have an idea where the painting is. Don't we, Hon?"

"We do?" Helen asked.

"Come on, my dear, think . . . you must have some ideas."

"Well yes, actually I do. I've been thinking about it, and I surmise that there is a possibility that the painting was not hidden in a rolled up state. It may have been rolled it up for a while, but on the day Gayle hid it, she may have laid it flat."

"Flat! Wow, Mrs. G., that conjures up all sorts of logical places for it to be."

Ben looked skeptical. "Name a logical place, Justin."

"A drawer, suitcase, trunk, briefcase, box, shelf, under a rug, under a floor . . . you know, places like that."

"*Or*," said Helen, "behind another painting."

As Nacho approached them he seemed excited. "Hey guys, I could feel the electric charge from a block away. Your investigative minds are working together on a problem, right? What's the problem?"

Justin poured Nacho a mug of French Roast and said: "The problem of where's the painting hidden, is it rolled up or flat? Is it inside or outside? You know, stuff like that."

Nacho looked thoughtful as he said: "Gayle promised Holden sexual favors if he'd steal the painting so, when he delivered it she was scared. She had only a few days, maybe only hours to hide it. Burying it would have seemed a bad idea - it would take too long and it might ruin the paint. I deduce that it is more her style to hide her cherished painting in a warm safe place."

Ben applauded. "Spoken like Sherlock Holmes himself! Careful, Nacho, or you'll cause another power outage."

"Just using the old deductive reasoning, my man. And further more, I conclude that the black leather ghoul sitting two tables over is trying to hear our conversation."

"She followed us here." Helen said.

"You mean you led her here. I know you two, and I can see a trap in the making. I like it!"

Ben grinned, leaned in close and whispered: "We want her to think we know where the painting is hidden. We have to do something!"

"Wait," Helen urged, "we need to have a plan before we do something."

"Right, my dear, you're always so reasonable. So, what's the plan?"

"I think what Nacho said about Gayle hiding the painting in a warm safe place is viable; however, almost any place she would have chosen to hide it would eventually change, over a period of 30 years. It could have been redecorated, burned down, torn down, restored, etc. So if the painting was hidden in the walls, under the floor or behind another painting, the chances are it would not be there now.

"You said *almost* any place, Helen. Do you have a place in mind where she might have hidden it?"

"Yes Justin, I think I know of two places that *could* be housing the missing portrait. So my plan would be for us to seem excited about something, then shout 'Hurrah' and leave, causing Lucille to think we've had a break through. Follow my lead."

With that said, Helen and Ben slapped a high five and everyone cheered and laughed. Then when Helen shouted 'Hurrah' they all got up and headed across the street to the Baldwin House.

"Wow, this place is beautiful!" Nacho exclaimed. "It's roomy and so New England-like . . . where's the kitchen?"

"The kitchen was in a separate building outside. Right there," Helen said, pointing to a small circle of stones outside the back door. As she began describing the dishes displayed in the dining room cupboard, Ben and Justin wandered off towards the north end of the house where, in the mid 1800's, Dr. Baldwin's office was located.

"Look at these old medical instruments, Justin. Is that a tooth-puller?"

"Yeah, I think so, and those little glass bottles must have been for medicines, pills, and potions."

"Hey, you two, we have work to do." Helen said. "The house is open to the public every day, you can take a tour any time you want."

Back in the living room she headed directly to the portrait of Rev. Dwight Baldwin, resident of the lovely missionary home from 1834 to 1868.

Martha, the docent, was at the front door welcoming a group of four tourists. As part of her tour, she pointed out the painting of Rev. Baldwin on the wall above the rocking chair used by Charlotte Baldwin to rock her babies to sleep. As Martha led the tourists through the dining room and towards the back of the house, the sleuths continued to stare at the portrait; gesturing, pointing and whispering.

The plan was working like a charm so far. Lucille Wonnaku was out on the front porch peeking in through the open window, observing with rapt attention the excited group of what she thought to be, weirdoes. Just then she heard footsteps clomping up the porch stairs, and turned to see Chief Johnstone approaching. Quickly she sat down on a bench and looked in the opposite direction.

"In his booming voice the Chief addressed the group of sleuths: "What are you up to now, my friends?"

"Hi Chief. Could we talk out back, in the parking lot? I think there's a tour going on." Helen said.

Nacho, Justin, Ben, Helen and Chief Johnstone left by the back door, taking the little ramp down to the lovely shaded parking lot.

"You're up to something." the Chief said. "The guys at Pineapples told me you were over here, and when I came up on the porch, I saw Lucille Wonnaku looking in through the window. What's going on?"

"Did you speak to her?" Helen asked.

"No, I pretended not to notice her. After all, I wouldn't want to mess up another one of your famous stings, now would I? What are you up to? "

"Actually Chief, we were just minding our own business trying to figure out where the painting is hidden, when suddenly Lucille showed up." Ben explained.

"Right!" Chief Johnstone answered sarcastically. "And when I was told that you guys were here, I rushed over to invite you out on my new yacht! Does that painting in there have anything to do with what you were doing when you were just minding you're own business?"

"Look," Nacho said, "we're on your side, Chief. We were just following our natural good sense in hunting down a missing artifact when, like a bird dog, Lucille shows up."

"Okay I give up. I will leave you here to do whatever it is you are doing." Then dripping with sarcasm, he continued: "I would hate to interfere with you when you're doing my job, anyway. Tell you what, just in the remote possibility that you might need the assistance of a lawman, I'll station an officer in front of the Baldwin House for the next 24 hours. Don't worry I'll instruct him to hide in the bushes or disguise himself as a tree – you know, something that will fit in with your scheme."

With surveillance taken over by the police, Justin and Nacho headed back to work, and Ben and Helen went up to the Master's Reading Room to check out the old paintings.

"That worked out well, don't you think, Helen? Now that there's a police officer stationed at the Baldwin House, we can relax and let him do all the work." Looking around Helen's office, he continued: "This is where Gayle worked, isn't it?"

"Yes, I think she and the others who typed all that history worked here at least part of the time."

Looking around at the walls of the room, Ben said: "Do you think any of these paintings were here at that time?"

"Possibly. I do know that this room and the Baldwin House are two places in which a painting could have hung on the same wall for 30 years without ever being replaced. There's only one way to tell if what we're looking for is here – we have to poke around the back side of these paintings."

With her heart pounding, Lucille ran down the porch steps of the Baldwin House, raced to her van and drove directly to her Uncle Hans house. She told him she was looking for a CD that Perp had borrowed from her a few weeks ago.

"All of Perp's things are in the closet in the back room." Hans said. "He's staying at Boys Camp, you know."

"I wondered where the little ra . . . kid was. Don't get up, I'll just go rummage around and get my stuff, okay?"

By the time Helen and Ben had checked out five of the paintings, it was beginning to get dark. "This is the one, Ben, I just know it. Look at the way it's assembled in the back. See?" Helen said excitedly. "Half the staples are in wrong and the other half are coming loose; this was done by an amateur."

"Is this guy in the painting, famous? It's such a dark picture, I can barely make out his face."

"He's probably a ship captain, Ben. Looks more like a mortician. I've never really thought much about the painting, or him . . . until now!"

Lucille climbed into the back of her van carrying a large paper grocery sack, the contents of which she dumped onto the floor. Good ole cousin Perp, the little twit, always had a stash of fireworks whether it was New Years Eve, Fourth of July or any other time of the year. There were cherry bombs, Roman candles, and a glorious assortment of other amazing explosive wonders. Just what Lucille was looking for.

The police officer stationed at the Baldwin home was standing under the grape arbor at the side of the house, trying to become invisible. Chief Johnstone had given him orders to meld into the scenery and to be on the lookout for anything from armed robbery to attacking cats. *Attacking cats?* Perhaps the Chief was becoming overworked . . .stressed out.

Is there always a cop here? Lucille wondered. No sweat. She knew the diversion scheme would take care of him, as well as anyone else who might be around. She would have to work fast.

Heading to the little seven foot by seven foot kioske on the Front Street side of the Baldwin lawn, she carefully kept the tiny building between her and the cop under the grape arbor. Gently she pried the window open with her trusty screwdriver. Without missing a beat she struck a match and lit the paper sack on fire. As soon as she tossed it inside, smoke began to billow out through the open window, quickly followed by a series of sharp little pops, probably one of the packages of ladyfingers. Lucille had counted eight packages, each one containing 2,000 of the little firecrackers.

As the cop approached to investigate the smoke and noise, Lucille crept around the opposite side of the kiosk. Keeping it between them, she made her way around to the side of the house and into the parking lot behind.

People were running towards the front lawn to see what all the commotion was about. Several cherry bombs, fountains, and the Roman candles blasted off all at once, breaking the windows, followed by red white and blue smoke. *Quite impressive*, Lucille thought.

It was an easy task for her to break into the house. She was getting better at it. This time she avoided cutting her herself.

"Ben, what's all that racket?"

"Judging from the whistling, popping and booming, I'd say someone is celebrating the New Year two months early."

Rushing out on the veranda of the MRR, they stood transfixed by the scene below, as the little building belched out blue smoke, gold sparks and balls of flaming red and green things. Loud exploding noises reverberated in all directions. The crowd across the street was applauding and pointing as a burst of spinning gizmos flew out onto the lawn. Traffic on Front Street had slowed to a standstill and the park next-door was filling with teenagers who were jumping up and down and cheering. The distinctive sound of fire trucks could be heard heading down the highway. Police sirens also added to the festivities as four squad cars, including Chief Johnstone's battered vehicle, screeched into the parking lot in back of the house.

"Helen, if we have any sense at all, we'll stay up here on the veranda and pretend that we are not involved in this."

"We *aren't* involved in this. . . are we?"

"Well, from what I can figure out, Lucille is trying to steal the painting of Rev. Baldwin, while diverting the cop's attention with an exploding kiosk. Why do you suppose she is doing that?"

"Well, because she overheard us shouting 'Hurrah' and then followed us and saw us staring at the painting. But that's not our fault. I mean, are we responsible for what another person does? Can't a group of friends stare at a painting without someone blowing up a kiosk?"

"Of course they can! You are absolutely right! We're *not* responsible - we're just innocent bystanders! So follow me, my clever one, and we'll disappear quietly into the night, leaving Chief Johnstone scratching his head. What's that kiosk used for, anyway?"

So that's how it came to be that Helen and Ben were strolling hand in hand down a starlit beach, minding their own business, when the last pathetic little pinkish roman candle plopped onto the lawn and Lucille Wonnaku was arrested. Charges included stealing a famous artifact, destroying public property, and violating city noise restrictions.

Despite a massive manhunt throughout the Baldwin Home and the surrounding compound and parking lot, Chief Johnstone found no trace of the four of them.

He even had Officer Jannola climb up on the roof. "No trace of them up here, sir. Can I come down now?"

Paying no attention to his officer on the roof, the Chief headed to Pineapples. Spotting Nacho and Justin eating what appeared to be their dinner, he shouted: "Just what do you two think you are doing?"

"Eating dinner?" Justin answered.

"And I suppose Ben and Helen are here eating dinner too?"

"Sorry, we haven't seen them since this afternoon." Nacho answered.

"Aha! Then they *are* over there at the scene of the explosion!"

"What explosion?" they asked, innocently.

Justin calmly dialed his cell phone, then handed it to Chief Johnstone.

"Hello?" he said, to the phone. "Ben? Is that you? Where are you? Where have you been? - - Hand in hand down a starlit beach? Yeah, right! - - So, you haven't heard about the little fireworks display? - - You know full well where! It was in the police satellite kiosk. Where are you now? - - On the patio with a glass of wine? Are you alone? - - Mambo? Put him on!"

Handing Justin back his cell phone back, the Chief turned and left the restaurant, mumbling something about when cows fly.

CHAPTER 26.

Thursday, November 11th

"Are you going to take Justin to the airport today, Ben?"

"Yes, and Nacho's coming too, and so are you. We're heading out early so we'll have time to stop at Boys Camp."

"Ah, so you asked Justin and Nacho what they think of donating $15,000 of our trust money to help with new appliances and building repairs?"

"Yes, and they are most enthusiastic. Both of them want to see the place. So get you butt in gear, and let's get going."

Keoni and a large group of boys were standing by the chicken hale when they drove up. He shook hands with Ben, Nacho, and Justin, and gave Helen a hug. Then he introduced every one of the boys by name, including Perp, now known as Michael.

"The boys are anxious to show you around so let's get started." Keoni said.

Off they dashed, excitedly pointing out every chicken, cat, goat and duck along the way to the vegetable garden. As soon as the adults caught up with them, the boys proudly pointed out their squash, melons, tomatoes, corn and beans, etc., then raced to the taro patch where they waited for Michael and two other boys, who were chasing a small herd of goats away from the vegetable garden.

After demonstrating how the lo`i is irrigated, they led the way to the bunkhouses. Justin and Nacho were impressed with the layout, which included a twin bed, dresser, and study desk for each boy. Everything was neat, clean and orderly. Screened windows let in the cool breeze, assisted by ceiling fans. Helen noted that most of the screens needed to be replaced and some of the siding was rotted. At each end of the two bunkhouses were bathrooms with showers in sad need of repair.

"We've saved the best for last." Keoni said. "Let's head to the corral and see the newest member of our family."

The boys approached the horse corral slowly and quietly so as not to frighten the beautiful little colt standing close beside his mother. He was fawn colored, adorable, and definitely the pride of Keoni and all the boys.

"Man, this place is so great!" said Nacho, as 9-0 leaped onto his lap. "My brother Nathaniel's coming for a visit at Thanksgiving, I sure would like for him to see this place."

Keoni turned to the boys and said: "You guys want to announce your big surprise now? Thomas, you can be the spokesman"

Thomas, one of the older boys, came forward and very formally invited all of the benefactors to come for a Thanksgiving Day feast. He added: "Everything we'll be serving, except the turkey, will be grown here on our farm; even the pumpkins for the pies! Then after dinner, we'll entertain you with our ukulele band and the Boys Camp Choir, who will be singing Christmas Carols. Kimo and Lelani will be Mr. and Mrs. Santa, so I guess you could say that we're kicking off the holiday season. Mr. Nacho, there will be plenty of food, so your brother can come too."

They were overwhelmed by the generous invitation and thanked the boys profusely, saying that they would be anxiously awaiting the feast. Keoni interrupted to say: "You're the ones who are being thanked. The donation you've made will help us in so many ways. I've already ordered the biggest refrigerator and freezer combo on the market – it'll be delivered tomorrow. I think Kimo's planning to declare it a national holiday!"

On the way back from the airport, after seeing Justin and his brothers and his cousin off for their ski trip,

Nacho said: "Justin's so excited to be going to Aspen; it's all he's been talking about for a week! I hope he gets this squirrel and raccoon thing out of his system."

Ben said: "My brother arranged to have the cabin stocked with all sorts of gourmet food, including chips, salsa, beer and lots of hot chocolate for those snowy evenings. I know they'll have a great time."

Helen sighed. "It's going to be too quiet here with Justin in Aspen, and Woody and Sam on their honeymoon. All the excitement of the past few weeks has ended. Oh well, it's probably a good thing, don't you think?"

"Here's what I think," said Ben "let's head up to town and see if the Arts Shoppe has finished removing the rest of the Englishman's portrait. Maybe they've uncovered the face of Princess Pualei, at last."

"Great idea Ben. You got time, Nacho?"

"Sure. It's my day off, and nothing could be better than seeing our latest adventure come to a fitting end."

Miss Hunter, from the Royal Hawaiian Museum, along with several other history experts, were gathered around an artist who was patiently using some awful smelling potion to remove the old painting of the Englishman.

Helen shook hands with Miss Hunter, then introduced Ben and Nacho, explaining to them that she was the archivist at the museum who had been so helpful in identifying the locket.

When they told Miss Hunter how they discovered the painting in the Master's Reading Room, she was amazed by their story. "After we're through here Mrs. Grant, I hope you can show me around. I would love to see the old buildings with you as my guide."

"I'd be happy to show you as soon as we check out the painting - I'm dying to know what's been uncovered."

"Take a look." Miss Hunter said.

Helen leaned over the shoulder of the artist, who was using a soft cloth to clean off the last remnants of smeared paint. What was emerging gave her a serious attack of chicken skin. For the first time, she looked into the extraordinary face of Princess Pualei; a face dominated by beautiful dark eyes. She had a resigned expression, as though she was enduring an experience that bored her, but was necessary. Yet when you looked closer there was a soft touch of humor showing in the curve of her lips, and there was definitely a proud tilt to her head. So much could be read in the artist's strokes.

"She's lovely! Look, she's wearing the *Aloha locket*!"

"Yes, indeed!" exclaimed Miss Hunter. Now all we have to do is hope that it can be located."

Helen gave Ben and Nacho a look that said: *Don't say a word!*

Turning to Miss Hunter and smiling, she said: "Miss Hunter, I have a wonderful surprise for you. It's something I ran across while searching for the painting. I guess you could say it's one of those weird little coincidences that happen in historical circles, from time to time."

She handed Miss Hunter the black velvet box. There was stunned silence as she opened the lid. Then, from the fascinated onlookers came a large group gasp. Everyone stared down at the glittering locket lying in the velvet box. Then almost in unison, all heads turned toward the painting, where it was depicted clearly, around the neck of Princess Pualei. It was one of those magical moments that connect the past directly to the present.

After they had recovered, Miss Hunter said: "We'll be taking the painting, and now the locket too, back to Oahu, where they'll go on display at the museum. Fortunately Mr. Hans Albright and his family have consented to donate the portrait to the museum. It could have been a sticky wicket if they had laid claim to it. We're very grateful for their generosity – and yours. Thank all of you so very much. By the way, do you have any idea how the necklace got to Lahaina?"

"Sure don't. Nope. No idea at all." They all said in unison.

Following a whirlwind tour of historic sites with Miss Hunter, Helen raced back home to join Nacho and Ben, who were flaked out on the patio enjoying the end of a rather perfect day. As Ben poured a glass of wine, Helen sat in her favorite patio chair, and slipped off her shoes.

Nacho proposed a toast with his beer can: "Here's to Hans for giving up the painting."

"And here's to us, for solving yet another complex mystery." said Ben, raising his glass of Merlot.

"Mystery? The mystery intruder? The mysterious missing painting? The stolen locket? The live dismembered body? The missing Myna? Which mystery?" asked Helen.

"All of the above, my dear."

As they sat basking in the glow of self-adulation, Nacho said: "You remember the tale of the howling dog and the screaming woman at Hale Aloha at midnight? Was that Galyle Reeves, do you think?"

"Here's what I think." Ben said. "I think that the howling dog belonged to Mrs. Sylva's neighbor, the very dog who barked at roosters and bayed at the moon. I think the scream was from Bonnie when she found poor Gayle laying there after the rape."

Putting in her two cents worth, Helen said: "Odd events tend to become urban legends and sometimes become a part of history. Usually they're based on some real event, but through the years they develop a life of their own. We'll never know the actual story because we cannot go back in time. Considering that it was at least thirty years ago, I am amazed that so much truth actually did come out."

Silence settled over the pensive trio. Waves lapped onto the shore. The light of day began to fade.

"I have news." Helen said, with a big smile. "My whole family is coming over for Christmas. This will be the first time we will all be together since I moved here."

"Sounds like a fun time, my dear. How about we take them all up to Makawao for the day, and stop at the Ocean Center on the way back. The little grandkids would love that."

"Wonderful idea Ben, and then on Christmas day we'll all gather here for a feast. Will your brother still be here Nacho? Love to have him join us."

"He'll be here if I can talk him into staying just a few days longer. But me . . . I'll be here. Wow, a real Christmas with kids, family and friends. It's been a long time since I . . ."

Mambo suddenly slammed onto the patio from somewhere in the bushes and raced for the swinging cat door.

It's unknown why at that exact moment Windy decided to gather up all her courage and approach the scary little door from the opposite side, in her first attempt to hop through it, but she did. Their heads, Mambo's heading mauka, and Windy's makai, collided in perfect precision.

Momentarily stunned, Mambo shook it off and, like the dignified feline he is, and sauntered off to the edge of the patio to lick his fur. Windy on the other hand, had a gross attack of fear and spent that night and the following day under the bed. She never tried hopping through the cat door again.

Ben, Nacho, and Helen, who had witnessed the catastrophic collision, were momentarily shocked into silence; then Helen noticed a muffled snuffing noise. She turned to Nacho and Ben, and said: "Stop that! It's not funny!"

To which Nacho, now laughing outright, replied: "Yes it is."

Wisely, Ben took on a more serious demeanor before he pontificated: "My dear Helen, you cannot expect *all* great events to happen at just the right time."

The End

A preview of the fourth novel in the
LAHAINA MYSTERY SERIES
The Wind Mists

. . .

"I take it Ben is still out of town? Where is he?" Justin
asked.

"I have no idea where he is." Helen answered. "He
could be in Timbuktu for all I know. That's part of the
problem. Not only do I not know where he is I don't know
when he's coming back. I'm worried about his house - it
needs to be secured before the storm hits, and I have to
get home to take care of my place. So I was hoping you
two could head to Ben's and check to be sure there's
nothing in the yard that could fly away, and check to see
that all the windows are closed and that sort of thing."

"Sure, Helen, don't worry I'll head right over there.
You coming, Nacho?"

"Happy to oblige, my man. Do you have emergency
supplies, Helen? Batteries, a camp stove, flashlights,
candles, canned food, cat food, bottled water . . . you
know, all the necessities of life?"

"Yes, Nacho. I just made a trip to the grocery store,
and already their bread and rice shelves are empty and
bottled water is almost gone. But I think I got most of
what I need and right now I'm anxious to get home - I'm
afraid Mambo and Windy will be scared and in need of
comfort. The wind is already beginning to gust and when
you look out over the ocean, you can see the dark clouds
coming. I wish Ben were here. It's not knowing where he

is that's the hardest to deal with. What if he's flying in the storm – in thunder and lightening?"

Justin looked concerned as he said: "I would think he'd call you on his cell phone. When's the last time you talked to him?"

"It was the day before yesterday. It was a terrible connection, but it sounded like he said he was bringing home a surprise and a guest."

"Maybe he said he was bringing home a super prize and a pest. You know if the connection was bad, he could have even said a nest or a vest. With Ben, you can never tell."

"If I didn't know you so well, Nacho, I'd think you had gone over the edge. But I understand that you're trying to be humorous in a misguided attempt to reassure me."

Justin interrupted: "If you two don't stop fooling around, we may not get to Ben's in time to tie things down. How about we come by and check on you and the cats when we get through? I'd feel better if we watched out for you while Ben is . . . wherever he is."

As Helen got up to leave, she smiled and said: "Come hungry – I'll fix dinner. I want to empty the refrigerator in case the power fails."

Back at Helen's cottage on the beach, just a mile or so south of town, Mambo and Windy had been feeling the electricity in the air all day, so rather than being scared, they were wired! When Helen opened the door and stepped into the kitchen, both cats attacked her, from the side and the rear, causing her to drop one of the grocery bags. "Hey you two, calm down." She looked into their coal black eyes. "Hoo boy, I've seen this before and no good can come of it. You know what? I'm going to put you both into the laundry room for a while, until I get things secured."

The wind had already knocked over a couple of orchid plants on the patio, and the wind chimes were a snarled mess, not to mention the hammock, which she untied from its palm trees and rolled up. She pulled the barbecue under the eaves and tucked the smaller potted plants under it for protection, then jammed the hammock and as much furniture as possible into the storage shed. When it was full, she hauled the rest of the stuff around to the side of the house under the big old mango tree. The carport was fairly secure except for a couple of Styrofoam ice chests and some stackable plastic chairs, which she tied down with a rope. Other than that, things seemed to be anchored down well enough.

As soon as the kitties were freed from their temporary prison in the laundry room, they raced to the big overstuffed chair by the sliding glass door. Standing on their hind legs, with their front paws on the back of the chair, they had a grand view of the ocean, which was crashing in large breakers onto the lawn. Leaves and debris were beginning to blow around and pile up in the corner of the patio by the storage shed. The sky and the sea were the same dark gray color, both churning wildly. Clouds scudded by and waves were topped with white caps. Mambo hopped up onto the back of the chair, mesmerized by the sight.

Helen began unloading groceries, taking advantage of the cat's obsession with flying objects. After hauling the three-gallon water bottles in from her car, she put a stash of canned food and other supplies in the pantry. Chili, soup, tuna, chicken, assorted fruit, beans, smoked oysters, olives, and little ears of corn on the middle shelf, and crackers, chips, and cookies on the top. Two large bags of kitty litter she put on the bottom shelf, along with extra toilet paper and assorted flavors of canned cat food and kibbles.

Then she remembered . . . no batteries and no wine! How could she have forgotten them?

Quickly dialing the phone, she said: "Justin? Are you guys at Ben's yet? - - -Oh good. Everything okay? - - - Oh, the one on the windowsill? Just water it, maybe it's still alive. As for the green fuzzy thing in the refrigerator, dump it. - - Could you do me one more favor? - - Raid Ben's corner drawer in the kitchen and bring all his batteries, especially the AA's. Then go to the wine rack in the corner of the screened porch and load all of it into a box and bring it here. - - No not an orgy . . . I think there's probably only three or four. I should have picked some up at the store, but with all the other stuff I had to remember, I forgot. - - Thanks so much. See you soon. Bye."

Somewhere between Oahu and Molokai, Ben looked out of the cockpit window at the threatening cloud formation ahead. He knew from twenty years experience as an airline pilot, that it was too risky to keep heading for Maui. He had to land at the nearest airfield. Once more he tried to reach Helen by phone, but could not get through. As he banked the to the left in a graceful turn, his passenger glanced over at him, waiting for some reassurance that they were not going down in flames. Ben winked and gave an okay sign. In return he got a huge grin from his "co-pilot," who relaxed and instantly fell back asleep.

No wonder, Ben thought – it had been an exhausting week. Fiji is still very removed from the mainstream of the world and spare parts for a DC-4 are very hard to come by. New Zealand was his best hope, and sure enough the wonderful Kiwis came through. Some of them were old time pilots who got caught up in Ben's dream of flying his newly found treasure back to Hawaii. They scrounged around for machine parts and even came up with two cannibalized windows and a couple of new tires. She looked like a relic from the Bermuda Triangle, but purred like a kitten – probably the only one of her kind in the whole Pacific Island chain.

Molokai was only a few minutes away now. What a shame it was to be heading away from home. He knew Helen would be anxious to hear from him and to find out what his big surprise was . . . oh, and his guest. He did, after all, mention that he was bringing a guest. My God, with her raging curiosity, she would be pacing the floor, imagining all sorts of scenarios. The thought of that made him chuckle.

Helen was indeed pacing and imagining things – like how she was going to kill Ben when he finally got back. *Oh please, dear God, bring him home safely* she prayed. Was he flying on New Zealand Air? Were they in the middle of the storm? Was there lightening? What was his big surprise? Who was this mysterious guest? In accompaniment to her increased state of anxiety, a gust of wind hit the house like an explosion, making Mambo jump and causing Windy to head under the table. It seemed that with each blast of wind, Helen's fear for Ben's safety was escalating.

To order other Lahaina Mysteries,
or to find out when the next book in the series is
available, visit our web site at
www.lahainamysteries.com

Would you like to know more about Maui?
Introducing '360⁰ Maui'
an interactive CD-ROM for your home P.C. See Maui's
Beaches in full 360^0 Spin & Zoom panoramas, photo
slide shows, full listing of all of Maui's tourist related
businesses, accommodations, activities, restaurants and
much, much more.
www.graphic-park.com/360maui
$19.95
Produced By Sharp Enterprises LLC

About the author:

Barbara Sharp was born and raised in Washington State. She attended the University of Washington, then married and raised three children. After they were grown and on their own, she moved to Maui, spending ten years as Research Director at The Lahaina Restoration Foundation.

Sharps books include **The Last Smythe**, **The Third Spy** and **The Right Time**. The fourth book in the series, The **Wind Mists**, is in progress.